Obsession

Obsession

by
Jules Clarétie

translated, annotated and introduced by
Brian Stableford

A Black Coat Press Book

Introduction

L'Obsession (Moi et l'Autre) by Jules Clarétie, here translated as *Obsession*, was first published in book form in Paris by Pierre Lafitte in 1908, having previously been serialized as "Moi et l'Autre" [The Self and the Other] in Lafitte's periodical *Je Sais Tout* between February and August 1905—the first novel serialized in that publication. It was the author's last novel and one of the last published works in a long and prolific career; it was written while he was the director of the Théâtre Français, a post he had taken up in 1885, three years before being elected to the Académie Française.

Clarétie undoubtedly owed his election to the Academy more to the influential position he had acquired—even Academicians need to suck up to influential gatekeepers—than to the renown of his works, but he was respected as a critic, historian and chronicler. In the last regard he made a notable contribution to the partisan reportage and analysis of the Franco-Prussian War and its aftermath. He was less celebrated as a novelist, his fiction tending to the popular rather than the prestigious, including conventional love stories and crime stories, and thus generally being regarded as lightweight fare. That did not, of course, inhibit Lafitte from boasting about the author's Academy membership when he serialized "Moi et l'Autre," the acquisition of which he doubtless regarded as something of a coup.

Born in 1840 in Limoges, baptized Arsène Arnaud Clarétie, and subsequently educated in Paris, initially at the Lycée Bonaparte, "Jules" Clarétie soon made his mark as a journalist, and became one of the most successful members of that profession in Paris. His career included a long stint at *Le Figaro*, regular employment as the drama critic of *L'Opinion Nationale*, and a column of contemporary commentary enti-

5

tled "La Vie à Paris" [Life in Paris] in *Le Temps* that ran for thirty years. He wrote plays of his own and the librettos for operas, but did not have a great deal of success on the creative side of theatrical work, being far more successful as a critic and manager.

Aided by collections of his journalistic essays, Clarétie became a very prolific author, routinely publishing more than half a dozen volumes a year from 1864 until the management of the national theater began to take up most of his time and cut his literary production rate in half. His early novels had some affinities with the Naturalist school, the most notable exercise in that vein being his lively study of contemporary leisure pastimes *Le Train No. 17* (1877), but his interests and methods were too varied to permit any simple pigeon-holing. One of the many writers of which he produced a major critical study was Jules Verne and in 1878 he published one of the earliest works of fiction in the Vernian periodical *Journal de Voyages*, "La Mer libre" [The Open Sea], but his interest in the *roman scientifique* was limited by the fact that his understanding of science was very rudimentary; he did, however, develop an abiding fascination with the development of psychological science, in terms of its cataloguing of phenomena and attempts to develop treatments for various mental disturbances. His novel *Les Amours d'un interne* [An Intern's Love Story] (1881), set in the Salpêtrière, was written with the active encouragement of the pioneering physician Jean-Martin Charcot, who was in quest of publicity for his work on "hysteria" and the use of hypnosis in treating it.

Clarétie went on to write several more novels on psychological themes. *Jean Mornas, ou l'Hypnotisme* (1885) is a further development of the notion of hypnotism, this time focusing on its possible uses for nefarious ends. *L'Oeil du mort* [The Dead Man's Eye] (1887) is an adaptation and extrapolation of the myth that the retina retains the image of the last thing seen in life, fixed as if on a photographic plate. *L'Obsession* is his most elaborate study of that sort, although—as the references contained in the text testify—it owes more to literary precedents than to scientific and therapeutic studies in its description and analysis of the psychological anomaly that would nowadays be called "multiple personality syndrome." It has an additional dimension of interest, however, in that the other obsession that it attempts to bring into focus is the obsessive quality of scientific research, thus also adding to the rich tradition of literary accounts of "mad scientists."

L'Obsession was presumably commissioned by Lafitte for *Je Sais Tout* while the periodical was still in the planning stage, the plan in question being to establish it as a French equivalent of the middlebrow English periodicals that had proliferated in the wake of *The Strand Magazine*. The periodical's early inclusions were deliberately cast in the same molds as those that helped to make *The Strand* and its clones so successful; the fiction featured therein placed a heavy emphasis on crime—Maurice Leblanc's Arsène Lupin stories began to appear there while Clarétie's novel was being serialized—and offbeat imaginative fiction, in a vein whose principal exemplar was then considered to be H. G. Wells. The other short fiction featured alongside "Moi et l'Autre" included translations of works by *Strand* stalwarts Arthur Conan Doyle and W. W. Jacobs.

"Moi et l'Autre" appears to have been composed while it was being serialized, and, like many *feuilleton* serials composed in that fashion, it loses its direction and its coherency as the author attempts to improvise a plot without ever really knowing where he is going or how to get there. After the brilliantly melodramatic early episode in which the heroine discovers her husband's multiple personality in awkwardly terrifying circumstances, the story struggles to make the most of that narrative capital, let alone to make any further progress in building dramatic tension or solving the problem thus defined. Even so, the novel's description of the hero's multiple personality is an interesting one, in terms of the literary history of the theme, by virtue of its avoidance of the simple moral polarization featured in such allegories as Edgar Allan Poe's "William

Wilson" (1839) and Robert Louis Stevenson's classic *Strange Case of Dr. Jekyll and Mr. Hyde* (1886). Although it remains, to a considerable extent, an "evil twin" story, its particular representation of the unfortunate aspects of the personality of the inconvenient "double" is unusual and striking.

Although Clarétie's story does not provide the kind of psychoanalytical interpretation of the double's behavioral tendencies and works of art for which they might seem to cry out, so that they remain essentially tantalizing, that adds to rather than detracting from the fascination of the story, and ensures that the novel itself appeals for interpretation at least as much as the fictitious situation it describes. It would be inappropriate to attempt any further analysis of the plot and imagery here, lest it should work as a spoiler, but I have taken the liberty of adding a brief afterword to the novel in which I have set out some of the thoughts that its intriguing convolutions prompted in me; doubtless they will prompt different reactions in different readers, just as rival schools of psychotherapy would probably offer different analyses of the hero's condition, the mentality of the scientist who "cures" it and peculiarities of their narrative representation.

Although *L'Obsession* probably cannot be reckoned as Clarétie's best work, by virtue of its relative incoherency, it is arguably his most adventurous and most interesting, partly for that very reason. It has some moments of remarkable dramatic intensity, even though they are not organized into the kind of disciplined crescendo that would maximize their effect, and it poses some authentically interesting questions, although the specific answers it suggests do not stand up well to rational analysis. It was certainly written with genuine intellectual concern and with feeling, and thus qualifies as a revealing narrative in more ways than one; it definitely warrants attention from literary connoisseurs of the unusual and the eccentric.

This translation was made from the version of the 1908 Lafitte edition reproduced electronically by the University of

Ottawa and available for downloading from the Internet Archive at *archive.org*.

Brian Stableford

Dedication

Do you like new novels, Madame and dear friend? Extraordinary novels, novels in which the truest adventures seem highly implausible? Open the books in which the scientists tell you what can happen in the human brain.

"Human heart, human body," cries a character in a comedy. The most astonishing voyage, which surpasses in its discoveries all the endeavors of explorers or inventors of airplanes, is the voyage around the human machine. And be sure that everything incredible that you will be told about the "double man" and stupefying research on the "eye" that is still lacking with regard to modern man is true, scrupulously and scientifically true. Science is the pursuit of the impossible. It will be attained.

In the meantime, the novel sees, foresees and prophesies. It is its right to divine the future, especially when its divinations are founded on facts.

Read this book, therefore, in which the dream is made absolute and fiction the truth.

To you, Madame and dear friend, with all my heart.

6 November 1908.
(Letter from Dr. Wells, of New York)[1]

---

[1] The book edition is dated 15 October 1908. The significance of the attribution of this "dedication" (which does not appear in the serial version) to "Dr. Wells" is enigmatic—presumably a private joke that the unnamed dedicatee would understand.

PART ONE

I. Doctor Chardin

Patients were waiting in Dr. Chardin's large reception room in the Boulevard Haussmann, having come at the appointed hour of consultation. Sunk into armchairs, in impatient attitudes, their faces sullen, or timidly seated on the edges of chairs, they maintained the irritated silence of accused persons in the antechamber of a magistrate. There were two old ladies with exceedingly sad expressions leading a pale child whom they scolded mildly, very quietly, whenever he coughed; a pretty young woman, visibly nervous, who was ruffling feverishly through the illustrated books—mostly accounts of voyages—laid on the table; a fat gentleman with a swollen and apoplectic face; and, in a corner, his legs crossed and his hat on his knees; and a thin young man, elegant and refined, whose interrogative gaze went from the paintings hung on the walls to the trees in the boulevard, perceptible above the windbreak of the windows, their leaves yellow and their branches half-stripped by the autumnal wind.

Occasionally, the oak-colored door with gilt decorations that led from the reception-room to the doctor's study would open and the long silhouette, emaciated and seemingly fantastic, of a man in a black frock-coat would appear on the threshold. A tapering skull was perceptible over a thin face, completely clean-shaven in the American style, and a tall, frail body that made a summoning gesture, as curt as the movement of an old telegraph signal; one of the clients would get up and disappear into the study, and the door would close silently on some confidence or dolor.

The young man, who had arrived last, having allowed the ladies and invalids waiting with him to go in ahead of him, thought that the long wait in the physician's reception-room vaguely resembled the other miserable pauses of everyday life. The gazes of the impatient stare with a kind of jealous anger at the clients who go in first. One might think that those the doctor summons are favored by fate, and stealing a little of the time and the life of others. The impatient young woman opened, closed, reopened and reclosed the decorative bindings of the worn volumes, handled by so many fingers, and the heels of her dainty feet beat a tattoo on the carpet.

"What's the point?" said one of his neighbors to the young man. "What's the point of hurrying, since one always has to wait one's turn?"

The sage in question—a forty-year old of military bearing—had only one thing on his mind: to avoid leaning back in the armchair in which he was sitting, in order to escape contact with its back; and he was sitting up very straight, on the very edge of the seat, gazing, with a sort of tender commiseration, at those who were letting their heads rest on their chairs or sofas. When his hand touched the arm of the chair he was quick to wipe it.

"They don't realize," he said, pityingly, "that they might catch alopecia. Yes, yes, the disease is everywhere. People are right to say that microbes are lying in wait for us. Breathe in a single speck of dust, and death might be entering into us." However, he repeated, philosophically: "Why hurry? One always gets there eventually."

The doctor's reception-room gradually emptied. The two ladies in mourning had shoved the little pale child into the study; the apoplectic fat man had hastened to see the physician, bumping into a chair; and, after the man preoccupied with microbes, the charming and, elegant young woman, arranging her fur stole prettily around her shoulders, had gone into the study, smiling courageously, as if heading for a rendezvous.

Now, alone with the paintings, which saddened him, going from a Diaz to a Ziem,[2] then, standing at the window looking out on the boulevard through the plane-trees, watching the trams and automobiles go by, the young man waited for his own turn, while a servant with a white cravat, opening the door to the antechamber, let in new patients, who took their places on the chairs that had been vacated.

Dr. Chardin's consultations were much in demand, and posterity, which begins at the frontier, had commenced for that bold innovator, as renowned abroad as in Paris, perhaps even more appreciate in America and Russia for his work on nervous diseases, encephalic afflictions, thought-processes and the life of the brain. The scientist did not confine himself to the various manifestations of that specialty, however; he also pursued active research in the most diverse directions, deeming, as a philosophical and encyclopedic mind, that only ideas of genius are important, and that in this vast universe, a man of the era ought to know everything and attempt to divine everything.

Stories were also told about Dr. Chardin, as if of some legendary character. Of unhoped-for cures produced by the gambles of a miracle doctor, without any publicity or advertising. Before Cailletet and Arsonval,[3] he had glimpsed the mar-

---

[2] Narcisse Diaz de la Peña (1807-1876) was a landscape painter best known for his forest scenes. Félix Ziem (1821-1911) was famous for his studies of Venice, although he painted many other landscapes as well as works in other genres.

[3] Louis Cailletet (1832-1913) was one of the first scientists to produce droplets of liquid oxygen in 1877. Arsène d'Arsonval (1851-1940) was one of the pioneers of electrophysiology (the effects of electricity on living organisms and tissues), but he did a course of public lectures at the Jardin des Plantes in 1901 that included one on the properties of liquid gases, which included a demonstration of the effects of immersing a steak in the liquid nitrogen. Clarétie probably attended the lecture, and it might have been his reportage that was responsible for re-

vels of liquid air; penetrated, almost at the same as Roentgen, the secrets of the human body by means of X-rays; applied and perfected the Dane Finsen's apparatus for curing lupus by means of light,[4] finding the cure in the famous red chamber in which other rays devoured and relieved diseases of the skin. There was much preoccupation in the scientific world with the research that Dr. Chardin was pursuing on the possibility of employing the properties of the Curies' radium curatively. Being free, however, and belonging to no academy, the doctor would not allow any visitor into the laboratory he had at Montrouge, and avoided the reporters that others sought out. He was an eccentric.

On the other hand, his study in the Boulevard Haussmann saw crowds flocking, his aristocratic clientele almost as numerous as the needy forming a queue at the door of a hospital clinic.

And while the young man watched the passers-by, walking rapidly, as if spurred by the first piquant cold of November, the reception-room filled up again with new clients, hastening to the consultation as to a vivid hope.

The study door opened. The doctor's bald head appeared, the long thin arm made a gesture of summons and the young man went in. The physician invited him to sit down in a leather armchair.

Behind at a vast desk covered with papers and books, with Japanese bronze crabs as paperweights, Dr. Chardin, impassive with his broadly-chiseled features, very pale and reminiscent of a face summarily sculpted in the white flesh of some giant nut, leaned his elbows on his blotter. Interlacing

---

ports that appeared in newspapers as far afield at American and New Zealand.

[4] Niels Finsen (1860-1904) was awarded the Nobel Prize in 1903 for his demonstration that the superficial symptoms of *lupus vulgaris* could be successfully treated with phototherapy, having published classic paper on phototherapy in 1896.

his slender fingers, he looked deep into the eyes of the patient sitting opposite.

The gray eyes, keen and piercing, as if the point of a scalpel were emerging from the pupils, became uncomfortable for the man supporting their gleam. It was like a kind of human ray, as penetrating as a cathode ray. For his part, the young man's own dark eyes, illuminating a pale face surrounded by a black beard, seemed to be examining the man whose gaze was examining him, with a slightly anxious curiosity, searching for thoughts as if with forceps.

"Well, Monsieur, will you please explain your case to me as concisely as possible. It's evidently a matter of some nervous malady?"

Tall, sturdy and handsome, the man interrogated did not have the appearance of being degenerate or defective, and it required the specialized eye of Dr. Chardin to perceive the invisible flaw.

"Yes, Doctor," the client said, his voice a trifle emotional, "and a rather unusual malady—but you have a lot of people in your waiting-room and I don't want to take up too much of your time. On the other hand, you'll see shortly that I couldn't put off my visit and that you cannot put off your judgment until another day. I ask you to listen to me patiently. The others..."

"You've waited for your turn, Monsieur; they will wait for theirs. What is it?"

"It is, as I said, rather strange. Anyone but you would take me for a madman, whose madness they would establish officially. I'm ill, undoubtedly—you can subject me to all the examinations and tests you wish—but I'm not mad. All alienated individuals, you'll tell me, claim that they're perfectly sane, but take note that I don't make that claim for myself—quite the contrary. There's a lesion within me, and I'll explain my case in order to ask you, not for an immediate cure, but for advice first, and a cure afterwards."

"I'm listening," said Dr. Chardin, who did not take his gray eyes off the speaker's black pupils.

"Before anything else, Doctor, you need to know who I am. Here's my card."

The physician looked at it. "André Fortis...the painter?"

"The painter."

The doctor smiled—and he expression of that unexpected smile in that glacial physiognomy seemed charming—and then offered a rapid, graphic and accurate comment on the beautiful landscapes exhibited by Fortis at the last Salon. "Your paintings testify, in fact, to an eye that is able to 'grasp' and an art that is able to express. You're a poet, but—judging by your work—you have a perfectly constituted brain. I wouldn't say as much about all of your peers. Let's pass on."

André Fortis smiled in his turn, but more sadly. "Doctor," he said, since your preliminary appreciation is so favorable, it put me more at ease in making a confession that I hope, in spite of its bizarrerie, will not modify your diagnosis. I've told you that I'm not mad, but my morbid state renders me as unhappy as if I were. I'm an individual who, at certain times and for a rather extensive lapse of time, has a double personality."

"What does that mean?"

"It means that suddenly, when I least expect it, while I'm walking, chatting, or working, in the studio or at table, a sudden attack of drowsiness takes possession of me, I fall asleep without cause, and I then become—believe me or not—another man: an entirely different man, a man who has his own life, different from the first, his own opinions, ideas and preoccupations, which are not mine; a man who lives within me and alongside me, and who cuts my customary existence in two, in order to recommence and continue another existence, suddenly, unexpectedly and almost overwhelmingly—to such an extent that, mechanically, in that second life, which, in reality, gives me a second consciousness, I am completely different from my habitual nature. Necessarily living with the same people, retaining the same body, the same voice and the same gestures, I must evidently seem to them to be incomprehensible and abnormal, since that double life really does make me

18

into two men enclosed in the same man. Take note, Doctor, that I would never even have found out about my condition, since I only remember my second existence when the crises overtake me, if an old friend of the family who died six months ago, Doctor Burke..."

"I knew him. He was a good man."

"If, as I say, Doctor Burke had not explained what was happening to me, and how a sudden sleep could precipitate me into another existence, completely different from my own, eventually returning me to the first existence with, I repeat, having any memory of what I have done, said and thought while in the second state... Second state, that's what you call—isn't it?—the species of somnambulism that takes possession of me, with the result that for a period of time I'm no longer me but *him*: an individual I don't know, who is not me but *the Other*?"

II. Two Existences in One

The doctor did not take his eyes of the young man, and seemed to be studying, simultaneously, his gestures, the sound of his voice and the movements of his face—a physiognomy that, quite calm a little while ago, seemed to have grown gradually anxious and angry, as if some third person had been introduced between the two men, and that André Fortis, divining the presence of the intruder, was irritated by him.

"I suppose, Doctor, that you think I'm completely mad."

"No," said the physician. "Ill, yes, and you've just described a quite extraordinary case..."

"Unique," said the painter, vehemently. "Yes, unique."

Dr. Chardin shook his head, smiling. "Behold human pride! It's found even among the ill—especially the ill. Nothing is unique in nature, Monsieur. Everything has a precedent. Science has only observed and studied half a dozen cases identical or comparable to yours, but the question of double consciousness, or the doubling of the personality is known, and even classic. I regret depriving you of an illusion, but you have had predecessors. There is even a famous observation cited in books of physiology and psychology—the story of Félida."

"Félida?"

"You don't know it? If you were to open a volume on hypnotism—and I don't advise it, given your nervous condition—you would find the story of that young woman from Bordeaux related, repeated and reassessed, who lived two existences in one. She had a husband and children, and a double life—a sad life when she continued one of her two existences, happy when she returned to the other, and astonished by that circumstances, which scientists had taken under observation. A charming and very erudite man, a professor of the Faculty of Medicine at Bordeaux, who I still see when he visits the Salpêtrière, short, pensive, modest, a good talker and a better listener, Doctor Azam,[5] who is very interested in hypnotism, has put his name to the extraordinary observation of Félida. Félida was a hysteric. Don't take that word in the meaning that the vulgar attach to it. You're neurotic, and neurosis is the hysteria of man. And if the phenomena that you've described to me are exact—and your precision persuades me that they are exact—you're a male Félida. How old are you?"

"Twenty-nine."

"Do you have, in your ancestry, any relative of bizarre inclination? Think hard."

"None," said the painter.

"At what age did your father die?"

"Sixty-four. He was robust. A chill caught on emerging from the theater carried him off."

"Your mother?"

"My mother died young. I hardly knew her. A smiling face, a Chaplin[6] drawing—that's all that remains to me of her."

"And in the family traditions, nothing that reminds you of any unduly exceptional individual?"

"Nothing."

"There must, however, be an ancestor to whom you owe this neurosis. Within us, there lives, or revives, some unknown

---

[5] Étienne Eugène Azam (1822-1899) published his account of the pseudonymous patient in question in *Hypnotisme, double conscience et altérations de la personnalité: le cas Fédida X* [Hypnotism, Double Consciousness and Alterations of the Personality: The Case of Félida X] (1887); it was widely discussed because of the questions it raised with regard to the nature of identity, challenging traditional notions of the soul. Azam did visit Charcot at the Salpêtrière on more than one occasion, and Clarétie probably talked about the case to Charcot.

[6] Charles Joshua Chaplin (1825-1891) specialized in painting sentimentalized pictures of young women, and gave art classes at his Paris studio that were restricted to female students.

ancestor who reappears and imposes his flaws upon us or brings us his genius. Did you have some kind of accident in your infancy—a shock or a fright?"

"Nothing," the young man repeated.

"Try to remember..."

"I'm searching my memory, Doctor, but I can't evoke anything, or recall anything..."

"In any case, the causes won't suppress the effects, and it's the effects that we have to combat."

André Fortis looked the doctor in the face; then, having seemed to hesitate, he said, slowly: "Combat, yes...but cure? Is there a cure?"

"There's always a cure!" said Monsieur Chardin, succinctly.

"But Félida, This Félida of Doctor..."

"Azam."

"Was she cured?"

"She lived, as I told you. She was a woman and a mother, and is probably still alive."

"Cured?" repeated André, emphasizing the word.

"One can always fall ill again," replied the doctor, in the same clipped tone in which he had mentioned a cure.

An abrupt gesture underlined the young man's reply: "But I don't have the right to fall ill again, myself, Doctor!"

"Why not?"

"Why not? Why not? Because I'm getting married tomorrow. That's why."

There was such an expression of haggard fever in the painter's gaze that the doctor, thus far observing a neurosis, wondered whether he might be in the presence of a dementia. With a singular precision, however, as if he were responding to the physician's mute preoccupation and thought, the young man hastened to add and repeat:

"Once again, don't think that I'm completely mad. Troubled, yes; frightened, yes; pushed as if toward a gulf, wanting to recoil and no longer being able to recoil, yes—and that's why I've come to consult you, to confess to you, in a sense, as

I said. As for being in my right mind, I *am* in my right mind: I'm really *me*. And for some time now, I've reconquered that me, and that's how I've been able to embark, without remorse, on the amorous romance that will terminate, or ought to terminate, tomorrow with a marriage.

"I adore the young woman who will be my wife. She loves me. I have an independent fortune and my paintbrush would make me almost rich if I were harassed by the need to work. We have every chance of happiness before us—but on one condition, which is that the doubling of my being does not render the new existence that I am going to create for myself, and which is my salvation, absolutely impossible. It is, in brief, that the other me, who is not me—in truth, Doctor, it seems that I'm talking like Sosie in Molière's *Amphitryon*[7]— does not thwart my life, my joy, my hearth, and change what ought to be my most delightful and, I assure you, most ardently desired refuge into a Hell."

André stopped, interrogating Dr. Chardin's hard eyes anxiously. He was reminiscent of a man awaiting the verdict of a judge.

Before pronouncing it, the physician asked: "How does this second state into which you enter commence? Do you have any sign or sensation—what we call an *aura*—to warn you of its coming?"

---

[7] Sosie was the part played in *Amphitryon* (1668; based on a similarly-named play by Plautus *circa* 185 B.C.) by Molière himself; like the name of the title character, which became synonymous with "host," the name of Sosie was adopted into the French language to mean "double," normally in the sense of "lookalike" but sometimes—based on the monologue that André is citing—to refer to a "second self." In the play, Sosie is a double of the god Mercury, and plays a role ironically parallel to that of the messenger of the gods—significantly, in that Molière was thought, probably rightly, to be using the play's characterization of Jupiter as a means of issuing subtle criticism of the morals of Louis XIV.

"Yes—haven't I told you? Generally, a sort of flash, a persistent luminous zigzag passes before my eyes; objects appear to me to by striped with streaks of light, or surrounded, as if by an aureole, a halo…and then a sudden somnolence, an invincible desire to sleep, a heaviness of the head that isn't disagreeable—no, on the contrary, which is engaging, attractive, as if sinking into darkness were something pleasant and good…

"Then I emerge from that vague semi-slumber to recover consciousness, doubtless to awaken in that second state and become the other person—to don, if I might express it thus, the livery and ideas of the other, to be someone else, to be the Other and to continue, in that state, the new existence that has nothing in common with the preceding one. But I've told you that. I beg your pardon—it's the obsession."

"Has it been a long time since you've been subjected to that second state?"

"Yes, Doctor, yes: two years. Dr. Burke even assured me that I was cured."

"He was right. Suggestion is very powerful in such cases. Anyway, Burke might perfectly well be right. It's quite possible that you're cured…quite possible."

A glint of joy traversed André Fortis' eyes, glued to the physician's.

"In that case, Doctor, this marriage…? This marriage taking place tomorrow…"

"Well?" said Chardin, coldly.

"There's no reason why it should not take place? I don't have to fear some kind of phantom interposing itself between my happiness and myself, taking my place, or expelling me, so to speak, from my own existence?"

"It's necessary, above all, to tell yourself, repeatedly, that what you fear is impossible. It's necessary to penetrate yourself and impregnate that conviction. It's necessary to expel all anxiety. It's necessary to persuade yourself that you've had a dream, and that the nightmare is over. You must persuade yourself intimately and absolutely, you understand?

You've come to consult me at a moment of your existence when it's difficult to draw back. It's tomorrow, you say?"

"Tomorrow, at eleven o'clock, at the Mairie of the Second Arrondissement, and at midday, at Saint-Roch..."

The doctor remained thoughtful, uncertain and hesitant, biting his lip. He had divined the disturbance of that soul in distress, the alarm of that mind. He felt that he was on the lip of a chasm. A master of human destiny, he had the right of life and death. A single word might become a sentence...

"Tomorrow," he said. "And the young woman loves you?"

"Profoundly, I'm sure of it. As I love her."

Then slowly, the physician said: "My God, Monsieur, if you had come to consult me two months ago, I would have advised you to reflect; I would have put you under observation, and my opinion would soon have been clear. But you've come at a time when it's a matter of the happiness and the reputation of a young woman, to interrogate me and to affirm that your own doctor, who has studied you and treated you, declared you cured. You're putting me in a difficult situation. Were you already engaged to be married when Dr. Burke died?"

"No."

"Had you taken him into your confidence with regard to your nascent love for the young woman that you're to marry?"

"Yes, Doctor. And when I expressed my anxieties, a perfectly natural anguish, as I told you, he reassured me. Given a certain existence, a profound affection and a craft that I love, he believed firmly that I could brave the future and that the past, the odious past, is indeed the past..."

"I hope so," said Monsieur Chardin. Very rapidly, André Fortis having gone pale, he added: "And I believe so, since he said it. The excellent Doctor Burke isn't just anyone."

"So?" asked the painter, whose voice choked in posing the question.

"So, between the certain scandal, which might give rise to some irreparable mishap..."

"Also certain, Doctor. Yes, if you tell me not to marry tomorrow, I'll go home, write me letter of farewell and kill myself this evening."

"That would be stupid," said the physician. "But it is the stupidities in life that one always enacts with the greatest urgency. I was saying to you that between a mishap—and the stupidity in question might perhaps open the door to many others—and a risk, or, to put it better, a hope, it is necessary to choose the less tragic solution. Give me your address. Whatever happens, you should come to see me again, and you can, if necessary, put on paper, for me—and me alone, of course—your sensations, and your anxieties, if you have any, if you anticipate the reawakening of that Other, as you put it. If he reappears in your existence, which I don't believe—look at me now"—the doctor plunged his gaze into the young man's eyes like a scalpel—"which I don't believe will happen"—he emphasized the words imperatively, dictating them like a command—"which I don't believe will happen, come right away, and we'll act accordingly. And we shall be the masters of the situation!"

"Truly?" said André Fortis, as if it were a cry of liberation.

"Truly!" said Monsieur Chardin, firmly.

"Oh, Doctor, Doctor, Doctor! You've saved my life!"

"I'm convinced of it. You're capable of having fired your revolver already."

The painter uttered a nervous little laugh, as if slightly frightened, not of the contemplated action, but by having been thus divined, reliably. "Yes," he said, "it's true. What do you expect? I adore my fiancée. Losing her seems to me an impossible thing. I can't resign myself to losing her. What's a piece of lead in the head?"

"Be certain that it's not a remedy," said Dr. Chardin. He stood up and extended his hand to the young man. "Go—and be confident!"

"Thank you, Doctor."

Then, as André Fortis made as if to deposit the doctor's honorarium on the desk, Monsieur Chardin stop him. "No, no. Later. This is a matter of a cure. We'll settle up when I tell you that it's complete. And it's you—yes, you—who will tell me, when the moment comes, that it is..."

"Oh, Doctor!" repeated the young man. "There is something more admirable than an artist who sells the illusion of color and dream, and it's the man of science who gives happiness."

"Good," said the physician. "I'll hold on to the phrase: merchant of happiness. It's a title. Well, I wish you happiness, Monsieur Fortis. And tell yourself: *I'm happy*, as you repeat to yourself: *I'm cured*. To believe it is to be it, and it's perhaps the only means of ensuring that one has what one wants."

André Fortis went down the doctor's staircase lightly, and, looking around at the boulevard, made his heels sound joyfully on the asphalt. He marched straight ahead, his head held high, filling his lungs with air. Life seemed to him to be better, or, rather, to have become possible. The desiccated leaves falling from the plane-trees ran before him rapidly, like harbingers of joy. On the horizon, in the pearl-gray tint of November, patches of blue sky—a pale Correggio blue—were opening like a woman's eyes. The sun appeared and disappeared, animating the slate roofs and tall white houses. The weather was very mild, spring-like—one of those of those melancholy *été de la Saint-Martin* days,[8] in which landscapes and people have the already-wounded joy of things that are about to end.

---

[8] The French use the term *été de la Saint-Martin* [St. Martin's summer] metaphorically in a manner analogous to the English use of the term "Indian summer," although that has a direct equivalent in French as well; the latter usually refers to a period of days, while the former refers to a singly unusually warm day before the advent of the winter chill. The literal reference is to the festival of the saint on 11 November.

For André Fortis, on the contrary, the joy was commencing. Two hours earlier he had taken, anxiously, the elevator that was to take him up to the doctor's apartment, but when the consultation was over he had come down placing the footsteps of a victorious conqueror or a liberated prisoner on the carpet.

Life seemed beautiful to him; the passers-by seemed joyful. On his pedestal, the statuary Shakespeare—Shakespeare, the poet of profound loves and sad follies—seemed to be saying to him: *Cast away that Doubt that kills, repeat to yourself the opposite of Hamlet's speech: Hope and live!*

Live? The painter wanted no more than to live. The blood of youth was pulsing ardently in his veins. The visions of art gave him beautiful dreams. Landscapes were like living poetry to him, which he fixed on his canvas with the joy of a creator, springs that smiled with all their whiteness, or autumnal tears with their rains of golden leaves. What! He had before him a future of glory, and abruptly, like a thief in the night slipping into his being, another, the Other, might come to snatch away all those dreams, to substitute new thoughts for his own, to bring the life that was opening triumphantly, happily, to a dead stop: a kind of stranger slipping into him and becoming him, as André put on a new personality, like a costume—in which costume he would feel himself choking, as if in iron armor that was too tight and too heavy!

But Doctor Chardin had just told him that one could shrug off the yoke of the intruder, and break that mental armor, as heavy as the instruments of torture in which victims were once enclosed! The physician had, with a word, rendered to the desperate man the pretext for living: hope! The joyful André Fortis mentally thanked the sky, the trees, the leaves, the entire frame of his happiness, associating with it the intoxication of an escaped convict.

Yes, if Dr. Chardin's verdict had been altogether different, he had resolved to die. Rather than write to Mademoiselle de Jandrieu that he was renouncing, for inexplicable reasons, the honor and joy of marrying her, he would have put a bullet in his head. It was not an impulsive temptation to suicide, it was a resolution made after reflection, the considered action of a man who does not know how to get out of an impossible situation. But—God, be praised!—he had got out of it quite naturally. The young woman he loved would become his wife tomorrow, and Dr, Chardin had, like Dr. Burke, declared that the Other could be chased away, expelled, dispatched or nailed to the threshold of the happy household like an importunate guest or a bird of ill-omen.

To marry Mademoiselle de Jandrieu! That was, for André, the desired union. A romance that, in its tenderness, would have been the simplest and most banal in the world, if the terror of a fearful tomorrow had not been lurking in the background, like a living anguish sitting by the hearth.

André Fortis had met Mademoiselle de Jandrieu in Trouville. A friend had introduced him to her parents: the father an old gentleman, a retired general, who had once been rich but whose land, the vines having been ravaged, was not worth today as much it had once been; the mother a charming, smiling, timid and pious woman who adored her only child, her daughter, and had taken great care in fashioning that soul. The hazard of walks, the promiscuities of the dining table, the games of tennis, and the conversations—rapid at first, and then, the particular intimacy of the beach succeeding the formal handshakes—had all come together, gradually, in the semi-liberty of seaside resorts, and the young people, whose meetings, under the eyes of Monsieur and Madame de Jandrieu, had no banal flirtation about them, had, on the contrary, engendered a grave and profound affection.

André had, in addition, exercised an absolute discretion in his relationships, and the disturbance that he felt with regard to his condition had imposed an anxious reserve on him. As if Mademoiselle de Jandrieu's gentle influence had had a particularly calming effect on him, however, in her presence, extraordinarily, he had never experienced any of the choking anguishes of old, any terror of the advent of the Other. Cécile de Jandrieu's clear gaze gave him the impression of a limpid lake whose bed he could see. He compared it to the blue water of Lac Leman, on which the young woman's thoughts—he smiled at the preciosity of the image—were swans.

She was tall, slim, pretty, very blonde, her nose slender and her ears pink, with the languid grace of an English miss. Monsieur de Jandrieu's mother had been Irish. Having the soul of an artist, Cécile was a musician, and a painter too—without any pretention—and that taste, a passion for water-colors, had brought her closer to Fortis. At the last Salon she had particularly admired "Ruisseaux des Vaux de Cernay," into which the landscaper-painter had put such a profound impression of melancholy, the water flowing between rocks amid sad trees like life through quotidian tribulations. At least, that was what Cécile had seen in the canvas. In a landscape, one perceives above all that which there is in oneself.

Rather timid, like her mother, Mademoiselle de Jandrieu had submitted her water-colors to Fortis. There was more than an amateur talent apparent in her studies of the sea shore, various studies of beaches or towns, at the hazard of her voyages: the solitudes of Port Royal; the deserts of the Crau, Mireille's homeland[9]; and the canals of Venice, the ideal homeland of Ziem. And while criticizing the young woman's water-colors, as a professor appreciates and corrects the pupils in his studio, André Fortis exchanged ideas with her, the memories and sensations experienced before the visions realized in some sunset over the lagoon or some gray olive-grove in Provence.

Nature and what it inspires is like a touchstone that brings souls closer together. It happened that the two young people had similar ideas on many issues, and that often, the same landscapes and the same times of day, radiant or melan-

---

[9] "Mireille" is the French title of "Mireio" (1859), an Occitan poem by Frédéric Mistral, which celebrates the popular traditions of the Provençal region; it was adopted into an opera under the French title in 1864 with music by Charles Gounod, Clarétie's favorite composer. It helped Mireille become a popular forename.

choly, had inspired the same reflections in those two individuals, who did not know one another. In such and such a place she had thought what he had thought in the same place. It was quite simple, but it appeared strange to them—strange and charming at the same time.

Thus, a sympathy was born. Mademoiselle de Jandrieu found in the artist a sort of exquisite guide, new ideas that touched her, the fraternity of admiration that leads to tender confidences. For André, it was love: a love compounded out of radiant joy and anxiety. For no matter how insistently he told himself that those appearances of an unknown being in his life, the doubling of his self that had overtaken him occasionally in his existence—all of that only-too-real phantasmagoria—belonged to the past, and was past, the memory and apprehension of that strange neurosis returned to him, not precisely, but with the vague and painful images that follow you after awakening when a dissipated nightmare leaves the brain disturbed, as a bad meal leaves a bitter taste in the mouth.

He remembered the first episode of that bizarre illness. At fifteen years of age, on a feast day, on emerging for a concert in which the maledictions of Schumann's *Manfred*,[10] the demonic or divine voices of the Byronic division had jangled his nerves and excited his sensitivity, he had felt a pain his temples, and dazzling flashes passing before his eyes. Dazed and half-asleep, he had followed his companions without saying a word; then, after a few moments of somnolence, his eye-

---

[10] The eponymous anti-hero of Byron's poem (1817), which inspired Robert Schumann's choral work of 1852, is a nobleman tortured by guilt regarding the death of a lost love, Astarte, who summons a series of spirits in the hope that one might grant him forgetfulness; they cannot, and he eventually commits suicide, in defiance of religious temptations to compensate for his unspecified sin by repentance. Heavily influence by Goethe's *Faust*, Byron's *Manfred* exercised an equally heavy influence on several works by Edgar Allan Poe, including "The Raven."

lids opened again, a completely new expression filled his eyes with flames and he had said things to his friends that astonished them, which were quite different from those of the morning or an hour before.

He had, in fact, become someone else, really and visibly.

His father, then still alive, had consulted Professor Charcot, and then Dr. Adam Burke, an old friend of the family, and asked them: "Is my son mad!"

He was not mad. The fit came to an end after a few days and André became himself again. The physicians had both pronounced the same name, and diagnosed the same affliction. It was the case of which Dr. Chardin had reminded Fortis a little while before. A double consciousness like that of Félida, arising from a double existence, or "second state"—the phrase was Dr. Azam's—also shared André's body and brain.

Without any mental illness there was a singular, incredible doubling, of a kind that had interested Chardin, and which Burke attempted to cure. The physician firmly believed that he had cured it, and Monsieur Fortis senior had had the consolation of dying with the assurance of believing that his son was saved from the threat, before André, having come of age, fell back into the grip of the malady three more times.

Three times, he had sensed his temples squeezed, seen the precursory flashes before his eyes, experienced the almost-agreeable, enveloping and seductive somnolence that took him away and caused him to slide into a kind of sleep.

Three times he had been "someone else" living an unexpected life under the same name and with the same face. Yes, the fantastic phenomenon had occurred. In order to escape the scrutiny of his friends, André had undertaken a voyage to Italy, taking his box of paints and his brushes, and, a kind of somnambulist, he had taken notes, made sketches and finished paintings in that abnormal state, of which no traveling companion, museum guide or stranger was able to suspect the existence, the intelligence or the speech, because the Other's reasoning, even though it was a new reasoning, very different from the artist's habitual opinion, was perfectly intact.

And it produced the result—which seemed incredible, and would have caused protests of absurdity or trickery if science had not been there to affirm the reality of the mystery and sustain the improbability—that André Fortis, awakened from that kind of annihilatory dream, read in his notebooks, found in his drawings and saw in his canvases thoughts, notations and landscapes that were his, canvases and ideas born of his preoccupations and his labor, that were unfamiliar to him.

And everything that he had thought, sought and found during those intervals in his personality filled him with astonishment and amazement.

Omnipotent nature has its ironies, for nothing was more different than the art and reflections of André Fortis during the distinct periods of his double life. The Other was excessive, carried away every novelty, feverish and paroxysmic. On the contrary, the young man's slightly melancholy gentleness was the charm of his gesture, his voice and his gaze.

It was that gentleness that had slowly seduced Mademoiselle de Jandrieu and inspired confidence in her mother and the general. It was, moreover, a gentleness that seemed to have become his very character, the young man's unique fashion of being, a gentleness that was found imprinted like a light silvery mist in his habitual works: placid visions that sometimes, without pastiche or influence, equaled Cazin's placid evenings of the villages, fields and hills around Boulogne.[11] And the sadness that André experienced in thinking about his condition, the threat of that confiscation of his personality by another, had melted, like a layer of snow hiding the tenderness of primroses, under the gaze and influence of the young woman.

Timid and hesitant at first, André had allowed his confidence to grow. He had lost hope, going through life like a man under threat of being arrested from one day to the next and thrown into prison, but a summer encounter, a naïve smile, the

---

[11] Jean-Charles Cazin (1840-1901) was renowned for the "poetical" charm of his landscapes.

caress of a woman's voice, had returned hope to him. He hastened to consult Dr. Burke.

"Can I marry? Am I mad?"

"You're not mad, my dear boy, you've been ill—and the secondary condition that you've passed through won't recur; you're cured of your illness."

"Cured? You can affirm that? You can swear it to me?"

"I don't swear, I believe. I believe it firmly—and above all, I order you to believe it. You are *you*. Your personality belongs to you. You're free."

That was the prescription and the instruction of Dr. Chardin.

"Free to love, to succeed, to be a husband and a father?" André had asked.

"Free in your destiny," Dr. Burke had replied, in all the plenitude of his conscience and confidence.

The André had let himself go, without resistance, in his love for Cécile. It seemed to him, in fact, that nothing could henceforth trouble his quietude, obliterate his joy. He felt young, healthy, full of confidence, cheerful in contemplation of the future. Dr. Burke's gaze was not one of those that can weaken. And, encouraged by Madame Jandrieu, after one last conversation with the doctor, he had dared to ask for Cécile's hand.

The engagement had last three months. André had rented a studio at Ville-d'Avray in order to be nearer to the Jandrieus, who, after returning from Trouville, were spending the first weeks of autumn at Marnes.[12]

---

[12] Marnes-la-Coquette, nowadays famous because its inhabitants have the highest average per capita income in France but notorious when the novel was written because local opposition has prevented Louis Pasteur from building his Institut there after he was given a portion of local land in order to continue his experiments on rabies vaccine, for fear that his experimental animals might escape.

The sudden death of Dr. Burke, carried away by an embolism, had terrified the young man momentarily. He loved the old physician, who had cared for him in his childhood, profoundly. Then too, Adam Burke was the confidant of his anguishes, the imperative master who enjoined him to hope, to believe. In losing him, André lost the great cordial support of his existence, and a bewildered distress had momentarily take possession of his mind. He felt surrounded by darkness again. The choruses of *Manfred*, with their satanic sonorities, came back to him like the echoes of a sinister beyond. He had the specter of the Other before him.

A glance or a smile from Cécile chased those night-birds away, and then he recalled his old friend's words: "I order you to believe. You're free. You're *you*." The dead doctor still spoke to him.

He believed, and he hoped He dreamed. He allowed himself to be lulled and drawn along by love, and to live. It had all disappeared; it was vain; it was dead. He had only to love and be loved.

Then, at the last moment, doubt and fear had gripped him. Tomorrow, he would marry Mademoiselle de Jandrieu; tomorrow, Cécile—all that grace and candor—would belong to him. He would smile at that virginal visage. He would bear away into the unknown that young woman who had said to him the previous day, from the bottom of her soul, while offering her forehead to be kissed: "My entire life is yours, and I'm very happy!"

Tomorrow? Atrocious anguish had gripped him at that thought, and he had been fearful of the iron band squeezing his temples.

Then he had thought of Dr. Chardin. He remembered that Burke had said to him: a master; *the* master.

He had hurried to the physician's home as toward a supreme hope. Had he the right to condemn an exquisite creature like Cécile to live henceforth with a being marked by an indelible flaw? Might Burke, in his affection, not have been mistaken? Might the physician not have lied, in trying to save a man, by saying: "You're free!" Might that freedom not lead to disappointment, a sinister revelation, ending in dementia?

In the fearful doubt of that thought, he thought of that joyful and honest family, the father emotional at the idea of seeing his daughter depart, the smiling, resigned mother, and the young woman gazing at the wedding-ring on her finger and trying on the following day's white dress. His decision was made, as clear and absolute as a judicial sentence. If Monsieur Chardin hesitated, he would not. Better a bloodstain on the wedding-dress than the kiss or the bite of a madman.

But now, a few words from the illustrious scientist had rendered to André, full of youth, the faith suggested by the dead physician. He was free to make his life as he wished. He was free to hope. He would hope. And the plane-trees with the autumn-bitten leaves outlined against a blue Italian sky—he, or rather the Other, had seen that sky in Parma—seemed to him to be a kind of golden aureole around the blonde hair and radiantly joyful smile of his fiancée.

III. The Marriage of André Fortis

It was an exquisite evening, that final evening when, alone in the small drawing-room, while Monsieur and Madame Jandrieu chatted about the future in the next room, the two young people—the morrow's spouses—exchanged the last thoughts and words of beings who, still strangers, would bear the same name and share the same destiny the following day.

Tomorrow! It was delicious, that word, which recurred in their speech like a joyful carillon saluting a dawn. Tomorrow! It was as if an entire poem of love were contained in those three syllables spoken and repeated with vocal caresses and pressures of the hand. They were sitting in the room, cluttered with trinkets, paintings, ornaments and lace, in which the gifts for the next day's reception were set out. The exhibition of fans and gold jewelry, with the cards of the donors laid out here and there, placed on cushions or slipped into silverware, resembled a luxurious display of disparate artistic bric-à-brac. There were marvels there, and mediocre offerings, in the taste of the friends who had chosen the souvenirs in question, and in the singular promiscuity of the little tables in the modern style, the antiques, the Gallé glassware and the Lalique combs, beside bourgeois crystals, ancient liqueur-decanters or old-fashioned adornments, two generations seemed to be rubbing shoulders, affirming their preferences by means of new vogues or past elegances. In accordance with the fashionable custom, changing a boudoir into a shop, the gifts had been put on display so that the guests, tomorrow, could estimate their value, and discuss their quantity and their weight.

André and Cécile did not care about that show of vanity. Hand in hand, they recalled their memories, and forged dreams. She gazed at him with her blue eyes, all of her delicate physiognomy smiling and bright, illuminated by confidence and love. And he, enveloping the slender creature whose supple body was extended on the sofa with an expression of protection and devotion, approached his lips to the little pink ear of the child who would be his wife tomorrow, and slowly, in a murmur, said: "I love you!"

It was the first time he had addressed her as *tu*, and the timid, anxious, slightly reserved fiancé that he had been became a passionate lover, speaking a language that seemed to Cécile to be an unknown music. She had blushed at that unexpected *tu*, which was like an assumption of possession of her entire being by the man she had chosen, and she allowed her pretty blonde head, as if it had become heavy with new thoughts, to fall upon the young man's shoulder.

"Yes, you love me!" she replied, in a scarcely perceptible voice. "And how happy I am!"

Their hands, which were to be joined at the altar, did not quit one another.

General de Jandrieu, paternal and cordial, interrupted the duet with a "Well now?" and then added: "My dear children, I imagine that time seems short to you, but it's passing. It's getting late. And Cécile has to get up early tomorrow. The dress! The famous dress!"

André got up. Cécile smiled.

"You're right, Papa!"

"I'm always right!"

The fiancé took his leave of Madame de Jandrieu, who held out her hands to him, her gaze emotional. Cécile accompanied him into the antechamber, alone, while he put on his coat, and he sought the young woman's forehead, posing one last kiss there, in order that she might say to him, in her turn, slowly and softly: "I love you too!"

André carried away a world of joy in those few words. He forgot everything else, thinking only of Cécile, absorbed in one unique thought: "I shall be the husband of that delightful creature!" All the rest, the anguishes and bad dreams, disappeared, dissipated, expelled and clarified by joy.

He slept like a baby and woke up to happy thoughts, as cheerful as the sun that filtered through the curtains, making motes of dust shine in the rays of light like specks of mica.

And it was with a light heart, an alert confidence and a sensation of gratitude toward destiny that he set off for the dwelling where his fiancée was waiting, beneath a white veil, in a white dress...

The doors of Saint-Roch were open now, and the cortege advanced on the carpet decking the stone steps, toward the altar. The organ hurled into the vaults the Wedding March that has saluted so many couples heading into the unknown in that manner, with smiles on their lips: the Wedding March of feast days succeeding on those same organ keys, beneath the same stone vaults, the Funeral March, which destiny had played in advance more than once for married couples avid for happiness.

Before the altar, when he placed the wedding-ring on Cécile's finger, André felt impressions of childhood returning to him, and it seemed to him that he was recovering himself as he had been a long time ago—such a long time ago!—when he had had faith. His finger squeezed the hand that the young woman placed in his with a tender gentleness, and emotion did not cause her to tremble as she gave herself to him, trustingly, certain of his affection and devotion.

Beneath the priest's blessing Cécile bowed her head with a fervor similar to the clarity with which the "I do" binding the two human creatures together had been pronounced before the Maire. And the relatives on the velvet-clad chairs gazed at the groom's black suit alongside the bride's white dress, in the light of the altar.

As the couple, now united, traversed the double hedge of guests, friends and curiosity-seekers, envious, interrogative or smiling faces watching the newlyweds go by, a ray of sunlight passed through the stained-glass windows, enveloping the blonde beauty of the new Madame Fortis like an aureole. A beam of electric light could not have brightened that pretty face more surely, which seemed joyful in that sudden illumination, and the superstitious smiled at the sudden intervention of the sun, saying: "It's an omen of happiness!"

Cécile leaned on André's arm, and that confident and charming pressure seemed to the young man to be a caress.

The cortege followed the young couple, truly beautiful in the unconscious pride of innocent love, and the sacristy filled up with the enormous crowd of guests, pushing and jostling through the chairs to the door. The disorderly throng formed a more orderly file there, with the obligatory handshakes and embraces, compliments and "all my best wishes": the inevitable sequence of banalities and salutations, indifferent faces sketching obligatory smiles, but among which there was, from time to time, a friendly gaze, a sincere word, or the appearance of some old comrade reappearing for one day, inserting their note of honest affection and tender cordiality.

Entirely happy with that urgency, one wave succeeding anther, the newlyweds and the relatives nevertheless found the file along which they made their way very long, and found the reception in the bustle of Monsieur de Jandrieu's drawing-rooms—the assault of the buffet, the inspection of the gifts, the compliments and "best wishes" reiterated among the bunches of white roses or lilacs—interminable.

In fact, a kind of fever, an intoxication, with all the noise and all the people, gave that second file-past the appearance of an unreal spectacle, and the guests around the glasses of champagne, iced chocolate and sandwiches, together with the buzz of voices, laughter and rustling silks, and the heady hot-house atmosphere, seemed to the married couple to be actors in some rapid-fire comedy, in which guests succeeded guests, staircases and elevators bringing and carrying away visitors who all repeated the same words in the same banal phrases with the same handshakes—which, replacing the fraternal accolade, have become the current and expected gesture of greeting.

Cécile came and went, radiant with the crown of orange-blossom in her beautiful hair, the color of ripe wheat; and when she passed nearby, André, whose gaze sought her perpetually in the elegant crowd, gave her an emotional, joyful and proud smile. He truly believed that he was living a dream. So that beautiful young woman who was standing there, admired and envied, as radiant in these apartments as she had been in the church beneath the gilded sunbeam, was his! She was his wife. She bore his name. He had chased away lugubrious thoughts and black dreads. He could hope, and live.

Then, all of a sudden, in the hubbub of the reception, as he was making his way through one of the drawing rooms in order to rejoin Cécile, he stopped dead. A singular impression—not a pain but, on the contrary, an almost agreeable sensation, something like a wave of drowsiness, like the gesture of an invisible soother drawing him gently toward her—traversed his brain, and it seemed to him that an unperceived finger was touching his head on the right side. And André Fortis remained motionless, rooted to the spot.

Abruptly, he felt gripped by terror.

Was it a crisis? Was the past, the frightful past, not dead after all?

Come on, come on...am I mistaken? The odor of the flowers...the noise...the crowd...it's permissible to have a headache. It's a migraine, nothing more. I have a migraine, that's all.

He tore his thoughts way from the anguish that had abruptly nailed him to the carpet. He went toward the next room. Cécile was laughing with her friends. One of them, armed with a camera, was determined to take a photograph of the newlyweds on the balcony.

In passing, André perceived a kind of pale, slightly haggard visitor in a mirror. It was his own image. Smiling a little while before, his features had taken on an expression of sharp anxiety.

I'm being stupid! Doctor Chardin told me that I'm free, liberated. Nothing more to fear.

And when Cécile's friend—and American, Miss Howe—repeated: "Yes, yes, I want to take a photograph of you; there

41

are memories that it's a pleasure to keep," he said, gaily: "Let's have our photograph taken, then."

On the balcony, far from all the noise that reached them through the window, he forgot the dispelled sensation. Bareheaded, in the fresh air of the beautiful day, which seemed spring-like, he no longer felt the pressure of that hand on his skull, nor any obsession or headache.

"There won't be any more fine weather," said Miss Howe. "This is St. Martin's summer. When you're very, very old, you'll be delighted to recover this summer in my verascope."[13]

"Oh! Very old! We have plenty of time."

They laughed. The American thanked them.

"It's done. Oh, it doesn't take long. As brief as saying *I do.*"

And they went back into the apartment, which gradually emptied, the buffet cleared out, the carafes run dry and the flower-petals fallen on to the floor. That solitude, for which they yearned in the lassitude of the day of official joy, seemed delightful to them.

Gradually, the evening entered the apartment, where the odor of liqueurs and roses floated. The melancholy of the dusk filled the rooms, invaded not long before but now deserted. Monsieur and Madame Jandrieu thought that soon—so soon!—Cécile would be going away, leaving the dwelling even emptier, especially the little bedroom with the blue-green flower-patterned curtains in which she had sent her last day as a young maiden.

---

[13] The verascope, invented by the Frenchman Jules Richard before 1900—long before the popular "stereo camera" marketed by Kodak in the 1950s—was a camera with two lenses, which captured images designed to be viewed through a device that would combine the two into a single three-dimensional image. Miss Howe is referring to the latter device.

She went from one item of furniture to another, harassed but joyful, sitting down and saying, with bright laughter: "I'm exhausted!"

The general, trying to smile, trying to smile and appear cheerful, replied: "Fortunately, one doesn't get married every day!"

The family meal was subdued, the parents thinking about the departure, Cécile of the flight of sorts that would soon separate her from those beloved beings to draw her into the unknown.

"Life is strange, all the same," said Monsieur de Jandrieu. "One brings up a child, who is the joy of all one's days, only for a gentleman one does not know, a passer-by—oh, I like that passer-by a great deal, my dear André—to take her away from you. She was everything yesterday, but will no longer be anything tomorrow. It's as banal as life. All parents have made that reflection, but when one has made it oneself, for oneself, oh, believe me, it's a trifle troubling! I'm not very hungry."

All the hopes of the parents were translated in gazes, as tender as blessings, benevolently fixed on the spouses. Abdication is the lot of the old; if the young do not forget them completely they are consoled for their loss and rewarded for their trouble.

Madame de Jandrieu gave her daughter one last kiss; the general shook his son-in-law's hand as if to crush it, and Cécile climbed into the coupé that was waiting at the door, with tears in her eyes, and André, happy and joyful, forgot his dreads.

"It's not from grief that I'm weeping," said Cécile, sitting beside her husband. "I'll miss those who'll be alone, but I'm happy, you know!" She addressed him formally, as *vous*.

"*Vous*? Why say *vous*?"

"I don't know..."

The informal form of address, which had seemed quite natural to her beneath her parents' roof, intimidated and troubled her in the privacy of the vehicle that was carrying them away, as if in flight—and yet she was not afraid. It really was the companion of whom she had dreamed who was beside her, whose devoted gaze she felt fixed upon her. When the coupé passed beneath a gas-lamp, the light came in through the window, momentarily illuminating André's smiling face and the white dress, and then disappeared...and Cécile allowed her blonde head to descend slowly on to the young man's shoulder, murmuring: "Yes, happy! I'm happy and I love you."

Then he hugged her to his breast and his lips sought the maiden's forehead, and placed an ecstatic kiss there.

They gazed at one another in the same way, holding hands, in the street.

"We'll live to be very old," said André, gaily.

"Very old?"

"Yes. I've just interrogated a sign. I told myself that if the first letter encountered was an O, it would mean that we would be together for a long time, and if it were an R..."

"And what did the sign say?"

"*Coiffeur! Virgile coiffeur!*"

"*Virgile?*" she started to laugh. "Good old Virgile.[14] You're superstitious, then?"

"Very. I only half-believe in those responses of chance, though. When the response is favorable, I'm content. *Virgile coiffeur!* We'll live to be very old..."

---

[14] Like André, Cécile seems to be content to ignore the fact that the R in *Virgile* comes before the O in *coiffeur* [hairdresser], thus failing to note the supplementary omen that Virgil was Dante to the *Inferno*.

IV. The Crisis Recurs

The coupé stopped in front of a house in the Rue Muril-lo, where the former Mademoiselle Jandrieu's chambermaid was waiting for Madame Fortis. Cécile went rapidly through the concierge's lodge, fleeing curious gazes, and only the rus-tle of her dress troubled the silence of the staircase as she climbed up swiftly, as if furtively, to the apartment in which they were to live. From the antechamber onwards, the electric light illuminated the flowers, whose arrangement Madame Jandrieu had supervised in order to give the new apartment as festive appearance. The bunches of white lilacs brought a hint of spring into it, a décor of joy.

Cécile smiled at the cheerful frame of light and flowers.

They remained silent momentarily, standing in front of the fireplace in their bedroom, their faces reflected in the mir-ror, their elbows leaning on the marble, their hands joined. They gazes had a fervor of prayer. The delightful solitude that was commencing their new life filled them with the same ex-quisite emotion, an anxiety that melted into tenderness.

"My wife!" said André. "What a word, which contains an entire existence, ours henceforth. My wife!"

Her only response was to take his hands, and the mute grip declaimed an entire poem of affection. She did not have to speak for André to understand. He read her soul like an open book, and quietly, leaving the seductive and graceful creature alone to take off the wedding dress that was molded to her figure, he went away, saying nothing, merely making a sign that he would be there, close by, in the next room, which was connected with the one in which Cécile would sleep.

It was a masculine sort of room with a bookcase, a desk and a few select paintings. André pressed the electric switch, and after having looked round, adjusted a frame that was not straight, took a book off the shelves and put it back without opening it, and let himself fall into an armchair. He was pensive.

The entire day seemed chimerical. That noise, that crowd, that file, all those faces, disappeared—had that really been real? Was he really in the Rue Murillo, a few steps away from that young woman, who was his wife, in the apartment he had rented, and whose furnishing he had supervised?

Yes, all that was true! Mademoiselle de Jandrieu was Madame Fortis. This abode was the nest, the hearth, the refuge. He had his studio upstairs, in the light, with the Parc Monceau for a horizon. He was going to work. He was going to love and be loved. It was a turning-point, a happy turning-point, a new life.

Or rather, life itself! he thought. *For have really I been alive until now?*

He could not even remember the dalliances that had preceded this true love.

He listened, wondering what Cécile was thinking now, what she was doing, whether she was thinking about him. He could not hear any noises; the next room seemed empty.

Perhaps she's praying.

It did not displease him, a freethinker, that the child might be praying for their common happiness.

He would have liked to tell her so, to speak to her, to see her again. He found the solitude strange after the hubbub of the day.

The clock chimed. The sound made him jump.

I'm so nervous!

He got up, took out a book a random. It was a volume of Musset: *Les Nuits.*

In the days when I was a student
I was staying up late one night...

46

He closed the book again, swiftly. That "Nuit de Décembre"[15] had always troubled him, finding therein a genuine sense of the fantastic. The doctor had even said to him one day that the man who had evoked that night was, medically speaking a madman.

These doctors! Such a poet!

He found it bizarre, though, that the hazard of his gesture had taken him straight to that item of verse, which made his nerves vibrate as if beneath the bow of a violin!

When a student dressed in black
Came to sit down beside me
Who resembled me like a twin...

And the lines that André knew by heart sang like a chorus, coming back into the young man's memory like a lament. He had sat down again and it seemed to him that behind him, behind the armchair, someone was moving.

In the mirror, he saw himself turning round swiftly, interrogatively, his face pale.

No one!

And who could it have been? It makes no sense.

He started to laugh, and head himself laughing.

That damned de Musset! It's his fault.

He got up, whistled some tune or other, and suddenly, invisibly, felt as if he were being drawn back, driven toward the same obsessive idea.

I was staying up late one night...

---

[15] The poem in question, a significant literary work dealing with the notion of a "double" or "second self," who presents himself to the poem's viewpoint character as a phantom, was published in 1835, as part of an impassioned and agonized sequence of four in which de Musset looked back on his life in the context of his recently-ruptured love affair with Aurora Dudevant ("George Sand").

He experienced the strange sensation that the person staying up late on the winter night was him, and that he was experiencing the character's anguishes and terrors. There was a noise in Cécile's room, the sound of a furtive voice coming through the door, and the obsessive sensation was abruptly driven away. But the room remained mute, to the point that André now feared some anger—a faint, an accident...

Should I call to her?

He tried to get a grip on himself. He wanted to leave her free. Soon, laughing, he would tell her about his fears...

Gradually, however, those fears took a different form. And it was for him, his own suffering, that he was now anxious. Could he not feel, in his temples, and there, on the right side of his skull, that singular sensation of pressure, that of an invisible finger pressing on the bones, touching the brain? Yes, that almost charming, tempting heaviness, like an attractive sleep, very soft, that particular sleep, cradling in its cruelty, the unhealthy sleep that made him another man, that imposed a new personality upon him, the sleep whose approach he had not felt for a long time, such a long time...it was coming, that sleep, like an unexpected, vanished specter, a melting fog that was taking on substance, looming up, sliding into his own individuality, or rather driving it away, transforming it.

"Ah!" said André, aloud. "Doctor Chardin was mistaken, then! Or did Doctor Chardin lie? The crisis is here! It's come back! But that's terrible!"

And, his voice becoming hoarse, he repeated that terrible word, full of horror for him: "The crisis!"

Then he stood up, very straight, gazed momentarily, with a wild expression and a frightful dolor, at the door that separated him from Cécile, and then, his tread unsteady, attempted to go to the little chest of drawers next to the bookcase, where he had placed a weapon—a revolver—a few days before.

He searched in his pocket for the key.

"Where is it, then, the key?"

His hand, becoming feverish, did not find it.

A torpor took hold of him, rendering his head heavy, and while he tried to connect up the ideas scattered by the prelude to sleep, his heavy head seemed to draw him forwards. Defeated, he finally sat down in the armchair…where—anxious in her turn, after an overly long wait, timidly, her heart beating forcefully—Cécile opened the door and found him sitting, not asleep, but dreaming with his eyes open.

She stopped. Expecting a smile or a word; then, a trifle surprised, she advanced slowly, while Fortis raised his eyes to look at her.

In her white peignoir, with the light of the lamps enlivening the fine gold of her hair, she seemed even rosier and more delectably frail and slender, with the elegance of a Jean Goujon Diana,[16] but a young Diana whose pride was still timid.

André's immobility surprised her; he did not even seem to have seen that she was there. She dared not move forward; and remained silent; a word from his lips would have seemed like an appeal. The slight sound of the hem of her peignoir sliding along the carpet ought to have alerted André, but he did not look at her. He was staring into the void, at some unknown image.

For a moment, she thought he was asleep, but he stood up abruptly, and this time turned to look at her. His eyes seemed astonished.

He made a gesture of great politeness, without affectation—the gesture of a gallant man greeting a woman and excusing himself for going past her. Very softly, he said: "I beg your pardon, Madame."

Cécile thought that she was dreaming. That voice was no longer André's. It had a singular sonority. The words pronounced were curt; the request for pardon seemed to be ad-

---

[16] The 16th century sculptor Jean Goujon designed "Diana with a Stag" (c.1549) for Henri II's mistress Diane de Poitiers, for display at the Château d'Anet; it is now in the Louvre, where Clarétie would have seen it.

dressed to a stranger. Madame! That word *Madame*, after the tenderness of the confidences murmured in her ear in the coupé that had brought the lovers, seemed like a word in a new, unexpected language. André had sketched the bow as if he were holding his hat in his hand, and he drew away at a hasty pace, opened the door abruptly and disappeared into the shadows of the next room.

Left alone, Cécile experienced a singular sensation of terror, as if she had suddenly slipped out of reality and found herself in a vision. Had she really seen the man who was her husband there, in that empty armchair? Had André really appeared, standing upright, looking at her with that surprised expression, which had surprised her in her turn? Had he really spoken? Had she really heard the words: *I beg your pardon, Madame*?

She examined the objects surrounding her: the furniture, the open bookcase, the book dropped on the carpet. Was that unfamiliar room in which she found herself alone a stage set, an image in a dream, or something tangible and real? The door open into darkness, through which André had disappeared, gave her a sensation of fear. She had a desire to cry out, alone in the house with the man from whom she had nothing to fear. Without him, however, she felt threatened by a confused danger, enveloped by an invisible menace.

Why had he gone? Why that change in his voice? She called out, then: "André! André!"

Through the open door, the next room was visible, still dark and empty. He did not come. He did not reply.

"André! André!"

He must have heard, though. The cry became strident now, the appeal for help that of a terrified child. And still there was that hole of shadow, that sensation of abandonment in an echoing emptiness.

"Oh, I want to go! I want to go!" Cécile repeated, and the appeals of her childhood returned instinctively to her trembling lips—those that even dying old men recover, to demand help, from the depths of their memory—*Papa, Maman*—the puerility of the cries sublimated by the peril.

She went back into her bedroom as if she were pursued. She had dimmed the lights a little while before. The white patch of her dress, extended on a sofa like a shroud, frightened her. She turned up the lights. The flowers were still framing the mirror over the fireplace, but Cécile saw a convulsed face in the glass that was her own, and, just as André had previously been astonished by his image, she was frightened by her own face.

Bewildered, she repeated her appeal, pronounced his name again, and heard it fall into silence again: "Andre! Where are you, André?"

She did not understand; she did not try to understand. She was simply in haste to flee, to escape that void, that solitude, to hear a human voice instead of struggling in that silence, as disquieting as a gulf.

What if she were to ring for her chambermaid? Yes! She already had a finger on the ivory button. But what would she say to her? What! Cécile was not going to ask her to leave the house, to accompany her to her parents' house, if she fled. And why flee? André was here. He would come back. He had not gone.

No, no—since, just then, on the threshold of her room, he reappeared, looking at her as if interrogating her, with a smile in his black beard.

Then a great cry of bewilderment precipitated Cécile toward her husband. "Oh, it's you! Finally, there you are!" And she ran to him as if to take refuge in his arms. But the same astonished expression that had surprised her before stopped her again, and André's eyes looked at her in an interrogatory fashion, as if he did not know, or did not recognize, the woman who was in front of him.

"Oh, if you only knew how frightened I was," she said, putting all her terror, tenderness and submission into her informal mode of address. "Oh, but you're here now, and I'm reassured. Was I mad? I thought about ringing for Marthe, of going away! Yes, can you believe it? I didn't know what was happening. I called for you, and you didn't reply. So, you understand..."

She drew nearer to him, waiting for him to hold out his arms to press her against him like a poor fearful bird. He did not budge. He stayed there, listening attentively to what she said, with the expression of a man striving to understand words whose precise meaning escapes him.

In the end, smiling politely and repeating the same words of apology, he said, slowly: "I beg your pardon, Madame. Why am I here? Why are you here?"

He looked at himself in the mirror. "White cravat...black suit...why? I have no soirée today. I have to work tomorrow. A painting that's expected. In order to start work earlier, I'll spend the night in my studio. I'll be better placed." Then he repeated: "But why are you here? Why?"

And the tone of interrogation was so profound, insistent and anxious that Cécile took a step back, certain that the man was mad. Yes, drunk or mad—and her terror returned, more intense, as if she were locked in a lunatic's padded cell.

The excessive politeness of the man who was her husband, but was treating her as a stranger, looking at her as if at an unknown visitor, seemed more frightening than an evident threat. He gestured an invitation for her to sit down, and he repeated his question: "Why are you here? To whom do I have the honor of speaking?"

To whom?

She looked him full in the face to see whether the interrogation might be some strange joke.

"To whom? But to me, your wife! Don't you remember, André?"

As if he were trying to understand something ungraspable, he repeated: "My wife?" He looked at her for a long time, with a kind of tender pity: an expression full of generosity, and forgiving. "But I have no wife. I'm not married. I like to live freely, to work in my studio, with complete liberty in the world. I shall never marry."

The tone of the words was cold, resolute and reasonable. She believed now that it was a test, whose meaning she could not grasp. She wondered if she were really conscious of what was happening around her, of what she could see and hear.

Sitting before that man in an evening suit, among those flowers, under the electric light, it gradually came to seem to her that she was speaking to a stranger, in an unknown house, and that the entire day—with the departure for the church, the file past the cortege, the sacristy, the afternoon, the crowd, and then the solitude of the tête-à-tête in the coupé—was a vision, something fugitive, that had appeared and disappeared like the bewildered phantoms caught in cinematic projections.

V. Is This Madness?

There was a dream-like sensation in what she was experiencing. It seemed that a yawning gulf had suddenly opened up around her. She felt dizzy. Either what had happened to her during the day was a vision, or what appeared to her now was a nightmare. That the exquisite fiancé of blessed hours, the tender lover of that flight into smiling joy was the distant, cold interrogator who was here now, with a different personality under the same features, a voice with a new unexpected and glacial tone emerging from the same lips, appeared to her to be impossible, incredible—and that caused a thought to rise to her buzzing ears, her throbbing temples and her aching head: *Either André is putting on some incomprehensible act, or he's mad, or I'm mad.*

Then the curt, decisive and seemingly sententious voice continued: "No, Madame, no, I shall never marry! An artist must have no impediments. I have my work to do. A great work. I have also to live—to live with all the intensity that modern life offers a man: to come and go, to travel and see…to see everything. Everything!"

"But I shall share that existence with you, André. I too want to see and want to live. I will be the most devoted of companions, in everything and for everything—you know that very well."

She waited for a response, but the young man remained mute, his face expressing increasing surprise—and the dark eyes arrested on Cécile's with a stubborn fixity.

"Yes, André, yes, everywhere and always. But I've told you that; I've said so. And the more beautiful the dreamed work is, the prouder I shall be of you! So proud!"

He got to his feet abruptly. "Truly, Madame, I apologize for not understanding what you are trying to tell me. Where do you think you are?"

"In your home…our home."

"To whom do you think you are speaking?"

"To my husband, André Fortis."

"I am, in fact, André Fortis—yes, you know my name—but I'm not your husband."

"You're not my husband? We weren't kneeling before the altar this morning? You didn't put this ring on my finger?"

She showed him her extended hand. The golden ring gleamed on her finger, under the lamp.

"That ring?"

"You haven't taken me from my parents' house and brought me here? Come on, André. What do you want? To test me, to scare me? I don't understand. But please, I beg you, stop this joke or I'll go out of my mind. You don't know how badly it's affecting me. I understand that it's a game, but why? For pity's sake, André, give me a reassuring word. I'm afraid—I swear to you that I'm afraid!"

She was certain that he would cease the frightful joke, that his mask was about to fall, that she would soon recover the exquisite being with whom she was to share her life. The absurd challenge was about to end.

He had wanted to scare her. Why had he wanted that? Cécile had no idea; but now, since she was trembling, what was the point in continuing?

"Oh, I'm afraid, I'm afraid!"

Impassively, André replied: "You know my name but I don't know yours. To whom do I have the honor of speaking?"

Oh! This time, there could be no doubt. The man had undergone some frightful metamorphosis. André Fortis was no longer the same, was no longer himself. A madman, no doubt. She was the wife of a madman!

She stood up, placing the armchair in which she had been sitting between them.

"You know my name, André. I was Mademoiselle de Jandrieu; I am Madame Cécile Fortis."

"There is no Cécile Fortis," said the voice, becoming strident. "There is no Madame Fortis. I'm not married! I'm free! Ah...Madame Fortis! Madame Fortis! A woman who would be a jailer, a spy every day! Oh, no, no! No, no, no!"

He strode back and forth across the room, with broad, staccato gestures, and his polite coldness was succeeded by an almost frantic agitation. Impulsively, his fingers searched for some bottle or trinket that he could hurl to the floor and smash, shattering it into pieces.

Cécile thought she understood that a sort of wrath had gripped him: the desperate wrath of a being free the day before who finds himself bound, as if imprisoned for life. She was frightened. André regretted having married her. He was recoiling from their first steps in life, ready to revolt against his duties. She had killed his happiness. Why? How? She did not know—but that happiness was lying there, more broken than one of the objects that André, resisting his impulse, wanted to shatter.

"Madame Fortis! A Madame Fortis! Where is this Madame Fortis? When you hear a Madame Fortis announced, you can say that she is lying. There is no Madame Fortis! There is a man named André Fortis—and that's me—who has no intention of being attached to anyone, and who, in fact, I can assure you, Madame, is not attached to anyone. Anyone!"

"I understand," she said, with great dignity. You want me to leave this house now, which I entered so happy. I shall leave. I shall leave tomorrow. Tomorrow, I shall return to my parents. You will be obeyed. There will no longer be a Madame Fortis."

Suddenly calmed down, he drew nearer to her, smiled, and shrugged his shoulders slightly.

"But that's not what I'm saying to you, Madame. I'm telling you that I'm not married, that there're is no Madame Fortis because there is, in fact, none. And I beg your pardon for having unwittingly frightened you, by announcing the simplest of truths in the most natural fashion in the world."

She would have preferred to see him as he had been previously, angry and insolent. This mildness, more in conformity with his nature, succeeding a fit of anger as if by an effort of will, appeared to the unfortunate woman to be a kind of insult. It gave his words the cold tone of a judicial sentence. He found that thunderbolt "the simplest of truths." With the studied correctness and artificial politeness of a man of the world, he was excusing himself for that revelation, that transformation, which, for Cécile, had something incredible, sinister and insane about it, but which remained for him a fact, and nothing more: a fact, as if the fantastic nature of the situation had escaped him.

It did indeed escape him. Through the disturbance of her own reason, Cécile divined an absolute conviction in André: the conviction of a dementia, as she increasingly saw it. She had married a madman! She had only one thought: to flee; to return to her maidenly bedroom, to become Mademoiselle de Jandrieu again, since there was no Madame Fortis.

She looked at the clock. It was about to strike two.

André divined her thought.

"It's too late for you to go, Madame. I repeat to you that since hazard has caused you to come here at such an hour, you may stay here until daylight. I shall sleep in my studio."

Once again he bowed, and disappeared into the profound darkness of the drawing-room, as he had a short while before.

Then, with an instinctive leap, Cécile raced to the door to shoot the bolt. She did not want to see him again. She was afraid of seeing him again. All alone, locked in that strange nuptial chamber, she wanted to try to take account of what had happened, to collect her thoughts, to figure out what to do.

Let's see, let's see... what? Is he mad? He must be mad!

She had sat down in the armchair from which, just now, she had been looking at him. Elbows on her knees, fingernails in her teeth, she thought hard. Two o'clock! Monsieur and Madame de Jandrieu, back there, were doubtless talking about her happiness. They would not have gone to bed yet. Her happiness? What if she went to tell them, right away, what had happened to her happiness! Poor people! What would become of them on seeing her reappear like this, as a fugitive, by night?

57

No, tomorrow. Let's wait until tomorrow. I'll go tomorrow.

She looked at the closed door. With that bolt drawn, she had nothing to fear. She was at home. She would wait for daylight. But what a long night it would be!

Her poor eyes, full of tears, went to the flowers on the mantelpiece—the sad flowers that had become funereal. There were bizarrely-formed orchids among them—flowers of macabre visions. The white corollas and buds of orange-blossom, were smiling, close by, in the light. Nothing was more ironically heart-rending that that festival adornment surviving crumbled hope.

She had married a madman! She was the wife of a madman!

Nothing in life frightened her more than that ferocious malady suppressing a being, making a human creature into a kind of puppet, whose strings were pulled by dementia. There was no doubt about it: the being that had spoken the words she had heard a few moments ago was certainly not in possession of his reason. And she bore his name! She given herself to him with all her heart, and she loved him! Even in her terror she felt an impression of pity giving her the desire to open that door again and go to him—whatever sacrifice she would be making—in order to find out whether he was suffering.

Where was he? In his studio? Upstairs. What if he called to her? What if he needed help? What if no one answered?

I'll go see. It's impossible that he won't come back to himself.

But she stopped, confronted by the terror she had that she would find him still impassive and resolute, repeating: "There is no Madame Fortis!"

Sometimes she felt a gripped by a shiver of cold; sometimes, opening the grille of the heater, she felt stifled, invaded by fever. She interrogated the clock. She listened to the sounds of the night. The hours chimed; the vague sounds of fiacres, rolling in the distance, seemed indistinct murmurs; a locomotive whistle, even more distant, tore the darkness like a sharp spike driven into her happiness.

She felt exhausted, although she did not want to go to sleep, and wrapped herself in her mantle—but gradually, in the drowsiness of fatigue, she let herself slide toward sleep, among the confused hypnagogic images that precede sleep, in which cheerful visions were mingled—the cortege, the music, her mother's smiles André's loving words, and the childish laughter in the carriage, the carriage that had carried them toward life, their happy life together. And gradually, forgetting the disillusionment and fear, happy, lulled by those consoling images of joy. Mademoiselle de Jandrieu—who was and was not Madame de Fortis—fell asleep in the closed room that had seemed to her, a little while before, to be as menacing as a padded cell, as lugubrious as a prison.

VI. The Awakening

When she awoke, it was daylight. The gray November light was filtering through the curtains. She got up, feeling the chill of the cold. She wondered how she came to be in that room, which was unknown to her. She looked round for familiar furniture. She had the sensation of dreaming. She looked through the window, which was prolonged by a stone balcony, leaning her forehead on the glass, at the Parc Monceau, an unfamiliar fragment of the landscape, the desiccated branches of its leafless trees outlined against the pallor of a snowy sky.

The solitude of the park, enveloped in a gray mist, gave her a sudden impression of distance, as if she had woken elsewhere than Paris, in the silence of an unknown city. Clumps of chrysanthemums, with yellow and brown leaflets twisted by frost, a long lawn where the silhouettes of evergreen yews stood out, the black trunks and twisted branches of large leafless trees, strange heaps of straw that provided armor against the cold for wrapped-up palm trees, and in the distance, Gounod's marble monument, seemed to her, with the cupola and the rotunda, like some cemetery through which no visitor was passing, nor any shade, on that icy morning...

She felt desperately sad, lost. The sight of the garden reminded her where she was, and who she was. What an awakening!

So, this was where that poor romance of love commenced in Trouville had led, to finish here, as if in an abyss. She was André's wife, and André, shaken by some neurosis, was here, somewhere, under the same roof, but separated from her by the strange malady that prevented him from recognizing her. What was she going to do now? Go back to the paternal home? Tell all to her dear parents, who believe that she was happy? Flee?

But that would abruptly break all the bonds that attached her to André. It would put something irreparable between him and the future. What if she were patient? What if she were to wait? Perhaps the crisis was temporary.

Yes, but she was afraid. She experienced a profound anguish at the thought that her husband—her husband!—might reappear before her and tell her in the implacable voice that seemed to be that of a judge pronouncing sentence: "There is no Madame Fortis!"

She had always had an instinctive horror of that atrocious malady, madness. On a trip to Dijon with her parents she had visited the Charterhouse[17] where the demented were accommodated. She had heard their lamentations emerging from open windows. She had seen one unfortunate brought in a carriage, crying out, appealing, his eyes haggard, foaming at the mouth, almost carried by the warders. She had heard those desperate cries in her ears for a long time. Had, she, then espoused one of those human wrecks, and would she hear André crying out and complaining like the lunatics of the Charterhouse?

She had a desire to ring for her chambermaid, and feared seeing her appear, announcing some new tragedy. She was a devoted girl, Thérèse, whom Madame de Jandrieu had yielded to her reluctantly. She had served Mademoiselle; she loved her. Her mother was glad to know that she was with Cécile.

Perhaps Thérèse can tell me where he is.

---

[17] The Chartreuse de Champmol, near Dijon was a monastery from the 14th century to the 1789 Revolution, when it was sacked and badly damaged. The remains were subsequently bought by Napoléon I's Minister of the Interior, who completed the demolition; in 1833 the replacement buildings he constructed were bought by the local municipal authorities for adaptation into a lunatic asylum; it is still a psychiatric hospital today, having long been famous enough to incorporate the phrase *aller à la chartreuse* [go to the charterhouse] into the French language as an approximate equivalent of the English "go round the bend."

She pressed the electric button—and the regretted having called. So soon? And what would the chambermaid think when she asked for news of Monsieur?

Thérèse's face did not allow any expression of astonishment to show, and in response to her mistress' question, the chambermaid replied that Monsieur Fortis was already in his studio and had rung for his manservant, François. Monsieur was working.

"Does Madame want me to do her hair?"

"No, I'll do it myself."

She wanted to be alone, to think, to make a decision. She felt that she would be gambling her entire life on the decision and the action that she was about to take. To return to her life as an unmarried woman would be to abandon André to his destiny, to abdicate, to divorce on the first day. And she experienced a tender pity—a maternal pity—for the unfortunate individual she had seen a few hours before, so different from himself. The terror of the poor woman, frightened by madness, was succeeded by a need for devotion, an appetite for sacrifice, which derived more from love than instinctive female charity.

He was working? She wanted to see him. Perhaps she would rediscover in him the delightful, gentle, confident and slightly melancholy fiancé, whose tenderness was almost timid, whose voice—do different from that dry, curt tone that she had heard last night—seemed to her to be music, to which she sometimes listened with her eyes closed, as if lulled by a dream. To that André, she had given herself with all her heart. In spite of the banality of their first meeting, he was not the random husband that a young woman marries to escape the monotony of the paternal home, to liberate herself and be free; no, he really was the elect, the husband for whom she had been waiting, and whom she had chosen, the one who was not a name but was *him*, the man with whom she had sworn to share her existence, with whom she wanted to share her existence.

She did not want, even after the frightful ordeal of that nightmarish night, to destroy that hope by returning to Monsieur de Jandrieu's house. Even if André had been struck by some sudden illness, if the frightful encounter had to be renewed, well, was that not her duty—the duty of a wife? Had she not promised her devotion through all suffering, as she had promised her affection at all times?

He's working! I'll go see him. And I shan't say anything to anyone. No one shall know anything—anything at all.

She got dressed, fatigue giving her pretty child-like face a pallor that added a charm of suffering to all her grace. She went out of her room, went through the empty drawing-room and reached the interior staircase, decked with works of art, paintings and armories that led to André's studio. She paused between steps. As she went up, she felt herself gripped once again by fear. What if she were to find, up there, the apparition with the dark impenetrable eyes, staring at her as if devoid of thought, indecipherable?

She leaned on the banister of sculpted wood. She felt her heart beating. She was tempted to go back down.

Come on! That would be cowardly.

She knocked on the closed door of the studio. A voice replied: "Come in!" It was André's voice—but it was the curt voice, the clipped voice, the hostile voice of the previous night.

It was not André that she was about to find there, behind that door; it was someone unknown, who had appeared to her like a specter of ill-omen.

"I don't want to see him! I don't want to see him!"

She pronounced those words aloud, which she had only intended to think silently, and with an impatient gesture, involuntarily, she opened the door; and in the vast studio, cluttered with precious works, in the distance, sitting in front of his canvas, palette in hand, she saw André, illuminated by the dreary daylight of the vast bay window.

His body half-hunched over his canvas, in an attitude of laborious attention, he did not even raise his head when Cécile came in. He appeared to be in the grip of a fever of endeavor, attracted and attached to his canvas, hypnotized by his own work.

Cécile looked at him. He had taken off his white cravat and his jacket, thrown on to an armchair, and in a black velvet waistcoat he had doubtless resumed his everyday life. His paintings, studies of landscapes, were hanging on the walls, among other works by friends, and throughout the vast studio, luxuriously and artistically furnished, the tapestries, draperies and curtains made a picturesque background for display cases full of choice trinkets, marble busts on their plinths, manikins covered with ancient or Japanese armor, knights of the Middle Ages or Samurai of the time of the *Ronin*—a décor in which every object had its price, its value and, as it were, its biography, revealing an impeccable collector and man of good taste. Among those canvases, wall-hangings and marbles, he seemed like a workman who had been toiling since daybreak, and he let Cécile approach to stand beside the stool on which he was seated without even perceiving that someone was there.

She paused before speaking to him, examining the canvas that André had begun.

She was amazed.

What the painter was seeking to produce, there on to the canvas, was not one of the landscapes whose penetrating poetry had made the young master's reputation—a poetry of gentle, dreamy sadness, extracting from Nature the consoling tenderness of which she was sometimes the harsh stepmother; it was a macabre vision in which, among gilts and colors, in an apotheosis of enchantment in which precious stones seemed to splash the eyes with dazzling pyrotechnics, there was Humanity, incarnate in the diversity of its races, wallowing before an immense idol with the head of a Beast, crushing bodies, pulverizing nudities, making the blood of the heaped up cadavers flow as a wine-press makes the juice of grapes spurt forth, trampling them underfoot like some frightful promenade of Jagannath.

And that monster with a bestial face was the Golden Calf, with, behind it, like two specters, Famine and War: Famine pale and sinister, as if anemic of all blood, of all the sap pumped by the pot-bellied beast, avid and gluttonous; War all bloody, howling, bare-armed, red with murder, as his blade was red, as his feet were red, paddling in the mud of the massacre.

And in front of the Golden Calf were laid down the traitors and the courtesans, the poor and the speculators, the pale-faced workers and the satiated obese... And a bizarre light, the light of a dawn or a blaze, enveloped that terrible scene, the display of the bodies crushed by the weight of the impassive Beast, whose muzzle and chops loomed over that crowd in the gleam of a vision of the Apocalypse.

Cécile was frightened by it. She recoiled instinctively before the spectacle. Was that, perhaps, the evocation that was haunting André's brain?

She wanted to save him.

"André?" she appealed.

He raised his head then, and the same expression that had frightened Cécile the night before passed over his eyes. Assuredly, he was astonished to see an unexpected visitor there, in his studio. He hesitated momentarily to interrupt his work, as if he were trying to take account of what was happening. Then, after a glance at his painting, he stood up, placed his palette and arm-rest on his stool and asked Cécile, in the same coldly polite, indifferent tone that had frightened her: "Did you want to speak to me, Madame?"

He invited her to sit down, and she did, wanting to try to find out what was going on behind that face, what was happening in that sick brain.

Then she evoked, with a precisions still charmed by memory, the entire exquisitely simple romance that they had lived until the end of the previous day, until that horrible night. She tried to reawaken in that mind, which seemed obstinately deaf to her words, cherished images and words, delightful humble fact, and strove to be tender, caressant and supplicant.

And still there was that impassivity of the visage, that pallor of the features, as if fixed in the black beard, that bleak expression in the profound eyes in which she could not read anything—like black lakes into which everything sang without any reflection or sound—that incomprehension in which André, doubtless involuntarily, stubbornly persisted. Gradually, it made her nervous, ready to cry out. She ran into an obstinate resistance, speaking to her husband, and speaking to him about herself, but soon realized that the memories she evoked did not recall anything in the man who was present, listening indifferently.

Having pronounced the name Fortis, Cécile had a frisson of veritable terror when André replied: "I know him well. He's my homonym. It's another self that you want; it's not me. The landscapes you see hanging there are his."

He pointed to the studies on the studio walls: views of Fontainebleau, Bas-Bréau, the rocks and streams of Vaux de Cernay, landscapes of Chevreuse and the Bièvre valley; impressions of spring or autumn, effects of morning and sunset; an entire series of exquisite sensations fixed there by the tip of a brush, on a panel or canvas.

"The two of us are sometimes confused in the newspapers. He has talent"—André said that in the tone of a man making a concession to an art that he does not like—"but what is a landscape? A sketch. Painting, like music, is made to express higher ideas, to give to human beings—who demand them, who live in them—symbols, the vision of great chimeras. A landscape is a state of the soul, it's said: so be it; but there's something superior to the painting of a corner of the earth that pleases us, which is to paint the soul itself. To seize the human soul by a symphony as well as by the palette, to paint mystery, the ungraspable—that's the ideal! André Fortis doesn't know the beyond; he confines himself to visible nature, that which photography can render rigorously. Now, there's only the invisible in art, nothing but dreams. A man who lives a common existence comes and goes, digests, sleeps, breathes and grows old. He doesn't live. That André Fortis, whose signature is the same as mine, can also exhibit at the Autumn Salon; he's an artist of talent, yes—but a painter for competition medals."

André spoke about his work in that manner, as if it had been done by a stranger. He judged it as a critic. He condemned his own efforts by virtue of a new ideal that he bore within him. If she had not had the terror of the fantastic situation in which she was struggling, Cécile might have been able to think that it was a humorous exercise in which the man was indulging, expressing that opinion about the works he had produced, as if the studies and paintings had been done by someone else—but the painter who was presently throwing on to the canvas that apocalyptic vision, that twisted flesh, that bloody anatomy, that sinister King of the World, was indeed another man, very different from the landscape artist of summer evenings and smiling dawns over silvery pools.

Cécile gazed at those studies with affection, as if they were the very images of her illusions: everything she had loved in the André who was no longer there—or who, although there, no longer appeared as anything but a stranger, almost hostile.

Suddenly, she uttered an exclamation, in which there was joy and sadness. She had perceived, among the studies of forests, the woods of Barbizon or Chailly, a recent canvas: a sea shore, an immense beach and, on the fine sand, silhouettes that she recognized immediately—her father, her mother and herself, beside a young man who was *him*.

"Ah!" she said. "Trouville!"

It was Trouville, with the costume she had worn on the day when he had seen her, with the weather that he represented, the beautiful clear sky, the color of Madame de Jandrieu's dress, the décor of villas and Norman houses where they had met.

Looking at André, indicating the luminous study with her hand, she said, trying to reawaken a cherished memory: "It's Trouville."

"A Parisian landscape," said André. "A subject for a water-color. I don't understand."

Once again, either he was playing an atrocious game or he had lost his mind. She did not want to prolong her stay in the studio any longer. She was stifling there.

"I beg your pardon for having come."

He stood up between her and his canvas, as if he wanted to keep the secret of his work to himself.

"Oh, I can be interrupted when I'm working." He put the slender index-finger of his right hand to his forehead, and said: "My work is here." And his dark eyes, expressionless a moment ago, flashed briefly, as if illuminated by pride. "Here!" he repeated, joyfully

And Cécile, before going down the staircase, saw him through the open door sitting down on his stool again, taking up his palette, and bending feverishly over the "work" and returning feverishly to activity, the canvas, the subject and the bizarre vision being possessed of an invisible magnet that attracted, summoned and held him.

VII. The Duty of Cécile Fortis

She went back to her bedroom in despair, and the problem posed itself again. Should she flee? Should she stay? Should she strike her parents in the heart by telling them the truth, or condemn herself to living in seclusion with a madman?

A madman? Was he really a madman? The precise tone of his words, the fashion in which he judged the Fortis to whom he seemed to be a stranger, retained the clearest expression, a form that appeared perfectly rational. Ignorant as she was of the characteristics of dementia, however, Cécile knew that lunatics—General de Jandrieu had talked about it one evening with regard to a late megalomaniac comrade—retained a disconcerting logic in their visions or manias.

She also knew, or hoped, that madness can be cured.

I shall stay with him.

Yes, that was her duty. Perhaps André would come back to her soon. And besides, it would spare her father and Madame Jandrieu a double grief. *So long as they don't find out—until later...much later.* To suffer a little, to suffer for them, even became, in her mind, a sort of bitter joy. She was one of those woman born to console others, nurses of the soul, who have an appetite for sacrifice. When very young, in a fit of religious exaltation, in a chapel in church, she had made a mental vow to become a nun—and the suspicion had subsequently occurred to her that she might be culpable in not having kept her promise. "A child's oath," Abbé Vibert had said to her. "I once swore to be a soldier!"

Well, that interior oath, that cry of a fit of mysticism, she would now keep. Beside the man who was her husband, she would be a Sister of Charity, watching over him at all hours. Was he suffering? What was certain was that she was there to prevent him from suffering.

I'll stay. I'll stay.

Her resolution was made. Of her life, which seemed to her to be ruined, she would make a duty, awaiting the end of the sinister nightmare, counting on the future.

She was only anxious as to what the servants might think about André's attitude, his speech and the strangeness of his state of mind. Could she hide the sudden change in her husband's ideas from those ever-present witnesses? They observed everything, sought to divine everything. They would soon perceive the disturbance of that unfortunate brain.

Then Cécile told herself that, if André was agreeable, they could leave on their own for the Midi, Italy or Egypt—he could choose—and in the privacy of that curative voyage, she would try to get him back, to find the man she loved within him.

It was an impracticable project. André, attracted by his work, hypnotized by the canvas that he was covering, up there, with a bizarre and terrifying composition, would never consent to quit his studio, to go with the person he addressed as "Madame" and did not even seem to recognize.

The poor creature felt as if she were lost in an opaque fog. No matter which way she tried to go, she ran into an impossibility. The best thing to do was to entrust herself to hazard in a life adrift. In the meantime, once again, she resolved firmly to stay. What fate dictated would come about.

Suddenly, as she was wondering whether she should send someone to inform André at lunch time, or go up to his studio and try once again to bring him back, rediscover and get a grip on him, someone knocked on the door of her room and, frightened, fearing some misfortune, she said: "Who's there?"

"Me," said a very soft voice.

She recognized that voice. It was André's—not that of the coldly impassive André who emitted his words in a dry tone, but the voice full of tenderness that, during the sweet hours of the engagement, had spoken quietly in her ear about the future, their mutual dreams, marriage and love.

Oh, there was no doubt about it! It really was the same musical and delicious caress, to which she had listened with closed eyes in her father's drawing-room when André had talked to her, hand in hand.

The name sprang from her lips then: "André!"

She raced to the door. There he was on the threshold, smiling, contemplating her with an indefinable expression of tenderness, simultaneously melancholy and joyful. It seemed that he did not dare to advance, being timid, or, rather, happy to gaze, in the frame of that flower-filled room, at the woman who was his wife.

She went to him, holding out her hands, ready to throw her arms around his neck, sensing tears of joy rising to her eyes.

"It's you! It's really you!"

He advanced, closed the door, and took her in his arms.

"It's you!" This time, she said *toi* rather than *vous*. And that form of address seemed infinitely sweet, like the conclusive proof of the disappearance of the nightmare.

"How was your night?"

She sensed in the tone of the question a vague anxiety, and the young man's dark eyes were interrogating her with a kind of slight anguish—which a radiant joy soon dispelled.

Those eyes had an enveloping and imploring tenderness, so different from the eyes with the glacial pupils had had stared at her, making her afraid. Their gaze had become once again the clear and frank gaze that sought a soul in the depths of other gazes, as it sought a sensation in the depths of a landscape: a gaze of piety and artistry; an amorous gaze that rendered all her rediscovered joy to Cécile.

She dared not tell him what she had expected. She did not know whether he had any memory of the crisis he had suffered. She did not want to question him; she did not want to know. He was there; he was smiling at her; he was talking to her. He had become himself again. Adieu to the memory of that frightful vision! Life had resumed, was continuing. She blessed life.

André, however, had an indistinct sense of a lacuna in the recent hours he had lived. His questions proved that to Cécile. He interrogated her, wanting to know if anything had happened to disturb her last night. As for him—he remembered it clearly...yes he remembered—he had fallen asleep in his study next door, and had just come to there, asleep in the same armchair, with a volume of de Musset at his feet.

How had he recovered consciousness there? What had become of the bizarre painting that had frightened Cécile? How had André caused the vestiges of his second life to disappear, as a criminal erases the traces of his crime? The only one who could answer that was the Other, who must, logically, have accomplished an action that the veritable André did not even remember, and, obedient to that other consciousness, had removed and hidden his work from view, and had then given way to a new being continuing a new life in the same body.

The same features, different souls.

"It's the first time that de Musset has sent me to sleep," said André Fortis, laughing. "A strange sleep that took hold of me suddenly...were you thinking about me, Cécile, while I was sleeping like that, close to you."

"Close to me?"

"Did you call out to me in your sleep?" he said, in a low voice, stroking the flesh of her pink ear. "It seems to me that I would have heard you!"

She shivered. This time, it really was André who was speaking—and the fit of madness was, therefore, nothing but a temporary somnambulism of which, on awakening, he had no memory. She did not even want to think about everything that was fearful about the crisis, which some unexpected emotion might renew. She had been so frightened last night, and a little while before, in running into some kind of ambulant manikin or moving statue, that she surrendered herself, without any analysis or anticipation, to the joy of rediscovering André as he was, with his charm and his smile.

"But it's absurd, that sleep!" he said. "And for a moment, when I woke up in the armchair, I wondered where I was. I had got cold; I was shivering. I warmed up my hands at the heating-vent. And I thought that I might in the palace of a fairy: the good fairy, the sweet good fairy that was you!"

She had taken André's fingers, which were still cold, in her hands, and warmed them with her breath.

"It's absurd," André repeated. "A kind of hand descending on the skull...a gentle torpor...and that awakening in the cold of the morning!"

He could not render an exact account of the sensation he had experienced, He seemed to be searching, interrogating his memory.

"Don't think about it anymore," she said. "I love you. Do you love me, André?"

"With all my heart."

"And will you always love me?"

"Always."

There was the same profound impression in the words repeated in the tête-à-tête in the coupé such a short time ago. Such a short time! A century for Cécile, who had glimpsed the fear of a catastrophe a moment ago. It was the same eternal duet of lovers on the threshold of life. She thought that she might have had a bad dream: a vision that had vanished with the night. Was she really certain that she had seen that other André, sinister and implacable?

"I'd like to see your studio," she said.

"My studio?" He seemed astonished.

"Yes. I don't know what it's like. I'd like to see the unfinished canvases, the sketches..."

"Oh, I don't have anything presentable, even to you. I haven't started anything since my painting for the last Salon. I was entirely yours. It seemed to me that giving any time to my painting would be stealing time that I owed to you." With a charming grace, he said: "It takes time, the profession of fiancé."

"It doesn't matter," she said. "I'd like to see it."

"Let's go see then, Madame!"

And, pronouncing the word "Madame" in a caressing tone, which the lips of the Other had made so hard and seemingly hostile, he offered his arm to Cécile, who leaned on it, and smiled as she went back up the steps of the stairway she had climbed that morning with a hammering heart.

She paused once to say: "It's really true, then? I'm not dreaming? We're at home?"

But she became scared as they approached the studio, of suddenly experiencing a profound disappointment in finding the other André, the redoubtable André, and seeing again the sinister, apocalyptic painting that had frightened her so much a short while ago. Had André not just told her that he had done nothing at all since the last Salon?

What about that canvas: the Golden Calf?

Although she tried to control herself, she uttered an exclamation of surprise on entering the studio and looking at the easel. The Golden Calf was not there.

There was no canvas on the empty easel. The stool, the brushes and the palette were a long way away.

"Here are my sketches," aid André, showing her the studies hung on the wall. "That's all I can offer you."

"And it's an entire existence of a poet of the paintbrush! Oh, I tell the truth. If I thought a painting unworthy of you, you'd know, André..." She stopped. "No, I'd be afraid of upsetting you..."

"Upsetting me? Me? Never. Oh! Well, if you didn't think a painting worthy of me...oh, grand words! You'll make me vain, Madame. Well, what?" He waited for a reply, drawing her toward him, placing his lips on her blonde hair.

Huddled in his arms, she replied: "Well, I'd ask you to erase it."

"Bah!" he said.

"Yes; I want my husband, my dear husband, to paint nothing but masterpieces."

"The assignment is to be a genius!" he said, laughing. "Damn! Well, I'll try."

She looked him in the face. "And truly, you have no other painting in the studio that you've begun?"

"Truly, No other painting."

"There wasn't a canvas on your easel this morning?"

"This morning?" he queried, a trifle anxiously. "Why this morning?" He had frowned, as if trying to figure out what Cécile meant.

She understood that she was about to disturb him, and make him anxious.

"I just said this morning...I could have said yesterday..."

"I haven't been into my studio for three days. No one has been in here. Has someone told you that there was a canvas on my easel? What canvas? Who saw that canvas? I haven't begun any painting—none. Why ask me that?"

"No reason," she said. "I think an empty easel seems sad, so I thought..."

"Well," said André, "my first painting on the easel will be the Trouville for which the sketch is over there, and if I can reproduce the impression of that moment of clarity...you remember, you remember...it will be the masterpiece you require!"

She looked at the landscape, of an exquisite finesse, the sea-shore, the beach, the villas, the study in broad daylight that she had noticed a little while ago, and which contained a moment of her life, fixed by André Fortis...

If she had not rediscovered that corner of Normandy, which the Other—for she could not give him any name but that—had declared a fit subject for a water-color, abandoning it to some English miss, she might have been able to believe that she had been dreaming, that she had never gone into the studio, and that the sinister vision, with that mass of flesh crushed by the Vile Beast, had not existed.

The lugubrious painting had disappeared. André was telling the truth; he had not stated a new work. Some sort of unwonted being, a passer-by, a fantastic visitor, had come, only to disappear. And it was now Cécile who was asking herself whether she had really seen the canvas that was no longer there, and whether all the anguishes of the night might not have been a hallucination, whether she might not have lived through a waking dream of a bizarre life.

It hardly mattered! She experienced such a joy in rediscovering André, as confident, as smiling and as amorous as the day before.

She was no longer in dread. With the facility that a happy illusion provides, she closed her eyes and abandoned herself to the joy of rediscovered wellbeing. The nightmare of that atrocious night? It was far away now—so very far away!

"Do you love me?" she asked, softly, leaning her fine blonde head on André's shoulder, in her habitual gesture.

And in a voice so very different from the harsh tone of the evil vision, he repeated the eternal phrase of eternal love:

"I adore you!"

"You really believe then, my dear doctor, that a man can have a double consciousness?"

It was at dessert, during a grand dinner that Madame de Vernière was giving, partly in honor of Monsieur and Madame Fortis, who were perfectly happy, and also glorious. At the last Salon, André Fortis had exhibited landscapes of an infinite poetry, and he had brought back delightful canvases from Italy, where he and Cécile had been traveling for several months, sometimes staying in Venice and sometimes in Palermo, in picturesque little villas in Umbria or exquisite corners of the Bay of Naples: an Italy viewed through a new temperament, no longer the theatrical Italy of the Romantics, but a rare and intimate Italy, of a modernity that seemed to be a new flower blossoming in the marbles of the past.

It was exactly a year since Cécile had become the painter's wife, and no allusion had ever been made between them to the strange crisis of their first night under the same roof, not a single word that could have enabled Cécile to think that André had any awareness of what had happened, or that might have made André suspect that Cécile had perceived anything abnormal. Perhaps, by a kind of tacit consent, they were both maintaining a secure silence about the mystery that there was—or had been—in their existence. Perhaps, too, the young woman had completely forgotten those hours of terror.

The last year had passed so quickly, with the sojourn in Italy, the return to Trouville, where André had completed the promised canvas—a scene of "high life" as profound, of a poetry as intense, beneath his brush as a view of Sicily or a corner of Sorrento.

That first year of marriage had had the happy rapidity of summer lightning. General de Jandrieu, proud of his son-in-law, often repeated to his wife that they had been fortunate in giving away their daughter, and the charming Madame de Jandrieu strove to be "the best possible mother-in-law" for the young household. She thought of nothing but the joy of becoming a grandmother and of hearing some delightful familiar name in the babble of a pink mouth.

"They have plenty of time!" the general replied.

"But have we, my friend?" she said.

Then, at the dinner given by Madame de Vernière, who was Cécile's godmother, André Fortis met Dr. Chardin again, whom he had consulted a year earlier, almost on the same date, and a question from a guest—a journalist ever ready to seek information about such matters—brought into the conversation the precise subject that had caused such dramatic anguish.

Across the table, while pursuing a conversation with his neighbor, a witty young brunette afflicted by contemporary snobbery, which consisted for her of demolishing all the art of the past and for him of defending certain masters, André listened to what Dr. Chardin—directly to whose right Cécile had been placed—was saying.

VIII. A Scientific Interview

The journalist repeated his question, as if he were interrogating the scientist in an interview.

"A man can have a double *conscience*, then?"[18]

"Indeed. There are numerous consciences, in accordance with estates and professions. The conscience of a money-changer is not that of a protestant pastor, for example. I started an argument once at a lecture by Desiré Nisard, and even got arrested for having jeered the professor, who told us that there were two moralities. Perhaps he was simply explaining himself badly; there are often as many moralities as situations."

"Oh, Doctor!" said Madame de Vernière.

"Understand me, Madame—there is, in reality, only one certain morality, but there are different ways of interpreting it. And without indulging in casuistry..."

"But Doctor," the journalist interjected, "it's not conscience that I mean—it's the double state I want to talk about. I'm interested in it. I want to publish a series of articles about the Salpêtrière."

"And you're asking me for copy? Just like that, over dessert, as if it were a cheese?" said Dr. Chardin, laughing. "Well, yes, the personality of a human being can be doubled, and he can, in consequence have two consciousnesses. Cases of periodic amnesia are known—which is to say, of periodic loss of

---

[18] In French, *conscience* is used as an equivalent of the English word "consciousness" as well as of the English word "conscience"—an ambiguity that permits Dr. Chardin to misinterpret, probably deliberately, what the journalist is asking him. In all Jekyll-and-Hyde stories, of course, conscience is very much at stake as well as consciousness, but the ambiguity innate in French considerations has to be resolved in English translation by separating the translated terms. There is perhaps a certain irony in that necessity.

memory, in which it is evident that the consciousness is different..."

"That's the question I wanted to ask you, Doctor. A man has, you say, his personality doubled...good. His life, then, is doubled, like his consciousness..."

"Yes—that's a scientific phenomenon that has become classic..."

"I know. One can compare the state of amnesia of which you speak to the state in which, for instance, a somnambulist exists, who moves around, reads and works without remembering anything when he wakes up.."

"Very nearly," said Chardin. "Although there are differences..."

"I know..."

"Journalists know everything," the physician remarked.

"Who is that gentleman?" Cécile asked her other neighbor.

"Frédéric Clement of the *Boulevard*."

"But this is the question I'd like to put to you, my dear Maître," said the reporter. "Suppose that, during the state of amnesia—of double consciousness, or unconsciousness, as you wish—the doubled man of whom we speak commits a crime...a murder, say...is he responsible? Is a somnambulist responsible for his actions in the somnambulistic state?"

At that moment Cécile experienced a kind of twinge, which resembled the anguish she had experienced a year before, and during the exchange, she looked at André, sitting opposite, in order to study in his physiognomy any impression that such a conversation might be making on him. Through the flowers in the centerpiece—camellias and chrysanthemums—André's face seemed absolutely impassive, merely paled by the electric light illuminating half his face, and the thin cheeks within his exceedingly dark beard. Perhaps there was a vague anxiety in the intensity of his gaze, which was seemed to be directed at Dr. Chardin, even though the mouth was smiling and replying to the young brunette, whose pretty teeth were

79

making a meal of the "black" paintings of the Venetian "ink-merchants" in the museum, the Tintorettos and Titians.

Frédéric Clément's question had, however, rendered the entire table attentive. Dr. Chardin became the focus of all gazes and Cécile awaited the physician's response as if the reporter's question mark had expressed her own preoccupation.

"The question has already been asked," said the doctor. "People have even written melodramas on the theme. I remember having seen one, a long time ago, in the provinces, in which it was a magistrate who committed a crime in a somnambulistic state, and had to preside at the Court of Assizes that tried the supposed murderer..."

"An innocent man?"

"An innocent man, naturally"

"And how did the drama end, Doctor?" asked Madame de Vernière.

"With a fortunate denouement, my dear Madame. In mid-trial, the magistrate—the unwitting murderer—was suddenly overtaken by one of his attacks of somnambulism, and before the eyes of the stupefied jury and his fearful colleagues, he reproduced with tragic precision the actions of the murder, handling his paper-knife as he had handled the dagger in the previous instance, and related the story of why he had killed and why he was avenged. Then, acquittal of the accused, embraces of the family, public applause. I'll skip the lowering of the curtain."

"And the magistrate?" asked Cécile.

"In truth, I don't know what the author did with him. I don't remember the conclusion, only the medically-interesting case brought to the stage."

"Good, my dear Maître," said Frédéric Clément, insistently, "But in your opinion as a spectator, in your appreciation as a man of science, was the magistrate who plied the blade guilty?"

It seemed to Cécile that an expression of anguish flared up like an unextinguished ember in André's fixed gaze.

"No, no, in my opinion he wasn't guilty. The man who had killed was, in a sense, very different from the man who judged. These amnesias, losses of memory, doublings of the personality, are absolute neuroses. The somnambulism creates, in an individual being, for a period of time, an entirely new being. Intoxication is similar; a drunkard is a temporary madman. The worthiest of men, on becoming drunk, can metamorphose into utter brutes, bestial and ferocious. People are not mistaken, who are being scientific without knowing when they say, for instance, of a coward that he's 'lily-livered' or of a drunk that 'he's out of his mind.' Like a man who drinks, a man who dreams has two quite distinct existences: his real life and his artificial life, each independent of the other. In consequence, he is not responsible for the duality of consciousness that the strange neurosis imposes on him, the doubling of his personality."

"Two being in one—two different human beings is a single human existence? But that's a tale worthy of Edgar Poe!"

"Not at all. It's not a matter of the American's extraordinary tales. I'm talking about recorded facts, scientifically classified and understood. Look…the other day, a soldier in uniform, with his trousers covered in mud, was found on a bench on the Boulevard des Batignolles, where he had fallen asleep. He was assumed to be an alcoholic. When, having woken up, he was questioned, he was unable to explain his presence in Paris. He was garrisoned in Limoges, and had come from Limoges without knowing why or how, having left the barracks under an inexplicable impulse, marching straight ahead, on and on, as if in a dream. He was brought before a court martial as a deserter. Deserter! The poor boy was absolutely innocent. It was not him who had abandoned the regiment and traveled from Limoges to Paris; it was someone else."

"What novels one could write with science!" said Madame de Vernière.

"And history too, Madame, if I tell you that the Wandering Jew—you know, the famous Wandering Jew of the ballad and the legend?—was doubtless simply a somnambulist."

81

"Old Laquedem?"

"Exactly. It has been observed that the particular neurosis from which the young soldier was suffering, and which is known as ambulatory mania—the need to escape, to march, to go forward, one knows not where—frequently afflicts Jews. In the villages of France, in various eras, Jews from Poland or Romania were sometimes seen to arrive, with their long beards and their fur-lined overcoats, with their traveling staffs in hand, and these Jews appeared there marching straight ahead, like the trooper going from Limoges to Paris, driven by an ambulatory mania.

"Appearing at various dates, appeared to the imagination of our peasants, and even the burgers of Brussels in the Brabant, to incarnate the Jew pursued by the malediction of Calvary. Struck by neurosis, these traveling somnambulists became, for the people, the legendary Wandering Jew: 'You shall walk yourself, for more than a thousand years...' And these wanderers who appear like that, from time to time, with their rags and fleshless faces, are somnambulists of a sort, individuals who have left their hearth without knowing why, without taking account of what they are deserting...

"Dr. Tissié[19] encountered one of these wanderers who covered more than seventy kilometers a day in that dream-state. He left after having taken banknotes from his money-box of which he did not even know the value in his secondary state, and traveled as a vagabond. He had passed through Germany, Turkey, Hungary, Russia and Africa. In Russia he had almost been hanged as a nihilist...in a dream-state. The scaffold would have seen him die an innocent, unconscious. And these wanderers take their ambulant dreams with them. They are beings who live a double life, and it's not Edgar Poe that they recall, but Charcot."

---

[19] Philippe Auguste Tissié (1852-1935) published *Les aliénés voyageurs: essai médico-psychologique*, [Traveling Lunatics: A Medico-Psychological Essay] from which these details of "ambulatory mania" are probably taken, in 1887.

"Have you encountered any of these somnambulists who live a double life, Doctor?" asked the journalist. "Tell us that."

Across the flower-laden table, in the warm atmosphere of the dining-room, it seemed to Cécile once again that André's gaze suddenly took on an anxious expression, something wild. She did not take her eyes off his. The face had paled; a slight tremor agitated the lower lip, and a singular gesture, of the right hand, slow and almost mechanical, seemed to be searching the white tablecloth indistinctly, for a knife.

André waited, attentively, his throat constricted, for the physician's reply.

"If I had encountered any," Dr. Chardin said, coldly, "I would not tell you, but if you want to write about the subject, my dear monsieur, it's not to me that you ought to address yourself, but to Dr. Klipper."

"Dr. Klipper?"

"Yes, an Alsatian, and a man of genius."

"Dr. Klipper," the journalist repeated. "That's astonishing. I never heard of him."

"Doubtless no one here has heard of him," said Chardin, his gaze seeking anyone among the guests who might contradict him by talking about Dr. Klipper. "He's an extraordinary man who, in his laboratory, is highly reminiscent of the alchemists that Rembrandt pained and evoked in his engravings. He lives in seclusion, researching mysteries, as Balzac's Balthazar Claës[20] researched the unknown, and he claims to have found, or to be on the brink of finding, some X-, Y- or Z-ray that will permit the human brain to be read through the skull like an open book."

"He's a madman," said Madame de Vernière.

---

[20] In *La Recherche de l'absolu* (1834; tr. as *The Quest for the Absolute*), in which Claës ruins his family purchasing chemical supplies in his obsessive quest to discover the philosopher's stone.

"Not at all. I've already told you that he's a man of genius. But attempts have already been made to prove that genius is a kind of neurosis."

"Oh, but it's necessary that I go to interview Dr. Klipper," said the reporter from the *Boulevard*.

Chardin shook his head. "You won't get to talk to him. I don't even know if you'll be able to see him."

"Oh, indeed! But what if I needed him, if I were suffering—if I *report sick*, as they say in the regiment?"

"Dr. Klipper doesn't take patients."

"What does he do?"

"I've already told you: research." The physician looked at the guests, who were listening, intrigued by the mystery. "And if I tried to specify what it is he's researching, you'd protest its implausibility, and believe it a story by Edgar Poe, Wells or Stevenson."

"Come on, Doctor!"

"You're making our mouths water."

"What is your Klipper researching?"

André, more than anyone, was waiting for Chardin's explanation, for which all the pretty women at the table were soliciting—all of whom fell silent, as if the master had taken the podium and was about to begin a lecture.

"In truth, it's rather difficult to explain it to you without being a trifle pedantic. I beg your pardon, Mesdames, but it might seem incomprehensible to you."

"You're insulting us, Doctor," aid Madame de Vernière, laughing. "I protest on behalf of these ladies."

"Well," said Chardin, "That astonishing man of genius, Jean Klipper—you can see that physicians sometimes do one another justice, and aren't always devouring ne another like wolves, artists and, beginning your pardon, Monsieur, journalists—is researching our third eye."

"What did you say?"

"I said our third eye."

"What does that mean?" asked the mistress of the house, on everyone's behalf.

"Quite simply that, like all vertebrates, we have here, behind the forehead, a gland that zoologists call the pineal gland, the pineal body, the pine-cone or the spinning-top, and that the gland in question, in spite of its name, is not in reality a gland, nor a nerve ganglion, nor a lymphatic ganglion, but a degenerate organ. The pseudo-gland in question can therefore be considered as a third eye, which is in a latent state in us—an unfinished eye, which has not emerged, which has not pierced the cranium, but which exists, and which physiologists have found at the tip of their scalpel."[21]

"So it's that eye," said the reporter, "which explains the fable of the Cyclops."

"Exactly. One can imagine that there was a time when the third eye appeared in the forehead of a few humans in primitive or fabulous times. I'm not speaking here about absurd things. It's certain that the rudimentary and degenerate organ in question, which serves no purpose today except to perpetuate within us the memory of an organ that existed in our distant ancestors, is an atavistic legacy, atrophied over the course of time. Oh, Dr. Klipper is not alone in having studied the pineal epiphysis. In 1882 Rabl-Rückhard[22] observed it in

---

[21] The notion that the pineal body is a vestigial "third eye" was popularized in France during the occult revival by Madame Blavatsky, who adapted the notion of a mystical eye associated with the *ajna* [brow] chakra from Hindu mysticism and attempted to give it a scientific gloss. The pineal body is actually in the center of the brain rather than at the front; it had earlier become famous in France thanks to Descartes, his followers and detractors, whose contribution to the mythology of the organ Clarétie sums up correctively via Chardin and Klipper.

[22] The neurohistologist Hermann Rabl-Ruckhard (1839-1905). Clarétie's subsequent references are to the Dutch zoologist Henri W. de Graaf and Walter Baldwin Spencer (1860-1929), although he or the typesetter misrenders the latter name slightly.

fish and declared that it really is an eye. In 1886 De Graaf studied it in the slow-worm—you know, that pretty reptile that can frighten you in the paths of Fontainebleau, but which is as inoffensive as a sparrow—the blind worm, a false serpent, a degenerate lizard. And Baldwin Spencer had, indeed, studied the third eye in lizards. It's also found, very evident and very characteristic, in birds—pigeons, for example. In pigeons, and in humans."

"Which is often the same thing," remarked a wit.

There was some laughter, but not much. Dr. Chardin's little speech had captivated attention.

"Except," he said, "that in pigeons the organ in question is apparent, while in humans it requires a preparation to perceive it, removing the upper part of the hemispheres. Let's not talk about that—it's not appropriate subject matter for dessert. Only Thomas Diafoirus[23] can entertain ladies with surgical matters."

"But you know, Doctor," interjected an old gentleman, slightly timidly, "that Descartes has spoken about it—the pineal gland, your third eye. My very knowledgeable friend Professor Pozzi[24] reminded me of it the other day. Descartes even claimed that the gland is question was the seat of the soul."

"Not exactly—I don't have his text present in memory, but you're right, Monsieur; Descartes did talk about it, and Galen before Descartes. Neither of them, however, thought about what Jean Klipper had imagined—which is to give humans the third eye of which they are deprived."

"A supplementary eye?"

---

[23] One of the physicians in Molière's *Le Malade imaginaire* (1673), who spouts impressive but meaningless jargon.

[24] Samuel-Jean Pozzi (1846-1918) was a prominent member of the Académie de Médecine who had strong literary interests; Clarétie undoubtedly knew him, although he did not know when he wrote this that Pozzi's fame would be further enhanced in 1913 when he was called upon to organize the amputation of Sarah Bernhardt's leg.

"Where? In the middle of the forehead?"

"That's amazing!"

"It's cyclopean!"

"It's frightful!"

"An eye in the forehead! Oh, that's horrid!"

The interruptions came from all directions, and Chardin enjoyed the amazement of the audience, quietly. The interjections amused the scientist, accustomed to such alarm in confrontation with the unexpected.

"Bah!" he said. "It's a matter of habit. If the idea catches on, it'll be regarded as a beauty spot. Its possessors would have less fear than today's blacksmiths of being blinded by sparks. One eye more would be an augmentation of life, and life in the most precious of human commodities, a loan of a few years that that has to be repaid, on an undetermined expiry date to the Grim Reaper. Now, this is why I told you that Jean Klipper is a genius. He lives with a pretty young woman whom he adores—and who is blind. It's for her that he is multiplying his labors and attempting the impossible. The unfortunate has lost her sight; he wants to give it back to her. She no longer has her two eyes; they're useless; they can only perceive light without distinguishing the form of objects. He wants the third eye to restore his wife to him."

"Get away!" said the reporter.

"What I'm telling you might not seem credible, but it's the pure truth. Dr. Klipper has invented a kind of electric lamp that projects its rays on the young woman's forehead, which has on the cranium, in a manner of speaking, a function similar to that solar radiation on the soil. The sun makes invisible seeds grow; the doctor hopes that electricity, penetrating the bone of a human being—I won't use scientific terminology to explain that; I'm trying to make myself understood, and, I repeat, it isn't easy because it sounds crazy—piercing, or, rather, enlarging the hole in the cranium through which the pineal nerve emerges, can provoke an unusual growth, making the third eye develop and blossom, which will render sight to his blind beloved. I'm not telling you a story, I'm citing a fact, an actual case. We've seen a great many scientific miracles; you and I will see many others."

"Where does Jean Klipper live, so that I can go to see him?" asked Frédéric Clément, joyfully. "What a revelation! What an article!"

All Dr. Chardin's listeners were exchanging incredulous observations. There were skeptical smiles on the lips of the pretty women. Cécile was probably alone in being interested, and also anxious, knowing that anything was possible. Madame de Vernière said to the scientist: "You tell stories like Scheherazade!"

"No, no, I tell stories like a phonograph. I'm a man of my time. The impossible is banal."

"So," said André, whose eyes were shining, "this Dr. Klipper really is capable of working miracles?"

"No, but he's capable of discoveries that will cause upheavals in knowledge and scientific laws. There are avantgarde scientists who catch sight of unknown lands. It's possible that he'll run aground, but he's not a charlatan who courts publicity for his work; he's a solitary worker in silent pursuit of a shadow. And that devil of a man has already made a host of observations regarding the human brain that astonish qualified scientists—including me, and I'm not timid."

"Has the man made a pact with the Devil?" said Madame de Vernière.

"No, he's a worthy Alsatian, devoid of conceit or malice, content to turn the world upside-down from the depths of a cave, in a laboratory the size of this tablecloth."

"He doesn't reside on the Brocken?"

"No, he lives in Batignolles. The fantastic is within range of everyone. To see sorcerers, one only has to buy a Metro ticket."

"I'll get that ticket, and I'll go talk to your sorcerer—and the *Boulevard* will publish his portrait on page one!"

"But you won't say that I told you about his genius. He *is* a man of genius."

"A crackpot! Starstruck!"

"Only idiots have no cracks!"

While these comments were exchanged, Cécile felt the sentiment of discomfort—the anguish that was gripping her—become accentuated and augmented. She continued to look across the room at her husband, without appearing to be studying him; his face, with its mat whiteness, seemed paler than usual, the back beard framing that Saracen head. The feverish gleam of the pupils did not escape the poor woman, fearful of finding there the strange flame that had been in André's eyes, those haggard eyes fixed on the exterior canvas, the vision of the Apocalypse, in the studio on that unforgettable night.

That entire conversation over dessert, half-scientific and half-Parisian, revolved around the disquieting case of André Fortis. For Cécile, he was the center of that discussion. She examined, sensed, with the acuity of an individual in love, everything that André would suffer if he became conscious of his condition, if he suffered the effects of a further crisis. She wondered whether the doctor's words, which amused the table as a curious anecdote, might not have awoken a memory, a sensation or a pain in the unfortunate man.

The feverishness of his gaze, the movements of his clenched fingers just now, permitted no doubt that André had been suffering and suppressing cruel sensations while the doctor was speaking, but all that disappeared when they got up from the table and, Dr. Chardin offering his arm to Madame Fortis, they went into the drawing-room. The men quickly went on to the smoking-room, where the journalist continued to interview the physician, while André remained with the mistress of the house, as if he wanted, by means of female conversation, to chase away obsessive thoughts and the dolorous dream of his life.

"So," repeated Frédéric Clément, "he's a coming man, your Dr. Klipper, and he has big surprises in store for us."

"If he isn't interrupted in his progress, yes. You know that Pasteur had a cerebral hemorrhage, which nearly carried him off, or left him paralyzed, which would have been even sadder. The attack was benign, in the end, but it would only have required a little more blood—a drop the size of a lentil—to have penetrated his brain, and that would have put paid to all the great scientist's admirable discoveries. It appears that the length of Cleopatra's nose influenced the history of the world; slightly shorter, and its fate would have been changed. One drop of blood more or less, and humankind would still have rabies. It still exists in politics, it's true, and the parties haven't yet found their Pasteur. As for Jean Klipper, if he remains, if he endures—endurance is everything in this base world—he'll amaze his century, and statues will be raised to him one day."

"Which doesn't prove, my dear Maître," said the journalist, "that he's an unmatchable man. Who doesn't have a statue nowadays? Who doesn't have his marble? Who doesn't have his confetti?"

Dr. Chardin laughed. "An incorrigible Parisian, always making witty comments."

"What do you expect? You're always talking science!"

When the cigar was finished and the doctor rejoined Madame de Vernière on the threshold of the drawing-room, he found Cécile, who appeared to be on the lookout for him. She smiled—a forced smile—suspecting that André would not take his eyes of her while she was speaking to the physician.

Striving to give the conversation the appearance of a banal exchange of insignificant comments, she swiftly said to Chardin in a low voice: "Don't be astonished by the smile, which will contrast with what I have to say to you, Doctor, and forgive me for saying it to you here, but I'm aware of one of those cases of doubling of the personality that you mentioned. Be careful—we're being watched!"

Dr. Chardin, who was used to conserving his impassivity in the presence of confidences or human suffering, did not allow his clan-shaven face to betray the slightest astonishment.

Slowly, he said: "Ah! You know."

"I've seen it," she said. She retained her smile.

"A serious crisis?" asked Chardin, who also affected to seem indifferent.

André's gaze never left them.

"A few hours?"

"When?"

"A year ago."

"And since?"

"Nothing. But I'm afraid..."

"Fear is a human being's worst counselor. Don't be afraid to be optimistic. I've been observing the person about whom you've just spoken, closely, and in my chatter I attempted an experiment of sorts. He listened without too much nervousness..."

"And yet..." she said. She stopped. "He's watching—he'll guess!"

The Doctor concluded, rapidly: "There might yet be a storm—there is, in fact, electricity in the air; I've seen it—but the thunder is drawing away. Besides, I'm here!" Bowing like a socialite thanking Madame Fortis for a cup of tea, he added: "And if necessary, we'll call Dr. Miracle."

"Dr. Klipper? That's serious...?"

"Very serious."

"A prince of science consulting a bone-setter!"

"Oh, it's not summoning a bone-setter. Anyway. I wouldn't scorn a bone-setter who could heal me!"

André seemed to be listening anxiously, from a distance, to that brief dialogue, the gravity of which was dissimulated by gesture of worldly banality. Cécile went to him, putting more expression into her smile than her joy really warranted.

"What did Dr. Chardin say to you?" asked the painter.

"He was talking about your views of Venice."

"Really?"

"What would you expect him to talk to me about?"

"I don't know," André said. Thoughtfully, he added: "Venice? Ah, an exquisite city for nursing forgetfulness!"

"And for love," said Cécile, whose gaze enveloped the seeker of dreams with tenderness.

André replied with a profound smile to his wife's smile, which was consoling and hopeful.

IX. The Illness Returns

Hope!

In the luxurious house on the edge of the Parc Monceau, Madame Fortis was indeed living suspended between hope and anguish. Nothing led her to believe that her husband might fall back under the claw of his illness, but, on the other hand, everything caused her to fear that the "unknown" might reawaken in the man she loved. André seemed to her to be more nervous than usual since the soirée at Madame de Vernière's house, and, in spite of the assurance of Dr. Chardin, she feared the reappearance, like that of a specter, of the Other she had seen, terrified by that living phantom, that stranger, that intruder.

She avoided making the slightest allusion to the doctor's words. André was working hard, with a kind of fever. She even feared that the relentlessness of that labor might stretch his never a little too far. She sometimes begged him to take more rest, a few days off.

"No, you now I'm only happy before my canvases—and with you, my love." One evening, he added: "And then again, what's finished is finished. One never knows what might happen."

"What do you expect to happen?"

"Nothing. I'm joking. An art-lover who'll steal my paintings."

She insisted, however, that he take some distraction. There were weekly artists' dinners at which, meeting his comrades, he could chat about the thousand-and-one items of gossip that were running round the studios, salons and theater wings, and make Paris the largest of provincial villages. He had neglected those meetings since his marriage, and Cécile urged him to return to them.

"What about your Club? Usually, wives are jealous of Clubs. I'm not. You can see your friends, chat, rest..."

"But nothing, my dear Cécile, is as good as an evening spent with you, beside you!"

"Oh, I'm sure of that," she said, with an affectionate coquetry, but you know the old song: "A legitimate wife/Can always be found,/Forever!"

She had a feeling that his unquiet brain needed a great many distractions. She persisted. "My parents are entertaining some tedious people this evening. I'll go there, and you won't have the trouble of sending the evening with people who have nothing to say. Or you can come to pick me up later, when the bores have left."

Then André got dressed and went out. Cécile, knowing that he was at the Club, was convinced that the painter, exhausted by the day's work, needed that change of environment, a different atmosphere. Solitude, favorable to work, could be deleterious to thought, if, by chance, André remembered...

He had therefore agreed to seek, in movement and change, a variation of that everyday existence, at the bottom of which Cécile feared that there might be an obsession.

"And I'm ambitious for you, you know. It's necessary to cultivate one's friendships. Do you see many members of the Institut at the Club? When I got married, I promised Papa that you'd be a member of the Institut. Oh, of course!"

"What!" André replied. "I've married a social climber!"

She came back one evening, rather late, from General de Jandrieu's house. André was at the Club. In the slumbering house, she felt slightly lonely, and, without knowing why, experienced a vague anxiety. She did not want to go to bed before André had come in. She looked out of her usual window at the Parc Monceau, which seemed be an entirely black ink-blot, with a few small branches barely visible beneath the slightly brighter sky, and the whiteness of Gounod's eternal marble monument more distinct. Every time she found herself standing there, with her forehead pressed to that same window-pane, she remembered the sad night of their first arrival at the dwelling, the terror of the next day's vision...

Let's not thinking about it anymore, she said to herself. *It was so long ago*.

She waited, wanting André to find her still up and about, or, rather, spending the time thinking. It was three o'clock in the morning—the clock was striking—when he returned.

"You're back very late," she said.

He looked at the clock. "Yes, that's true. How time flies. I didn't think it was midnight."

"Did you have fun?"

"In truth, no."

"Who did you see?"

"A crowd of people. I didn't know half of them."

He seemed tired, and had no desire to chat. His eyes went to the clock, staring. He seemed astonished. "Three o'clock!" he said. "That's odd!" Taking out his watch, he looked at the hands. "Yes, three o'clock. That's astonishing."

He passed his hand over his forehead, as if he had a headache.

"Are you in pain?"

"No."

"There's nothing worrying you?"

"Nothing."

He went to sleep, as if harassed.

The next day, Cécile found him anxious, his expression weary, drawn and pensive.

He had put his wallet down on the mantelpiece the night before, mechanically. Cécile, from inside her dressing-room, saw him standing in front of the fireplace. The open door of a cupboard, fitted with a mirror, transmitted the image of her husband, who, with a gesture of amazement, opened the wallet and stood there, immobilized by astonishment, looking at a wad of banknotes that he had taken out of it.

André's whole attitude expressed such amazement that Cécile, huddled in the depths of the dressing-room, stayed there to study him silently, holding back the questions that rose to her lips.

André was now turning the wallet over and over, like a man encountering an unknown object. He touched the banknotes with his fingertips, stroked them, counted them, and then interrogated the wallet again: a dark green leather wallet with silver initials; his own wallet. It really was the one that Cécile had given him. Yes, that monogram in old silver, it was his fiancée who had designed it herself.

His wallet?

How, then, did that wallet, which had contained three hundred francs the day before—three hundred-franc bills—come to contain a wad of banknotes this morning?

Fifty-two bills! Fifty-two thousand francs!

André's thin hand passed over his brow with the familiar gesture. He looked at himself in the mirror, and found that he was very pale.

Cécile, as immobile as he had been a few moments ago, pressed against the wall in her dressing-room, saw him look round, his eyes seeking to know whether he had been seen. Then he rapidly slipped the wallet into the inside pocket of his jacket, which he buttoned up with a curt gesture, and all of his anxious physiognomy expressed the fear of being watched, the desire to escape any surveillance. That face had the expression of a thief who has just brought off a coup and wants to flee.

Now Cécile was trembling from head to toe.

She had seen those movements of palpitating fingers, stroking the bills, and the banknotes, which she had counted while André was counting them. Where had they come from? How did they come to be in the wallet that she knew so well? André's amazement had not escaped her, any more than his final desire not to be seen, to hide the bills. She found herself confronted once again by something mysterious and troubling. But she would find out...

She came out of her dressing-room.

André, his features visibly taut, tried to smile. Then he excused himself, with the necessity of going up to his studio. He wanted to add a few strokes of the brush to a scene of Sorrento before lunch, to finish it off.

"You're not tired? Don't work too hard.

"One never works too hard."

"You haven't told me what you did at the Club yesterday."

"Nothing. Chatted. A banal evening—a wasted evening."

He did not mention the bills, the wallet, the astonishment that had struck him, which she had read clearly in him a little while before.

She let him go. She would interrogate him during lunch.

At lunch-time, however, Monsieur and Madame de Jandrieu came to visit their daughter. The general was coming back from the funeral of an old comrade in the Army of Metz, at Saint-Honoré d'Eylau. He had stopped off at the Parc Monceau, with his wife, who had accompanied him.

André begged his parents-in-law to stay.

"No, no—the old belong with the old, the young with the young!"

"You never visit," said André.

"I don't want to be a mother-in-law to you!" replied Madame de Jandrieu.

"Have I ever called you that?"

Cécile noticed that her husband was putting a particular persistence into getting Monsieur and Madame de Jandrieu to stay, as if he were trying to avoid being alone with her. He was not, however, preoccupied or sad. She even thought him excessively cheerful during the meal, with a slightly forced gaiety. He seemed to be cudgeling his brain for conversation, talking about the latest fashions, the theater, various exhibitions.

"And are you working on new masterpieces for us?" asked the general.

"Oh, masterpieces! No. But I'm working feverishly. The brush flies hither and yon, the colors catch fire, the canvas feels good—and I'm even going to leave you in order to do some more work."

"Go, go, dear child..."

He kissed Cécile on the forehead and went back up to his studio, leaving his wife with the general and Madame de Jandrieu, both of them delighted with their son-in-law's good humor.

"What a charming fellow! You resemble two turtle-doves."

"Very nice, and in a delightful nest!"

The mother, however, noticed a latent preoccupation in Cécile's gaze. She asked her whether she was experiencing some vague anxiety. No—except that André might be working too hard. Such a nervous nature needed breaks.

"But you're happy?"

"Very happy."

"Truly?"

"Truly, Maman—I swear."

She was impatient to be alone. She wanted to know the truth. Her parents had not reached the far side of the Parc Monceau when she went up to André's studio and knocked on the door. He was finishing his Italian landscape, reviving the hours that she had lived with him out there.

"Oh, that's beautiful," she said, looking at the canvas. "Yes, it's superb."

She did not know how to interrogate him, to demand explanations of what she had seen, and André, absorbed in his work, appeared to want to avoid all questions. Then she feared wounding him, perhaps irritating him with some false step. She soon aid: "I'm getting in the way. I'll go."

He did not say a word to hold her back. She would wait, then—but the idea of seeing the man standing in front of the mirror and counting the banknotes with an expression of amazement would not let go of her.

They had planned to spend the evening at the Opéra. *Samson et Dalila*[25] was playing. André listened, telling Cécile

---

[25] By Camille Saint-Saëns, first performed in 1877, especially celebrated for the love-scene featuring Dalila's aria "Mon Coeur s'ouvre à ta voix" [My Heart Opens at Your Voice].

how the music was a stimulant for him, his imagination invoking dream landscapes while the orchestra cradled his visions.

"A man needs a little smoke and an accompaniment to his dreams, pipe-smoke or the echo of old tunes. That's why I like to listen to you play your piano. When you play, it seems to me that you're dictating sketches to me."

"Except that I no longer play. I honestly believe that young women get married primarily in order not to have to play the pieces they've been taught any longer." Suddenly, she added: "On Sunday, at Colonne's there's a performance of Schumann's *Manfred*. I don't know it. We can go, if you like."

She was struck by his convulsed expression. "No, no, no," he said. "Not *Manfred*."

The sonorities of old, the voices of the beyond that had shredded his nerves, suddenly came back to him. He changed the subject, picked up his opera-glasses and paraded them around the room.

Cécile went back home without having had the courage to ask him what he had done the night before. She was late going to sleep, still anxious.

The next day, André went to work early in the morning. The fortunate fever by which the work was growing continued. When Cécile had finished dressing, she rang and asked for the mail and the newspapers. The *Boulevard* was among them. She flipped off the rubber band and looked at the first page.

X. The Card Game

In the Paris news column signed by Frédéric Clément, one name struck her immediately: André's. She unfolded the paper and read it avidly, fearfully.

The journalist related a scene that had occurred the night before last at the Club in the Rue Boissy-d'Anglas. A young painter who normally never appeared at the gaming tables had, with a kind of intelligent virtuosity, risked a game for high stakes against Prince Stalinski, famous for his bold fashion of challenging fortune. For hours, there had been a kind of duel of chance between the Parisian painter and the great Polish lord. At one time, the Prince, smiling, gallant and courteous, had been more than a hundred thousand francs down, but the artist had not wanted to get up from the table until he had lost all his winnings. Having won back two thousand five hundred francs, the Prince had left the table himself, saying: "Let's leave it at that. I'm no longer interested."

And the painter, trying to convince him to continue the game, had said: "No, no, a loss of fifty thousand francs is the precise figure I'd fixed for myself tonight. One more hand, and no more."

In relating the anecdote, the reporter added: *The composure of the two opponents was noticeable, both of them playing as if their minds were elsewhere, the prince ironically indifferent, the painter calm, with a gaze that did not even seem to see the banknotes temporarily accumulated on the table. That tourney around the Queen of Spades interested the aficionados.*

And Frédéric Clément concluded:

Is it necessary to name the victor? More used to manipulating a paintbrush than handling cards, perhaps he had signed one of those landscapes during the day that the art dealers sell very dear, but we doubt that his afternoon was worth as much to him as his evening. Like the Roman emper-

or, Monsieur André Fortis can boast of not having wasted his day.

After having read the article in the *Boulevard*, Cécile read it again. She was scared. In her absolute conviction, André had engaged in that game of cards without being aware of it, in the unhealthy dream state that removed his own personality in order to substitute another. The journalist had noted the significant feature that André did not even seem to see the money he had won, the piled-up bills. The article explained the surprised expression of the reawakened man, counting the paper money with astonishment, which he seemed to be interrogating by feel, André amazement before the sum he had in his wallet, without knowing how it came to be there.

At the Club last night, André had had a further crises—doubtless temporary, but certain—during which, without calculating the sum he was risking against Prince Stalinski, he had gambled, like a madman, at hazard, not knowing how he was winning, remaining at the gaming table without knowing why, haggard and panicked, as he would be the following day on finding his unexpected winnings in his home.

Thus, for hours, out there, far away from her, André had become the Other, of whom he was afraid.

He was not cured. For a year she had hoped that the Other had disappeared, but André was not cured. He had gambled, probably not even remembering having gambled—no, certainly not remembering; she only had to recall the way he had held the bills between his fingers.

He had gambled! He could have picked a quarrel, made threats, killed someone—and he would not remember it!

Cécile reread the article in the Boulevard with frissons of terror, as if learning it by heart.

...both of them playing as if their minds were elsewhere, the prince ironically indifferent, the painter calm, with a gaze that did not even seem to see the banknotes temporarily accumulated on the table...

Well, no—he couldn't see. He couldn't see anything. He wasn't himself! It's terrible! He might come back to me with

blood on his hands, and wouldn't be aware of it! He would be
responsible for what the Other had done...

But in truth, did he really not know? Was it possible that
the nocturnal dream—not a dream but a reality, lived in the
second state of his being as if in a mist—had not left any trace
in André's brain?

Now that she knew where the banknotes had come from,
now that the newspaper had reported the nocturnal adventure,
she would not hesitate to interrogate him.

And when Fortis came down from his studio, she did indeed interrogate him.

"You know," she said, "I've had an idea, a whim. I don't
have many caprices, and I never ask you for anything, but
today, I'm going to ask you for something."

"What?" said André. He seemed delighted; it was his joy
to make her happy.

"But you might not want to..."

"Why not?"

"It's very expensive. Oh, it's not a matter of a pearl
necklace; mine is sufficient. Once, wives asked their husbands
of a coupé, a pair of horses. I'm a woman of my own time. I'd
like an automobile."

"An automobile?"

"It's necessary to keep up with fashion."

"You can have an automobile," André said, "but later,
when I've delivered a few more views of Venice to Telasco. I
don't have the disposable cash."

He had pronounced the last words in the most natural
manner in the world, and Cécile felt that he was, in fact, telling the truth. He certainly did not remember the adventure at
the Club; he had forgotten Prince Stalinski—and that was
what threw the unhappy woman back into anguish.

If the memory of something that had happened only a
few hours ago had escaped André's brain, it was because there
was a lacuna in him, because, for a while, he had been living
that other life again: the life of which he no longer had any
knowledge now, but which was as real, in its strangeness, as

his own life, his everyday life. He was not cured. At any moment, he might be afflicted by the amnesia, the suppression of his personality.

At the risk of giving his main, Cécile got straight to the point, tearing away the veil, wanting to know.

She looked deep into his eyes, mildly, not like an interrogating judge but like a mother, smiling as she asks a question. "But what about the banknotes you brought back yesterday?"

"Banknotes?" he started to laugh, good-humoredly. "What banknotes?"

"You counted them in front of the mantelpiece and put them in the monogrammed wallet—the one I gave you.

"Banknotes?" Like a man searching for a memory, he stared at Cécile, making a mental effort. "Banknotes?" he repeated.

"Yes—the ones you won from Prince Stalinski."

"What Prince Stalinski?"

"At the Club, the night before last."

"Me?" he said, striking his breast forcefully. There was such sudden doubt and pain in the cry that Cécile was afraid, regretting the test.

"Come on," he said, reassembling his ideas, his forehead creased as if in confrontation with a problem to be solved. "Who told you about Prince Stalinski, and winning money?"

"Gambling, the night before last," she said. "Look!" She held out the newspaper, which was lying on the table.

André became momentarily angry on reading Frédéric Clément's article. "Is it possible?" He raised his hand to his forehead. As if dazed, he stammered: "Yes, possible...it's possible!"

The article in the *Boulevard*, which he reread, had the effect on him of some fragment of cinematography in which he had suddenly perceived himself moving back and forth, bent over a gaming table, dealing cards: an agitated, active phantom, who was himself...

His lip trembling, he repeated: "It's possible! Yes, it's possible..." Then, throwing away the crumpled newspaper, angrily, he said: "And you saw me counting the banknotes? Where are they?"

"In the wallet," she repeated.

He did not have the wallet in his pocket. Where had he put it? He did not remember. About what he had done, of what he had said, back there in the Club, and then, on his return, when Cécile had seen him holding the bills between his fingers, he no longer knew anything. It was not him who had lived those feverish hours, it was the Other.

Then he uttered a cry of rage, threw himself into a armchair, put his face in his hands, and, among sobs, violently repeated: "*The Other! The Other!*"

Sometimes, he stared ahead of him. A brief gesture of his closed fist seemed to be threatening some vision in the empty air. He had a murderous flamboyance in his eyes. And Cécile regretted having unleashed that dolor, reawakened that memory.

"Where is it, this wallet?" asked André, suddenly straightening up. "How was that money won? I need to find that money! Prince Stalinski! I scarcely know him. I've only talked to him twice in my entire life!"

He reached out to Cécile as if to draw her toward him, and when she came to him he let his head fall on to the young woman's shoulder, begging her pardon, whispering in her ear, into her neck, between kisses, as if some witness might be spying on them and listening: "Forgive me! Forgive me! You forgive me, don't you?"

"Forgive you for what?"

"For having lied. For not having told you everything. You, my darling, you! For having made you marry a sick man, a madman...is that what I am?"

She calmed him down, hugging him like a distressed child who issuing a plaint while weeping.

"No, no, you're completely sane. You're good, you did the right thing, I love you! With all my heart, I love you, André. I adore you."

Furious, amid gasps of pain, he said: "Dr. Chardin lied to me! He was mistaken, Dr. Chardin! Oh, science! Their science! They don't know anything! They lie! They say to themselves, *Let's console this person who's suffering—and anyway, he might be cured!* So he consoled me—assured me, in fact, that I was a man like any other. What another scientist had told me, he repeated to me, the day before our marriage. He was afraid that, if I lost you, if I renounced you, I might kill myself. I would have done it. He didn't say to me what he should have said: 'Better to disappear!' Some people don't have the right to love, don't have the right to be happy. They have a flaw, here! And that's it! And I've given you my name, and you've given me your life, in complete confidence! And we're waking up to that reality..." He looked at the newspaper, pushing the copy of the *Boulevard* with his foot. "I'm incapable of knowing what I did the other night, and I'll be dishonored, because, although unconscious, I'll be responsible! It's idiotic, insane, stupid, atrocious! Oh, my poor Cécile how unhappy I am."

The sobs rose into his throat again; he was like a little child. She tried to calm him with caresses, the tender words whispered to small children when they have to go to sleep. There are nursery rhymes to assuage dolor too.

André felt in desperate anger beginning to melt away under those soft words. She found delightfully soothing words. The Sister of Charity dormant in every woman quickly became, for the unfortunate, a mental field-hospital, fully equipped with all devotion and gentleness. The wounded man felt a coolness on his injury.

She told him to hope. She did not tell him, as the physician had, in affirming that will-power could do everything, that one is cured when one wants to be cured. She changed André's tears of rage, excited by the idea that he was once again prey to the Other, into tears that were almost gentle.

"It's necessary, though," he said, "that I find those bills. I want to return them. They're not mine."

"Return them? Was Prince Stalinski playing with you or a phantom? He was playing with you. Give the money to the poor if you want to. Lose them in another game with the prince—but don't tell yourself that the person who was gambling the other night wasn't you. Your secret, André—our secret—must remain between the two of us. Don't let anyone suspect, or let anyone guess...and I swear to you that we'll get rid of the one you call the Other. I promise you, I promise you, we'll get cast him out!"

"Oh yes, of course, there's exorcism!" said André, brusquely, his voice strident. "In the twentieth century! A man possessed! It's ridiculous!" Suddenly, obsessively, his brow furrowed. "Where's that money?" Tearing himself away from Cécile, he said: "In the studio! I'll get it."

She tried to follow him.

"No, I beg you, let me go! I need to be alone. I need to relax my nerves, to weep."

"Weep with me: it will be a pleasure like any other," she said, trying to laugh.

He was already on the staircase, running up the steps.

And once he was alone, he tried to remember.

XI. Desperation

About the card game, Prince Stalinski, his return, the wallet that Cécile had seen in his hands, he did not remember anything. There was a lacuna in his life—and the excision did not date back very far...it was a matter of yesterday.

"Come on, come on...I came in here...I put that money in some drawer..."

He searched, rummaging through the dressers, the chests of drawers. His memory was blank. If Frédéric Clément's article had been an invention from beginning to end, André would have thought it absolutely natural on the part of a reporter. No circumstance to which he could attach a past sensation came back to mind. There was a gap.

Seeking truth in that black hole, he felt a fever gradually taking hold of him; the veins were throbbing in his temples; a vague sensation took possession of him, as if objects were taking on phantasmal appearances. He had to make an effort of will to maintain his composure, to conserve his reason.

Then, suddenly, the money turned up, in a folder into which he normally slipped his drawings, proving to him that the Boulevardier had not invented anything, but had reported a fact.

He counted the banknotes.

"Fifty-two thousand francs!"

Of the fashion in which he had won them, he could not remember anything. It was a kind of somnambulist, not a conscious and active being who had gambled against Prince Stalinski. Before the absolute reality, however, André bowed down, crushed by the evidence. For hours, his habitual life had been suppressed. That human being made of flesh and bone, which was his self, had fallen prey to the Other. It was the Other who had won the banknotes.

"The Other! The Other!" André repeated the words aloud, and looked around, as if he ought to be able to see the specter of his own person.

He held the bills between his fingers, stroking them, wondering if the banknotes might suddenly turn into dry leaves, like the money the demon of legend gives to those whose souls he buys.

"Someone else's money!" The other of whom he was thinking, this time, was his opponent, Prince Stalinski. It seemed to him that he was in possession of the wad of paper illegally, that the sum was stolen.

"Let's see—where does the Prince live?"

He searched for the address in *Tout Paris*. "Stabad...Stanbard...Stalinski, Prince Ladislas, 70, Avenue des Champs-Élysées... Good! I've got it! I'll find out what impression he had of me, the other night."

He put the bills back in the wallet with the monogram, went back down, and asked for his hat and gloves.

Cécile was waiting for him.

"You're going out?"

"Yes."

"Where are you going?"

"To see Prince Stalinski."

"Why?"

"I want to know what I said, what I did...what *he* did, *him*...the man that is *me*. Oh, the atrocious comedy!"

He tried to laugh, and Cécile tried to calm him down, to prevent him from going out.

"No, no—anyway, the fresh air will do me good."

Walking did, in fact, momentarily dissipate the migraine of sorts that was squeezing his head. He went up the Champs-Élysées on foot, trying to forget, the eye of the landscape-painter embracing with its gaze the long avenue of slender trees, like the smears of Japanese prints, which terminated, in the distance, in the mist, in the hole of the Arc de Triomphe.

Before Nature, the artist recovered his self-possession. He had arrived, almost having forgotten why he had come, at Prince Stalinski's house.

He stopped dead, abruptly asking himself a question that frightened him.

What am I going to say to the man, whom I hardly know? He gambled, he lost. I can give him his revenge at the Club. But why interrogate him? Why, and about what? If he tells me that he found me strange the other night, am I going to tell him that I wasn't responsible for my actions and that the person who won his money was...what? A madman!

"No, let's wait."

He did not go up to the Prince's apartment. He would see him at the Club.

He resumed walking, but this time aimlessly, accelerating his pace, going toward the Bois, telling himself that the winter wind would calm his nerves; and as he walked, the obstinate thought came back to him, as if impelled by magnetism: he was not cured, then; not the master of his thoughts and actions; he was, therefore, still the prey of that frightful psychoneurosis, since, for hours, in the midst of the Club, at a gaming table, among those Parisians who were watching the game, he had been able, an astonishing automaton, to play, to chat, to ask questions, to reply, without even the shadow of a memory remaining to him of what he had said, his responses, his actions...

It's terrifying—simply terrifying.

Now an anger was growling and growing within him: an anger that saw Dr. Chardin as guilty of not having told the truth, of having been mistaken, and of having deceived him.

If I have to go back to that torture, to fall into that evil uncertainty again, why didn't he tell me that I should not— could not—marry? He lied; he failed in his duty!

Yes, undoubtedly, as he has cried out to Cécile a little while before, Dr. Chardin had been afraid of the nervousness of the desperate man who had talked about loading a revolver after the consultation and ending everything right away. Dr.

Chardin had taken pity on him. He had refused to condemn a man to death. He had spared him.

Spared me from what? Spared me from a painful step that would have been a liberation? I should be dead; it should be over!

André plunged into the pathways of the Bois, walking rapidly, talking to himself, fleeing noise, finding a charm in the deserted by-ways, in the chilly atmosphere of a damp December.

It was one of those rotten December days in which arthritis twists the limbs of rheumatics like vine-stocks: gray and lugubrious weather, with damp cold falling from dead trees from which droplets hang, as if the branches were weeping, pleased the painter hungry for solitude.

He went on, without knowing were, carrying his thoughts, driven by them; and the poignant sentiment of his impotence in confrontation with the illness from which he was suffering became sharper as he repeated: *He lied! The doctor lied!*

So, at any time, in any circumstances, he was at risk of the reappearance of that "double" who would expel him from his life? Definitely, he did not belong to himself. He could smile at Cécile and suddenly, a stranger might loom up between the two of them. Everything for which he had hoped—a cure, forgetfulness—was impossible.

Sick! I'm sick! Oh, my father-in-law, with his dreams of success, his ambitions of honor. The Institut! Poor general! It's at Sainte-Anne, your Institut, my dear André Fortis. At Sainte-Anne![26]

He became excited in that rapid march, which he wanted to be exhausting, as if he wished to tame the beast, to chase away the obsessive, dolorous thought that griped him more forcefully at every step: the possibility of being separated from the wife who was his, who bore his name, who was proud of

---

[26] The psychiatric hospital created on the site of Sainte-Anne Farm in 1867.

it, and whom he adored, with all the strength of his being, as an ideal creature, the best and most devoted.

To lose her! To be thrown into a padded cell one day and leave her, a widow without being widowed, the widow of a living dead man, to a future with no exit—or to another man who might perhaps love her!

An unreasoning jealousy—the jealousy of the future— tortured him. Rather than submit to such an obsession, to live with that tormenting threat, would it not be better to end it right away? Was that really living?

He went on, like a wanderer, passing beyond the paths of the Bois, still walking, walking determinedly, taking no account of the route he was following. Even fatigue did not affect him in that continual acceleration. A human machine, he resembled one of those iron machines the hectic sped of which intoxicates its driver. Moving aimlessly, he had a kind of mania of velocity, the fever of a jockey whipping his mount. And as he went further, his excitement took another form: objects, houses, trees, the background of the landscape, drowned in mist, underwent metamorphoses into unexpected appearances.

He was going through suburban streets that were familiar to him, through woods he had sketched, but he did not find any of their accustomed aspects. The houses seemed to be watching an unknown passer-by with open eyes. The trees, blackened by winter, extended twisted limbs toward him, hostile and menacing. Whether it was the fog, the dusk or the winter twilight he did not know, but he had the vague sensation of being surrounded by darkness, enveloped by one of those dense, cold atmospheres that he had sometimes traversed in London.

And he went on, and on, gradually losing even the sentiment of his personality, having before his eyes those rapid flashes, stormy zigzags, that used to precede the strange crises from which Dr. Burke and Monsieur Chardin had declared him liberated.

He wondered now where he was, and what unknown city he was entering. An immense, broad and seemingly sovereign avenue opened up, tall trees forming dark masses to either side. Trams were passing by, sounding their horns. He had gone through a set of railings cutting the avenue in two. Men in képis had gazed at him, and the uniform of customs officers had seemed as singular as that of foreign soldiers. In the distance, at the end of the avenue, in the mist, the silhouette of a large château blocked the view.

He knew it well, that château. He had seen it before. Certainly, he had seen it.

What was that building growing on the horizon with every forward step he took? Where was he?

He interrogated the houses bordering the avenue. Some of them, constructions of the last century, overlooked high walls bordering the avenue. Vast buildings, solemn in style, loomed up with enormous portals and sculpted blazons. All of it was familiar. The château in the distance, appearing in a mist of dream, he also recognized.

It was Versailles. He was in Versailles.

What was he doing in Versailles?

He continued on his way, aimlessly. Now he was going across the empty main square, swept by the winder wind. He went straight ahead, went into the park, gazing, as if they were new apparitions, at the avenues, the horizons, the bronze tritons in the empty fountains, the immense garden depopulated by the cold and that astonishing solitude. It seemed to him that he was visiting a cemetery. The statues of demigods, heroes and goddesses appeared to him on their pedestals like images of death rising over tombs. And the north wind, the December wind, whistling through the leafless trees, added a note of complaint to that majestic sadness.

He was going over the lawn, still walking, when the sentiment of hunger made him change course, instinctively returning toward the city. The hungry beast suddenly woke up in the wanderer. He would find a restaurant and stop there. He went into the Réservoirs[27] via the exit of the park, and sat down at a table in the large hall.

---

[27] The Hôtel des Réservoirs, constructed in 1751 for Madame de Pompadour, with a corridor connecting it to the palace, was combined with a neighboring building and converted into a luxury hotel in 1870, which function it served until it was bought by the state in 1934.

XII. An Affair of Honor

Diners were installed, finishing their meals, chatting: English people, including a young blonde who bore a strange resemblance of Cécile, the sight of whom brought a question into André Fortis' mind. *Where have I seen that face before?*

The new man that he became in that second state only had a confused recollection of who his wife was.

At any rate, he experienced a sensation of wellbeing at pausing in the ambulatory fever and sitting down, and he ate with a good appetite, only irritated by the noise of his neighbors, who were dining merrily. Their laughter seemed to him to be ironic. He wondered whether they might be laughing at him.

Why? He could not explain that—but he would have preferred to be alone, not to see anyone, not to hear any noise. Young people at the far end of the room, recently disembarked from their automobile, appeared to him to be darting sly glances at him from time to time. A pretty young woman, of whom he could only see the back of the neck and the black chignon, turned toward him from time to time. And still there was that same question, that eternal question: Why?

Did he look ridiculous, then?

He experienced a kind of embarrassment at knowing that people were looking at him, and, impulsively, he was tempted to go straight up to the strangers and ask them the question. Lines of verse he had once heard returned to his mind: *Par le sambleu, Messieurs, je ne croyais pas être/Si plaisant que je suis!*[28] Then his thoughts drifted toward the memories of the

---

[28] This quotation from Molière's *Le Misanthrope* (1666) was well-known by virtue of being cited in Littré's dictionary as a key example of the employment of the meaningless oath "sambleu." An approximate translation would be "Crikey, chaps, I don't think I'm as funny as all that."

theater that those words evoked, and he forgot momentarily the gazes fixed upon him, the irony that he thought he had detected a little while before. He felt an impression of relief, as in a restful pause. In a kind of singular wave, reality seemed to be enveloped in a mist, but that mist now had the charm of those light fogs that resemble bright smoke, or silvery gauze.

He no longer paid any attention to his neighbors. In fact, he no longer paid any attention to anything. Without worrying about why he was there, in the gentle warmth of that restaurant dining-room, he allowed himself to live.

Having finished his meal, he asked for the bill, got up and left, the waiter having brought him his coat. He left without knowing where he was going, pausing momentarily on the threshold and looking at the broad, almost deserted streets in front of him.

As he was standing there, an automobile coming into the Réservoirs came toward him, and he heard a brusque voice call out from inside the vehicle: "Look out, imbecile!"

Instinctively, he adjusted his position, stepping back against the wall. The large red vehicle passed close to his feet, nearly running over them—and he experienced the irresistible anger of a pedestrian threatened by a danger that takes on an appearance of violence and insult.

The voice emerging from the automobile seemed to him to be a brutal order, and he sensed a kind of revolt, as if he had been subjected to a personal insult. He took a few rapid steps toward the interior courtyard in which the automobile had stopped. A kind of Eskimo dressed in animal skins got out of it, holding hands with a package of furs that resembled a hairy sack, which was a woman, probably a pretty woman. The Eskimo had not taken off the enormous blue-tinted goggles that made his face into the mask of a Neapolitan Pulcinella remodeled in the American style.

"You could be more polite," said André Fortis, advancing toward the worldly Samoyed.

The two living furs exchanged a movement of the head that signified *What does he want?* and a voice emerged from beneath the mask and goggles.

"What's that you say, Monsieur?"

"I'm saying that you nearly ran me over, and that your only apology was to speak to me like an uncouth boor."

With his furry gloves, the motorist took off the goggles that hid his face, and the masculine face of a young man appeared within the animal skin, with a powdery blond moustache beneath a slender nose, and two very blue eyes beneath eyebrows gray with dust.

"I'm not in the habit of hearing myself described in that manner, Monsieur," said the traveler. "I allowed myself to make a remark to you in passing that was merely addressed to a barely-glimpsed obstacle, but you have put an evident intention into your words, and you will take back the term that you have just pronounced."

The woman enveloped in her sheepksin coat, her head in a kind of grey hood, placed her furry hand on a sleeve swollen by wolfskin, and repeated, in a supplicant tone; "Henri! Henri!"

"I shall not take back anything at all," said André, looking the young man in the eyes. "Speed does not exclude politeness."

"Monsieur!"

An arm as hairy as a bear's paw rose up in an impulsive gesture to threaten André. In his turn, however, with a similar instinctive moment, the painter pushed that raised arm away. His fingers brushed the stranger's cheek, and the traveler, similar beneath the apparent bristling of his furs to a wounded animal, would have leapt upon him if the young woman, frightened, had not stopped him by repeating the same cry, the same name: "Henri! Henri!"

The noise had attracted the waiters; the chauffeur, enveloped in goatskin, came running. There was an abrupt silence, and the motorist, having become very pale, said as he rummaged in his overcoat: "I hope, Monsieur, that we shall not leave it there!" And, reaching into his wallet, he took out a card and handed it to André.

The painter did not even look at him. He too handed over his card, bowed to the young woman, who was huddled against her traveling companion, and said, with a nervous gesture: "I beg your pardon, Madame."

Then he went away, going straight ahead, without knowing where...

XIII. *After the Crisis*

André Fortis found himself—or, to put it better, recovered self-consciousness—on a wooden bench, in the cold bleakness of a railway station in which rare travelers, like shadows in the gleam of the gaslight, were asking for tickets of Paris. He had arrived there an hour before, driven by instinct, mechanically, and as he had been told that he had nearly forty minutes to wait, he had sat down on the bench, after having tried to kill time by looking at the old multicolored posters of last summer's seaside resorts, as sad as vanished joys, in the half-light. Exhausted by fatigue, in spite of the meal that had just refreshed him, he was gripped by an invincible numbness, asleep and dreaming about some monstrous beast, some colossal cave-bear extending its claws toward him at the end of enormous hairy paws...

And he stayed there, drawing his garments over his knees, instinctively seeking the angle of the wall in order to sleep in peace, indifferent to the noise and the cold or, rather, lulled by the sound of footsteps, and the distant the rumble of cars and trams. He had remained in that reparative state of slumber, which had become profound, until the moment when a keener sensation of cold, almost an impression of suffering, woke him up—and his amazement was profound on finding himself there, in that station, without the slightest suspicion of how he came to be there.

Damn it, where am I now? What's happened to me?

He now resembled a drunkard whose intoxication had dissipated, a sleeper extracted from a nightmare. He had gone to sleep in the second state that made him another person; he woke up in the plenitude of his own personality: crisis past; dream effaced. He was André; it really was André Fortis who now had a clear perception of place, people and things, of the surroundings in which his self was operating.

By virtue of that very fact, he realized that there had been a lacuna in his existence, that he had not come to that station of his own free will, that it was not him who had come there but the Other.

How long had he been here? When had the frightful crisis gripped him? He could not remember anything. No image, however vague or fugitive, remained in his brain of what had happened at the Réservoirs or elsewhere. Of the traversal of the Bois that had brought him to Versailles nothing remained in his memory. He had woken up by night in an unknown railway station, shivering with cold, his feet icy and his head aching—that was the only perception he had of exterior life.

He only remembered that he had left the Rue Murillo in order to go and see Prince Salinski. What had happened after that? After that, there was another lacuna in his life, and what had happened—whether for hours or days, he had no idea— escaped him, as if it were a matter of someone else's life. And it had, indeed, been the life, the actions, thoughts, gestures and deeds of someone else.

Then an atrocious, desperate dolor shook his entire being. He had hoped for liberation! He had believed that he might get a grip on himself again, escape the claws of the neurosis. And so rapidly, after so short a time, the evil had returned, an ironic demon, to sink its talons into his distressed brain!

In the presence of people, who could hear him, André choked back the sob that swelled his bosom. He only had one thought: to go home, to find Cécile, who must have been waiting for him, distressed, if he had been wandering for days on end.

First, though, he needed to know where he was. He recognized that provincial railway station, that wooden staircase going up to the waiting-rooms. He took a few steps out of the station, looked at the banal monument with the clock in the middle, as luminous as the eye in the forehead of those Cyclopes Dr. Chardin had talked about the other day, at Madame de Vernière's house.

It was Versailles station. He had come to Versailles, without even being aware of it. How much time he had spent in Versailles, on that wooden bench, it was impossible to tell, Only in Paris, from the unhappy Cécile, could he find out how long it was since he had left the house in the Rue Murillo.

As for himself, he did not know anything. There had been a brutal interruption of his normal life, a substitution of a secondary existence for his customary consciousness.

Oh, poor, poor wretch! Is this living?

The train was leaving. He asked for a ticket to Paris. For a moment, he was afraid that he might not have any money on him. What would have happened to him if he had found himself without a sou in that town? Like a tramp, he would have had to knock on the door of a friend, some painter or acquaintance—or, if he had not dared to do that, set out on foot on the road to Paris, in the nocturnal cold, his limbs weary, exhausted by fatigue.

In the carriage, he experienced a haste to arrive, to know sooner. The wintry horizons, bathed by bright, chilly moonlight, rested his landscape-painter's eyes. Viroflay, Chaville, Ville-d'Avray, familiar locations, went past, illuminated by a spectral glow, with the reddened windows of houses dotting the horizon.

It was not very late—nine o'clock. At ten o'clock he would be home, reassuring Cécile, who must be worried. And as soon as he arrived at the Gare Saint-Lazare, he leapt into a fiacre in order to get there sooner.

The porter told him that Madame was in the studio, and, as he was tired, in spite of the respite in the railway carriage between Versailles and Paris, he took the elevator that went up to his workroom. As he opened the elevator door the electric light came on, and he let himself fall, tiredly, on to the yellow leather seat.

It's not very far, but I need the rest!

The elevator rose up slowly, shadows dancing on the glazed window during the ascent. When he arrived at the level of the first floor André heard a door open and saw two silhouettes suddenly profiled on the frosted glass: a man's and a woman's; and he heard Cécile's voice thanking someone. So she was not in the studio, as the porter had affirmed!

The two silhouettes disappeared, sinking as if into a trap-door as the elevator continued its rise, but André could still hear Cécile's voice, fading way. He emerged from the cage, sent the elevator down again by pressing the brass button, and leaned over the stairwell. On the floor below Cécile was still bidding farewell to a small, thin man of strange appearance, with long white hair, who was going downstairs, hat in hand.

He did not know the visitor. Some stranger—perhaps an art dealer or a client?

He went down in his turn and rejoined Cécile, who seemed astonished.

Where had he sprung from? She interrogated him. She had been waiting for him all day and all evening, wondering whether something might have happened to him. Accidents often happen abruptly in life.

He explained that he had gone to Versailles, but without daring to mention the further lacuna that he had suffered, and of which, this time, he was ashamed. In his turn, he asked: "Who was that old gentleman you were showing out, to whom you said thanks?"

"He's not a old man His white hairs aren't those of old age. That's Dr. Klipper."

The name reminded André abruptly of the conversation that had troubled him at Madame de Vernière's house, and he looked at Cécile in astonishment.

"Dr. Klipper, here?"

"Yes, I wanted to consult him. I wasn't able to get through the door of his laboratory. I wrote to him, and he came to apologize."

"Consult Dr. Klipper? On your own behalf?"

"No," she said, "on behalf of someone else."

André tried to laugh, but Klipper's name caused him to feel a sick sensation, as if it recalled past anguish. "And you didn't say anything about it to me? You have secrets from me."

"First, I wanted to find out whether we could have recourse to the scientist in question, and Dr. Chardin offered to take us to Klipper's house personally. It was Monsieur Chardin who gave me a letter of introduction to his colleague.

"And I only learn that by chance, listening to a conversation through the glazed door of an elevator!" he said. "A scene from a vaudeville...or a melodrama. A husband comes home and he sees two Chinese shadows emerge from his dwelling. He emerges and kills. Or he divorces. Othello in an elevator!"

He took her hands, touched by the knowledge that she was thinking about him, but also anxious in knowing that she was anxious. Oh well, since she had summoned Dr. Klipper, he would go with Chardin to consult Dr. Klipper. In any case, he was curious to see that man of genius at close range.

"What if I had arrived a little sooner?"

But he experienced a need not to talk any longer about that obsession, which Klipper seemed to incarnate. He even avoided answering Cécile's questions. She was astonished to see him weary, his clothes dusty and his boots muddied by the effects of the long journey.

"Have you walked a long way?"

"Yes. The fresh air does me good."

He avoided all explanation, having the tragic impression that he could not explain anything and experiencing the need to spend one of those evenings of calming conversation with Cécile, under the lamp, in which people who love one another find in togetherness, even in silence, the supreme tenderness of absolute love.

"Are you hungry?"

He was not hungry. He would have a cup of tea if Cécile was having one—and there, together, she forgot the day of anxious waiting she had just spent, and he obstinately chased away any recurrent thought of that cold waiting-room at Versailles. They stayed there until late in the night, glad of the solitude, in the great nocturnal silence of sleeping Paris.

"To stay like this," he said, "huddled together every evening, after having worked all day, would be happiness!"

"It is happiness," Cécile replied, as if to bring the painter's thoughts back to the reality of the situation.

By virtue of a singular phenomenon of forgetfulness, however, André did not experience any anxiety. His entire life seemed to him to be contained in the present moment. He concentrated in the warm enjoyment of an unanticipated repose all the joy of savoring the exquisite quality of an impression snatched and stolen from his phantoms. The tea whose fumes rose up like an exhalation, the pretty pensive blonde head, those soft blue eyes, so tender under the light of the large lampshade, that halting conversation, even its silences, with tender gazes exchanged at length, seemed to him to be the life he had always lived. There was nothing else in the world. The rest disappeared, fading away. A fog lighter than the one trailing beneath the trees of the Parc Monceau glimpsed in the moonlight beneath the pale sky; visions more fugitive than the fumes emerging like mist from the porcelain tea-cups; nothing was as true as that repose, that silent evening in the familiar drawing-room, far from everything, close to his beloved.

"Do you know," said the painter, "that I produce my most beautiful paintings on evenings like this, without touching a brush, chatting to you, dreaming in your company? Oh, the beautiful visions there, the lovely landscapes, in gazing at you, in placing you, mentally, in the midst of those imaginary pictures that I shall probably never paint, but are worth more than all those I have painted!"

"But which the dealers wouldn't want!" Cécile replied, laughing.

"Oh, yes, they'd want them, if they saw them as I see them! We're all like that. Our best works are those we dream. 'My most beautiful paintings,' Julien Dupré said, 'I paint for myself alone, in the corner of my fireside, smoking my pipe.' I'd gladly do the same in contemplating you and looking at the fumes from the teapot. Of, how good it is! I shouldn't ever say that I'm happy—no one should ever say that they're happy, because it brings bad look—but what a dear, sweet evening! In life, it's only these moments that count."

And after having gone to sleep on that sensation of exquisite quietude, André woke up the next day with an ardor for work, a confidence and a gaiety that reassured Cécile and reminded her of something that Dr. Klipper had said: "If your husband can believe that he's cured, he will be cured."

"I'm going to work hard today, my darling," said André Fortis.

"Real paintings? Not those one paints while smoking one's pipe or watching tea fume?"

"Naughty!"

He kissed her eyelids slowly, as he had when they were engaged, and went up to his studio, alert and glad to be alive.

Oh, the joy of labor, the pleasure of making up his palette, displaying his colors there—the painter's joy in scenting the oil mixed with the paste in the tubes; the writer's joy in the flow of ink from the pen on to the smooth paper, like blood from a vein. André experienced that joy in the fever of delight that an artist promises himself who has before him a day of ardent and resolute work, good, free and absorbing work.

He had set on his easel and painting that evoked, in a sort of apotheosis of the setting sun, the crumbling Campanile of Venice[29] that no longer perceives the ships coming from the sea.

He was sitting on his stool, glad to have long hours of good solitude before him, in a fever-free activity of joyful work, when a series of raps on the door extracted him from his first moments of active delight.

---

[29] The story is set before the Campanile di San Marco collapsed in 1902, but was composed afterwards.

XIV. Two Unexpected Visitors

He knew that fashion of warning, which his manservant Aurèle[30] had orders to use only in grave circumstances, when it was a matter of an important request or decisive news.

"Come in," he said, anticipating one of those inevitable visits that cut off inspiration, casting away the thought of the caressed idea.

The servant apologized, knowing full well that Fortis' initial reaction in such circumstances was one of nervous abruptness.

"What is it, Aurèle?"

"There are two Messieurs who desire to see Monsieur."

"Two Messieurs?"

"I told them that Monsieur was not receiving, that Monsieur was not at home. They insisted, repeating that they would come back and that it was absolutely necessary for them to know at what time they could see Monsieur. They told me to give you their cards. Here are their cards."

Aurèle held out a tray bearing two cards, which Fortis examined. The domestic added: "Oh! They also said: tell Monsieur Fortis that we have come on behalf of Monsieur de Morlière. I thought it best to let Monsieur know..."

André looked at the cards, repeating the name *Monsieur de Morlière* while rereading the other names engraved on the pieces of cardboard—the Comte de Lartiges and Commandant Vignal, of the General Staff—wondering what this double visit signified, of unknown people coming on behalf of a third person.

"You're certain that these Messieurs asked for Monsieur Fortis?"

---

[30] In an earlier chapter André's manservant was called François, but it is possible that this is not the same one.

"Yes, Monsieur, perfectly sure," Aurèle replied. "One of them, the taller one, even said 'He must be in his studio'— proof that they know that Monsieur is a painter."

"Monsieur de Morlière? Who is Monsieur de Morlière?" wondered Andre aloud,

"Should I send them up, Monsieur?"

"Send them up."

Two men coming on the part of a third, Andre thought. *No one does that for any reason other than a duel. On the other hand, two people might come to see paintings that a third art-lover has mentioned.*

He was in haste to know what it was about, and, setting down his palette on the stool, he gazed with a slight sadness at the flamboyant sunset from which the unexpected visit was snatching him away.

Aurèle reappeared on the threshold of the studio, ushering in two elegantly-dressed men who bowed to André in correct, slightly solemn, diplomatic fashion.

It was not the visit of art-lovers.

"Is it Monsieur André Fortis to whom we have the honor of speaking?" said one of them.

"Yes, Monsieur."

He invited them to sit down, even pushing forward an armchair, enveloping them with a glance and studying them swiftly, and waited.

One of them—the one who had spoken—was a slimly-built man of about fifty, bald, with a thin moustache that was still blond, stiff-necked, wearing a blue cravat, in a tight frock-coat of the latest fashion. As he spoke, he advanced shiny boots with gaiters, as if to show off his feet: an elegant club-man, a gentleman hunter.

The other, still young, was thin and stuff, with a Don Quixote profile and a Russian moustache; he had to be a cavalry officer.

"Monsieur," he said, emphasizing his words, clipping them with his teeth as if by a coquetry of diction, "our friend's name will inform you sufficiently clearly of the purpose of our visit."

"Your friend's name?" said André, a trifle surprised.

"Monsieur de Morlière has asked us to demand an explanation—or, since it is necessary to speak clearly, an apology—for the altercation that took place between you yesterday, at Versailles."

André listened, scrutinizing every word, like a man having difficulty understanding the syllables of a foreign language.

He found himself abruptly confronted by a reality of which he knew nothing, which loomed up before him like an unexpected vision brutally materialized. What, and whom, was it about? Who was this Monsieur de Morlière, and to what unknown altercation as the visitor alluding?"

The two men were the seconds of some adversary of whose very existence he had had no suspicion.

Come on, he said to himself, *let's summon up all our composure, and maintain our reason.*

What he wanted, knowing nothing of what is was for which he was being called to account, was to discover the cause for the sending of seconds, without letting Monsieur de Morlière's representatives see that he knew absolutely nothing about the object of their mission.

There was a kind of fencing-match, in which André, not giving himself away, dominating himself by a powerful effort of will in order not to let his amazement show—his incredible ignorance of an action that, evidently and certainly, he had been the agent without knowing it—sought to learn indirectly a secret for which he was responsible without being conscious of it.

"An altercation with Monsieur de Morlière?" he said, coldly. "I do not have the honor of knowing Monsieur de Morlière."

"We are well aware that you do not know Monsieur de Morlière, any more than he knew you yesterday," said the Comte de Lartiges. "Personally, at least, since our client is not unaware of the name of a celebrated artist. However, although the insult was not addressed deliberately to Monsieur de Morlière, it was nevertheless an insult, and, in the presence of a lady, it takes on a sharper quality, for which our friend requests, I repeat, a reparation."

"I'm ready to give Monsieur de Morlière any reparation he wishes," said André, suppressing his emotion, "provide that he tells me in what way I have offended him."

The Commandant, who had not unsealed his lips, interjected brusquely: "What, Monsieur, because an automobile passed close to you, and you do not shout a warning quickly enough, someone hurls at you—perhaps excitedly, too excitedly, if you wish—an exclamation, an epithet that displeases you, and you reply with a gesture, almost brushing the cheek of a man you do not know, who has, perhaps, putting matters in the worst light, almost run you over, but whom you have materially insulted...and you ask how you have offended Monsieur de Morlière!"

Andre Fortis' eyes never quit those of Commandant Vignal. He tried to read there what the soldier was not saying, completing the scene himself, the details of which he was ignorant, but which was being revealed to him as if it had happened to someone else.

And that eternal word, *the Other, the Other*, came back into his mind: the "someone else" who had incurred the debt for which these men had come to him to demand payment.

That frightful lacuna in his life gaped wide, full of mystery.

"Are you certain," he said, slowly, dominating himself by a powerful effort, suppressing the beating of his heart, fearful of seeming frightened when he was actually thunderstruck and dazed, "that I really did make the impulsive gesture in question?"

"The staff of the Hôtel des Réservoirs witnessed it," said Monsieur de Lartiges.

"And we're astonished that you're trying to get out of it by dilatory means," added the Commandant.

André replied curly, determined now to cover up the Other, the guilty party, in order not to have to make a confession that seemed to him to be shameful, revealing of himself.

"I beg your pardon; I'm not seeking a way out. I was simply asking exactly what happened between Monsieur de Morlière and myself."

Monsieur de Morlière's seconds exchanged a surprised glance. "Well," said Commandant Vignal, "although I've already made it clear, I'll make it clearer still. Yesterday, at quarter past seven Monsieur de Morlière, returning from an automobile excursion with Madame de Morlière, shouted at you: 'Get out of the way, imbecile!' You came toward him when he got out of his car, and, words having been exchanged, you raised your hand to him—and you took the card that he gave you, while you handed him yours."

I didn't find that card, André thought. *It must still be in my pocket.*

The Comte de Lartiges held out the piece of cardboard bearing the painter's address. "Is that card really yours, Monsieur?"

"Indeed."

"*André Fortis, Rue Murillo.*"

"It's my card, my name and my address."

"In that case, Monsieur, it only remains for us to return to the object of our visit. Monsieur de Morlière demands, as we have had the honor of telling you, a formal apology or reparation by arms."

André smiled. He had come to find the tragic situation ironically comical: a human being becoming responsible for actions of which he was not even conscious."

To fight on another's behalf! he thought. Another thought passed through his mind as he looked at the two men sitting in his studio, demanding an apology or a duel. *After all, that's what war is! Poor fellows fighting on behalf of others, for the sins of others!*

"Messieurs," he said, "if I have by means of an unreflective action, offended Monsieur de Morlière, whom, I repeat, I do not know, I express all my regrets to you—but do you really believe that I owe him the apology that you're requesting of me, you must admit, in a rather imperious tone?"

"Our client's tone," said the Commandant, "is adequate to your action."

"Regrets are insufficient," said Monsieur de Lartiges, as if regretting the fact himself.

"And the apology would consist...?"

The Commandant completed André Fortis' question: "of a letter in which the apology demanded..."

"Or requested," the Comte put in.

"Would be clearly and formally expressed."

André might have placed himself—like a shield, so to speak—in front of a kind of specter, but he told himself angrily that the apology would be made by the Fortis whose visiting card Monsieur de Lartiges was still holding in his fingers, and the mere idea of putting his name to such a letter caused his blood to rise, as if in a surge of anger.

"No, Messieurs," he said, "once again, I'm sorry for what has happened—a reflex action, nothing more—but it's impossible for me to write the letter you're requesting or demanding...the expression hardly matters. I can deplore the action, declare that the gesture was accomplished mechanically, without any intention on my part, but I cannot say or do any more."

"Monsieur," the Comte de Lartiges concluded then, coldly, "When one is no longer master of oneself, as you have been, one pays the debt of one's impatience or unconsciousness."

Without knowing it, he had pronounced the nub of the situation. Consciousness must bear the penalty of unconsciousness.

"A debt to pay?" said André Fortis. "Well, Monsieur, that is what I shall do."

"By apologizing?"

"By placing myself at Monsieur de Morlière's disposal."

"We shall have the honor of awaiting your friends," said the Comte de Lartiges, bowing.

"Our salutations, Monsieur."

They went out with the same official politeness and the same bows that had marked their entrance, and Fortis, slightly sunned by the adventure, found himself alone in that strange situation, to which he was subject without having created it.

There could be no question of explanation or attenuation with the seconds he was about to select. He would have blushed to admit that, at certain times of his life, he became suddenly irresponsible. No, he would recognize the insult made to Monsieur de Morlière and would fight in order to repair it. Except that he wanted to get it over with quickly, very quickly, fearing that the nervous effects consequent upon the stupid adventure might themselves bring on a further crisis.

What if, for example, the Other reappeared on the way to the duel and took possession of his being? What if the Other, who had no consciousness of his actions, recoiled before his own responsibility? What if the Other did not go to the encounter of honor that he, Fortis, had accepted?

That incredible complication was possible. André, brave to the point of temerity, was terrified that someone else, who did not have his courage, might be substituted for him. He did not know him, that automaton who became, at certain times, his double, his living—and very much alive—phantom.

Come on, he said to himself. *Don't think about that. I'm master of myself; I feel it. It's necessary to hurry, that's all, and that no one should have the slightest idea of that anxiety.*

He did not want to say anything to Cécile. Why trouble her? If he were wounded, she would learn the truth soon enough.

He asked two friends from the Club, a painter as celebrated for his exploits under arms as for his powerful and decorative portraits, and the captain of a ship released by the Ministry of Marine, to arrange a meeting with Monsieur de Lartiges and Commandant Vignal.

Monsieur de Morlière, in the capacity of the offended party, demanded a duel with pistols. André would have preferred épées. They would fight with pistols.

André, having got up at dawn, spent the morning writing his last will and testament for Cécile, which he then hid and locked in the drawer of a small Hispano-Moorish cabinet. Then, his mind quite free, making a violent effort of will to dispel the thought of a possible and sudden interruption of his normal life, he had taken an automobile with the artist Pétrus Hardy, the captain, and Dr. Wyns, the surgeon who was to witness the duel. On the way, in spite of the noise of the automobile, they had chatted. Dr, Klipper's name had chanced to come up in the course of the conversation.

"Oh, yes," said Wyns, "a madman—but a madman of genius. He's one of those men who oscillate between the Panthéon and a padded cell, who are capable of working miracles."

Fortis then saw Klipper's silhouette again, going down the staircase of his house. Cécile must have spoken to him. If the duel did not prove fatal—anything can happen, alas, and bullets are crazier than people!—he would consult this Klipper, and ask that madman for a remedy for his own madness.

Monsieur de Morlière and his seconds having already arrived at the Sablonnière de Viroflay, the rendezvous chosen the day before, when he got out of his automobile, André Fortis bowed to his adversary and, turning up the collar of his overcoat, placed himself in the position indicated to him. Pétrus Hardy measured the distance and Commandant Vigal, clapping his hands, gave the signal for the combat.

Monsieur de Morlière fired first. André, with emotion, heard a small abrupt sound, like the detonation of a child's toy, in the moist air of the December morning. Then, having to respond, he raised the barrel of his pistol and pressed the trigger.

The formal statement was about to observe, according to the formula, that two bullets had been exchanged without result. With a charming courtesy, however, Monsieur de Morlière advanced toward André, who gallantly took the hand extended to him.

"Monsieur," he said then, "I now have the right to regret an action, for which it seems to me that I was not responsible, and I beg you to believe that my sentiments are sincere."

"Monsieur," said Monsieur de Morlière, "I would have been sorry to wound a man whose talent I admire, and I hope that we shall meet again elsewhere than the Réservoirs or the Sablonnière."

They bowed. The ship's captain made the remark that on the very spot where, thank God, the encounter had just terminated with a handshake, a student had been killed by his friend one autumn morning.

"There, by a pistol bullet—I saw the marks, still visible in the sand, at the spot."

"And why did they fight?"

"Why does anyone fight? Why this meeting with Monsieur de Morlière? Over nothing."

André went back to Paris very happy. It was as if there were now one veil fewer before his eyes. Not that the duel troubled him. What had to happen had happened; she was something of a fatalist. But the anguish of telling himself that it really was him and not another who had to go to that duel had finally dissipated. He had even been able to observe that his composure had not abandoned him for an instant.

At one moment he had asked Dr. Wyns to take his pulse, and asked, quietly: "Is it beating more rapidly?"

"No—it's very calm."

His brain, too, retained the most complete lucidity. He had, while Monsieur de Morlière's pistol had taken aim at him, noticed the effect of a black human silhouette upon a winter landscape. The painter alone, in that perilous moment, had been interested in what was happening around him; the man had not experienced any weakness.

Yes, for an instant, in his mind, he had seen Cécile: Cécile, all alone in the house in the Rue Murillo, waiting for him without knowing that, at that moment, he was risking his life—and if his adversary's bullet had hit him, it would have been in sending a last adieu to his beloved that he would have fallen.

He embraced her with an almost dolorous effusion of tenderness when he saw her again and she, divining that some new sadness had occurred in his life, interrogated him, wanting to know, smiling and pleading.

"What's happened? You're hiding something from me."

"No. Nothing. Later."

Taking her blonde head in his hands, he covered it with kisses, repeating the eternal words: "I love you! I adore you!" and no longer seeing, forgot about the specter that sometimes took his form, his name, his thoughts, his life...

But an idea, a violent idea, took possession of him, and in his turn, he wanted to interrogate Cécile.

"I have something to ask in my turn," he said, softly.

"What is it, my darling?"

"Why did you summon Dr. Klipper?"

She smiled, slightly embarrassed and ad, as if she feared hurting him. "You know why..."

"Yes, yes, I can guess," he said. "And I've thought about him too. A madman, it's said. It's possible—but what does it matter to me, if he can cure me? There's also a mental...cerebral homeopathy; and genius is that which goes further, and higher, which sees what cannot be seen. I shall go to see Dr. Klipper!"

XV. The Two "Manners" of André Fortis

In any case, a further amazement determined André Fortis to summon someone to his aid again. In his studio, one morning, he found a canvas placed of his easel, placed there by an unknown hand, which frightened him. A sinister vision, something akin to the frightening symbolism of the modern school: an automobile racing through the air, piercing the clouds with its two incandescent eyes, and pressing a heap of crushed bodies into a sort of bloody pulp.

Fortis had seen the paintings in which the old masters had imagined their visions of the last judgment, Hell and the apocalypse. He had once smiled at the bizarre inventions of the painter Wiertz[31] representing, attempting to fix on canvas, the last thoughts of a suicide or the supreme terror of a man being decapitated, But who, penetrating into his studio, could have replaced on his easel his usual landscapes, his exquisite woodland scenes or melancholy views of Venice by funereal images?

Whose was that canvas, illuminated by a spectral light, with patches of color as dazzling as arc-lamps: a kind of challenge, a duel of intensity between the palette and the electric light? What hand had placed that ferocious evocation, that apotheosis of matter, making skulls burst and bones shatter

---

[31] The Belgian painter Antoine Wiertz (1806-1865) was known as a "Romantic" painter, because the Symbolist school only developed after his death; he was, however, one of its key precursors, and it is not entirely surprising that Clarétie should compares the Other's painting to such works as *Faim, Folie et Crime* [Hunger, Folly and Crime] (1853) or *Le Suicide* (1854), even though another writer of the same period would surely have referred to more a recent Symbolist, such as James Ensor, Fernand Khnopff, Fécilien Rops, Odile Redon or Gustave Moreau.

beneath the wheels of a monstrous iron machine, accumulating horribly disfigured, atrociously piled up bodies, like the cadavers of combatant in a battle, in poses that were comical and terrifying at the same time?

There was, in those scenes of terror in which André did not recognize the hand of any painter known to him, a rare power in the manipulation of horror, in the spectacle of a frightful dream. The automobile, animated by a formidable speed, really seemed to be advancing toward the spectator. The canvas had the fearful magnetism of a machine growing larger on the highway, seeming to swell, to inflate, to be magnified by every spin of its wheels, with its enormous locomotive eyes.

The artist who had fixed such a nightmare in sinister color was a master of his genre—the horrible.

But no one had entered the studio, and it certainly was not Cécile who had bought such a vision of terror.

Perhaps some painter, in quest of buyers, had sent his canvas to a colleague in order to obtain artistic advice or material support. André asked. No, no one had come.

Then he was gripped once again by his quotidian anxiety; he asked himself tragic questions, as an invalid gripped by intermittent fevers feels his pulse.

Days had passed since the adventure of the duel, during which he had tried to reconstruct the scene at the Hôtel des Réservoirs, of which no consciousness remained to him. He knew that Monsieur de Morlière had got out of his automobile that evening, when the quarrel had burst forth. And, remembering certain uneasy feelings, warning signs that had afflicted him in recent days—the temporary dazzlements, the feeling of heaviness, the mild torpor on the right side of his skull—he told himself, with a new anger and a new fear, that fits of the intermittence in his life might, or must, have seized him with his even perceiving it, and that perhaps it was during those sorts of absence that the Other had come, enclosing himself in the dear studio that was his refuge, in the same place, in the very place where he usually worked, with his own colors and his own palette, to throw on to the canvas this fantastic scene of cruelty, terror and blood.

Reasoning with an implacable logic, studying, in the healthy state, the actions that he might have committed in the second state, he explained by the remembrance of the quarrel in Versailles, the canvas in which motoring became a kind of crazy Moloch. Impressed by the machine's flamboyant eyes, the painter had fixed the vision, attempted to express the impossible, seize a nightmare on the wing.

And what painter, if not the one who had the right to come in here at any time, who was at home in this house, who lived in this luxurious cell a fraction of his own life?

Before that almost insane canvas, André stood, amazed, as troubled in his mental beings as he could be materially, in his body. What a challenge to any theory of art was that doubling of talent in the same individual! A poet here, a visionary there. A landscape artist disengaging from Nature the charm that she reveals to her elect, and a seeker of chimeras sticking, in a way, to untranslatable subjects, visions in the manner of Callot in which the metal monsters of contemporary industrialism played the role of the winged dragons, animate toads or caricaturish demons of the engraver of the temptations of St. Anthony.[32]

So, the same brain could conceive such different scenes! The art of that lunatic of genius who was here launching an automobile over cadavers, was he very negation of that of the painter who, with a fragment of landscape, the corner of a village, or the first star lighting up in a pale sky, awaken in the soul a whole world of exquisitely sweet dreams!

A kind of dolorous irony caused a comment of rise to André Fortis' lips: "The 'manners' of André Fortis!"

He tried to mock himself, but he experienced a dolorous anger at feeling himself thus condemned to the sinister duality in question.

---

[32] Jacques Callot's depiction of *The Temptation of St. Anthony* (1630) is in the Hermitage.

Then he searched the studio, opened the folders, the cupboards, and interrogated the dark corners, in order that he might perhaps find other sketches and canvases by the "André" who was not him; and behind a large oak dresser, as if hidden from all eyes, he discovered the Golden Calf that had frightened Cécile, that grim allegory of the power of money, the composition that resembled a hypnagogic vision, the dream of a sick man realized by an artist gripped by fever in the depths of some lunatic asylum.

The temptation suddenly came upon him to smash those paintings, to destroy and burn them—but then a singular scruple stopped him, a bizarre, ironically unexpected sentiment.

Have I the right to reduce those works to ashes and smoke? If they're mine, by a self that I don't know, are they really mine?

The respect of an artist for the labor of another artist, for a work of art, whatever it might be, imposed itself on the man before those productions which were undoubtedly by his hand, but which did not belong to him, which came from someone else, forming no part—even if he had given them birth—of his work, nor of his life.

And, speaking aloud, as if instinctively replying to himself, he said: "I don't believe that such a doubt has ever been imposed on a man before. Never!"

Yes, they belonged to the Other, those works of a disquieting paroxysm; they had a master, those excessive compositions; and that man was the individual who substituted himself for André at certain times. Had André Fortis the right to destroy what that Other had invented?

"Yes, I have every right," he said, raising the palette knife over those bloody visions.

He was about to cut and carve. He recoiled again.

No, it seemed to him that he would be attacking the work of a human being. Besides which, he wanted to keep those canvases in order to show them to Monsieur Chardin and Dr. Klipper. He sensed an absolute need to be finished with this terrible double life. He was tired of these suppressions of his own self, this usurpation of his personality by a being so different from himself. He felt that before the contemplation of those frightful canvases, his thoughts collided, becoming confused; that a fever of folly, a derangement, was beginning.

And what if, in a period when the Other was the master of his own self, the Other sent these symbolic paintings to the Salon for exhibition? What if, just as he had taken responsibility for the action of the other André Fortis, he also had to answer for these paintings, inscribed in the catalogue in alphabetic order: André Fortis?

That would be insane.

And he was afraid now, materially afraid, that the insanity that there was, indeed, in that possible future might affect his brain, changing his doubt into dementia.

Oh, let someone rid me of this obsession! Let someone save me! Let someone give me back to myself! I've had enough! I've had too much of it! I want to escape. I want to resume possession of myself! To regain possession of myself, or put an end to it!

The old thought, the morbid temptation, gripped him again. Why not die? Suicide was so simple, so prompt, so facile.

But might that mad genius not be able to cure a madman? André believed in the exorcism of science.

"What if I go tell Dr. Klipper everything?"

PART TWO

I. The Laboratory

"Dr. Klipper!"

Since André Fortis had heard Monsieur Chardin, and then Dr. Wyns, talking about that eccentric—a crazy physician—he had only had one desire: to put his fate in the hands of that seeker of the impossible. And Cécile had had the same thought, since she had, after having written him an imploring letter, gone to consult the scientist. The difficulty was getting in to see Klipper. In vast, noisy, tormented, urgent, hungry Paris, avid for money, activity, luxury and noise, the dreamer of infinity obstinately pursued his quest in an unknown corner, as if in the cell of a cenobite, forgotten in the very heart of the hectic city.

There was in the hubbub, in the formidable dust of the city of social climbers, politicians, financiers, newsmongers, businessmen, tricksters, rogues, and courtesans of both sexes, a sacred corner in which, finding absolute calm in relentless labor and continuous work, a man suspected by men of science of pursuing certain discoveries that surpassed the most astonishing of an era accustomed to marvels, spent his days and passed his nights in a laboratory into which no one ever penetrated: a scientist of another epoch, an enemy of renown, suppressing everything in his life that might distract him from his goal; lurking in his home, cloistered in his work, nourishing his body just sufficiently to maintain the health of his mind—his brain free, his thought intact—closeted with Nature, intent on extracting from her a secret that she was hoarding like a miser, as if he and she were engaged in a perpetual duel.

And it was from that man, that slightly fantastic and Hoffmannesque being, that André Fortis wanted to request his cure: help that the official science of Dr. Chardin could not offer him.

But he did not want to offend Chardin. He did not want to attempt anything without having informed the physician, and, before going to knock on Jean Klipper's door, he went back to consult the scientist of the Boulevard Haussmann. He found himself once again in the reception room in which he had waited, so emotionally and impatiently, on the eve of his marriage to Cécile.

"Why, what's the matter?" said Monsieur Chardin, embarrassed and hesitant, on seeing him arrive.

André feared that he might wound him by talking about Klipper, but Chardin, a free spirit who was also curious about everything, stated laughing and said: "You put me in mind of one of those people who, weary of the prescriptions of some prince of science, goes to consult a bone-setter! And I don't blame you. I've often been tempted to seek a remedy from a wise woman myself. You believe that Dr. Klipper has special remedies? Go see Dr. Klipper, then. And as he doesn't open his door to just anyone, and I have some credit with him, I'll put in a word for you with that eccentric. Listen and watch—it's worth the trouble."

And, sitting down to his desk, Monsieur Chardin had written a brief note on his prescription pad, addressed to Jean Klipper, saying to André: "This should serve as an Open Sesame!"

He wrote the address: *Monsieur le Dr. Klipper, 4 Place de Valois*, and put on the envelope: *On behalf of Dr. Chardin*.

"And you must keep me up to date, my dear Monsieur!"

Fortis was in haste to see this Dr. Miracle. For a bizarre and seemingly fantastic malady, it seemed to him that a singular cure was required, outside of any category that had been depicted by Strasbourgian medicine. Rapidly, he sought out Klipper's abode.

And, remaining an artist even in his visits, he experienced an unexpected impression, a curious joy, on finding the house that Chardin had designated to him in the old quarter in which the scientist lived.

Like the majority of Parisians, André did not know Paris at all; he only knew the Paris of his habits and friendships. He had gone through the Palais-Royal a hundred times without stopping at the ancient Cour des Fontaines where he went in search of Klipper. He was quite astonished to go along that sort of unknown corridor, the Passage Henri IV, dark and narrow, as if passed through soot, with sacks of coal and vegetables, black walls, and puffs of vapor emerging, like the warm breath of a factory, from the grates in the gutter: a strangled corridor, like a hernia of the great and solemn Cour, into which he went from the Place de Valois, pierced by various passages, in order to find the doctor whom the reporter from the *Boulevard* had sworn to disinter there.

What! It was in this quarter that Klipper had established his laboratory? Here, a few steps from the passage ending in the enormous Arcade des Bons-Enfants, which looks like the opening of a gaping market-gate; the vault holed by a central stairway of which one could see the superimposed flights, as one can see the flue rise up from the opening of a colossal fireplace. It was in this black paste of houses, with wine-merchants' shops, bits of meat hung up on butchers' hooks, in his corner of the Paris of old, dark and muddy on rainy days, with bars over the windows and bars and the entrances to passages, shadowed in the evening and shadowed by day; and dwellings also maintaining the solemn appearance of a majestic Paris, a Paris of luxury and authority, tall house with zigzag staircases, the appearances of convents or barracks and large slate roofs crowning the high stories of gray stone; it was in this Paris of Louis XIV, invaded, jostled and smudged by the laborious Paris of the twentieth century, an old, abolished capital Paris a few steps from the movement of life, the feverish crowds of the Louvre, the Rue de Rivoli, the Paris of automobiles and the Metro, that Dr. Klipper pursued his research, of which the official scientists spoke in whispers as marvels?

André Fortis would willingly have imagined Klipper working in the shadow of the new Sorbonne, over there, in some back street of the old Latin quarter, but here, in the hubbub of the Saint-Honoré quarter, so close to—and yet so far way from—the Institut; here, in this shadow, and doubtless in a cellar, where only printing presses brought cerebral labor to mind, it seemed a challenge, a paradox. But anywhere that a man pursues his dreams can be rendered solitary.

The Place de Valois, moreover, the Cour des Fontaines, solitary and silent, where a passing carriage was an event, was for Klipper like a corner of a provincial city in which no one would guess that a scientist had taken refuge, in the heart of an unknown Paris.

"4 Place de Valois!"

André had looked for the building. It was the one that seemed to be united in body with the buildings forming the initial arch of the Passage Henry IV: a tall house with a broad staircase with iron steps, whose windows looked out over the square itself, on views of the readapted palace.

He asked for Dr. Klipper. The concierge, huddled in hr lodge, seemed astonished. Dr. Klipper was not there, and in any case, Dr. Klipper never saw anyone—no one at all. But the visitor had a letter that ought to open any door.

"Go up to the second floor and ask," replied the concierge, doubtfully.

André went up two floors. It seemed to him that he was climbing the stairs of an old, abandoned seigneurial dwelling. On the red-tiled landing, there were two doors one unexpectedly bearing the title of a sporting newspaper that was printed there; the other mute and nameless, had to be Dr. Klipper's.

He rang. No one answered. He rang again; the door opened inwards, as if worm-eaten, and an old Alsatian serving-woman asked André what he wanted.

"Dr. Klipper."

"He's not here."

"I have a letter to give him."

"Leave it with me; I'll give it to him."

"It's to him that I need to give it."

"He's not here."

But André was resolute, and would not go away without having seen the doctor. He insisted, saying that it was a serious matter, and that the very important letter was from Dr. Chardin. The name was doubtless familiar to the old Alsatian woman, for she softened on hearing it and said: "Oh, in that case..." Then, opening the door fully that she had only opened by a crack, she said: "If Monsieur will come in, I'll inform Madame!"

II. Extinct Gazes

She allowed André to pass. Having come through the antechamber he found himself in a drawing-room with high windows looking out on the horizon of the slate roofs of the square: a drawing-room of old, with a large and beautiful cupboard whose open battens allowed the perception of piled-up books above doors ornamented with mythological paintings—and everywhere, on the walls, more books—old books with worn bindings, the books of a researcher, not a curio-collector or a bibliophile—with framed engravings of the streets of old Strasbourg, the Munster of red stone, the statue of Kléber, a file of French soldiers, in front of houses on which storks were perched.[33]

André was looking around at all that with an artist's rapid circular glance, when the door of the room opened and a young woman came in, very pretty, very blonde and very pale, with large blue eyes that gazed before her with a bizarre fixity. She was petite, clad in black, and what immediately struck the painter in her regard was the gilded hue of the hair crowning a visage of a sad gentleness, and very small, slender hands, which she extended before her as if seeking a point of support.

The apparition was exquisite. There was still something of the young woman and the child in her, with a caressant charm, a tender voice.

"You've come on behalf of Dr. Chardin, Monsieur?"

"Yes, Madame."

"The doctor never refuses anything to Dr. Chardin, who has been very obliging at the Académie de Médecine in speak-

---

[33] Clarétie's contemporary readers would have realized immediately that these images had a particular nostalgia attached to them, knowing that when Klipper had been born Strasbourg would have been a French city, whereas it had been under German rule since the Franco-Prussian War.

ing about my husband, but the doctor is in his laboratory and when he's working, it's difficult to disturb him—oh, very difficult. What name shall I day, Monsieur, when he comes back up?"

"Monsieur André Fortis."

"Ah!" she said. She wore an indistinct smile while her beautiful blue eyes, fixed on André, continued to gaze at him without changing expression. "You're Monsieur Fortis? Oh, Monsieur, Madame Fortis has already worked a miracle. She caused the doctor to leave home and pay a visit. That's the rarest thing in his life!"

When she said *the doctor*, her voice, delightful in its timbre, took on a very particular tone of respect. In that musical fashion of pronouncing a very simple word there was a respect, a tenderness and a sentiment of absolute and devoted admiration.

"And I ought to tell you," the young woman added, "that the doctor, too absorbed by his work to take on any clients, is interested in you. Yes—and in Madame Fortis, whose sadness touched him. He told me so. We have no secrets, and, although ignorant, I have the confidence of his research."

André had taken Dr. Chardin's letter out of his wallet.

"If you would care to take cognizance, Madame, of this letter of introduction..."

He held the paper out to the young woman. Smiling softly, however, her beautiful blue eyes, the color of periwinkles, remaining fixed, she said: "You don't know, then? I can't read the letter."

"Why not?"

Without sadness, softly, as if it were the simplest thing in the world, she said: "Because I'm blind."

He let an "Ah!" of pity escape, and began to say something, which she interrupted with a wave of her hand.

"Oh, it's no sadder than anything else! And then again..." As if talking to herself, her eyes not seeing anything of what surrounded her, but her internal gaze perceiving, as it were, some distant apotheosis, a deliverance, a light, she added:

145

"And then again, the doctor is here. The doctor is searching. He'll find it. I'll be able to see, one day. I'll be able to see."

She had spoken, in her singsong voice, as the faithful speak, following the Master. And Fortis felt his heart warmed, and comforted too, in the presence of that suffering, expressing thus the certainty of being consoled.

If the blind woman believed that Klipper could restore her sight, why should he not hope that he could cure a neurosis?

André contemplated her youthful face, retaining on her lips the smile, not even resigned but glad, that certain blind people have, as if their blindness were preserving them from the sight of human ugliness. He gazed at something that had struck him immediately: a round, reddish-brown patch in the center of the very white forehead, like a large medallion, which resembled a strawberry birthmark, but which seemed more like a burn, or a recent wound.

The young woman, who did not seem to be suffering in consequence, added: "Will you follow me, Monsieur."

She walked straight ahead, as if her eyes were guiding her, toward the mantelpiece, from which she took a small lantern whose candle she lit without any hesitation. André, seeing her action, would not have suspected that she was blind.

As if she had divined his thought, a trifle sadly, she said: "Habit. It's not for me, who can guide myself on the stairway without seeing it, but for you, who won't be able to see there—for we're going down into a cellar. The cellar of the house is the doctor's laboratory."

She went ahead of Fortis, and the painter admired all that living grace, the unhesitating tread of the blind woman, and, in that tender virginal face, the melancholy, resigned and seductive smile.

They went down the broad staircase, the young woman holding on to the iron railing, until the lowest floor, where, groping with her hand along the wall, she opened the door that opened on to dark steps. To illuminate the somewhat worn steps of that new subterranean staircase, the lantern was useful to André. Madame Klipper guided herself by means of the thick, solid damp-free side-walls, and the artist, thus preceded by a blind woman carrying a light that she could not perceive, had the vague momentary sensation of being in some fantastic tale, of moving through a dream of a Hoffmann, a Poe or a Hawthorne.

They did not go down very many steps. The cellars of the building, opening here and there, were banal, but at the end of a long corridor, they came to an entrance, apparently vaster, closed by a heavy lock, whose slightly rusty iron the lantern caused to shine.

III. Unknown Things

The young woman knocked on the door, with a series of raps evidently arranged in advance as if by a Masonic ordinance. After a few moments, a man appeared on the threshold, illuminated both by the lantern and the vague gleam of some kind of ventilation shaft, which, coming from the floor of the Cour behind him, gave him a kind of pale aureole. Between those two different lights, short and thin, with long white hair framing a thin face, clean-shaven, with an aquiline nose and strange dark eyes, shining ardently with an inner fire, was Dr. Klipper, enveloped in a black overcoat. He seemed like some dream-creature, a being from another time or another, forgotten race, there in the heart of modern Paris.

The face of the scientist, astonished to be interrupted in his labor in the depths of that subterranean cell, expressed a kind of sulky anger. His scornful lips, like those of the bust of Machiavelli in the Uffizi, were beginning to say something when the young woman explained, in her soft and musical voice: "This is Monsieur Fortis...André Fortis, whom you mentioned to me yesterday and whom you wanted to see."

Then the surly, almost severe, expression vanished from the face, and the little man's terrible dark eyes searched in the gloom for Fortis, in order to interrogate him immediately.

A subject! An extraordinary case! A phenomenon! Dr. Klipper only interrupted himself for exceptional circumstances that presented themselves to him as astonishing problems.

"Aha!" he said, with the slight Alsace accent that he had retained. "André Fortis! Come in, come in!"

André attributed that enthusiasm to Cécile's confidences. She had consulted the doctor, and the explanations that he would need to give the doctor would be simplified by that circumstance.

The painter became a painter again, almost forgetting that he was a patient who had come to interrogate a doctor, in gazing at the environment surrounding the scientist: the hidden corner in which Jean Klipper conducted his research. André experienced the joyful sensation of a voyage to an unknown land, an unexpected encounter.

Dr. Klipper's laboratory under the vault of the basement of the old Parisian dwelling immediately evoked the image of the dusty corners in which Rembrandt had depicted alchemists and rabbis in a strange penumbra. Flasks were outlined against the wall, fitted with tubes twisted like serpents; wires were dangling from the ceiling or hanging from the walls, or departing from some bizarre item of apparatus to end at some electric socket: electric wires that played the role here of the spiders' webs in the paintings of the great Dutch magician, science thus achieving the same picturesque quality as art.

It was the scientist who had set up the wooden benches on which various glass vessels, a furnace, squares of faience were set: all the décor and apparatus of the cave-like cell in which he imprisoned himself, pursuing his relentless dream of the solution to the problems posed, living the intense life of a recluse, like a hunter glued to the track of the impossible, among these instruments that he had constructed or perfected with his own hands, photographic darkrooms that he had made the instruments of his research, and there—André questioned him immediately and Klipper replied with the naively proud satisfaction of a man who feels admired in his work, in his efforts—between the compressed air stored in a canister, the electric lights distributed over the area, the spectroscope that assisted him to decompose metals by means of light,[34] Klipper spent hour after hour, and had done for many years, in pursuit of research that resembled a combat with the impossible.

Daylight only reached the subterranean laboratory through the ventilation shaft that opened into the Cour, but

---

[34] The original has *sthetoscope* [*sic*], a word only employed as a variant of stethoscope, but the context makes it obvious that Clarétie means a spectroscope, used for studying the spectra generated by burning metals, so I have made the substitution.

between that light from outside and the light within, subservient to him, Klipper had placed a screen of black cloth in order to produce, when needed, complete shade, permitted the scientist to work in the absolute darkness that the rays provoked by him would traverse.

André studied the spectacle, storing the vision in his memory; for him it was both disquieting and touching to see that small, thin man, as if lost in the host of those instruments of copper and glass, those retorts and rubber tubes like black snakes, and that poetic, delectably pretty young woman standing there with her light in her hand, who seemed like a Muse, the living Muse of that poet of science, working in the dark to match himself against infinity.

"So, my dear Master," said Fortis, emotionally, "this is the hole in the ground from which a scientific revolution will emerge?"

Beneath his long white hair, Jean Klipper started to laugh. "Oh, a revolution! A revolution! I know that because I work in a cellar the official scientists have jokingly dubbed me the Marat of science, but I don't want to revolutionize anything. I'm only searching for the truth, and the universal truth." He became excited, his gestures feverish, placing his thin fingers on his instruments, which he caressed amorously. "Yes, yes, I want to find in electricity and in light all the unknown that Nature keeps hidden. The Rays, all these Rays that seem to spring from the ground, are as many torches that illuminate all obscurities. Radium is a symbol, and there are other radiums in the vast universe; there are other forces, other mysteries. All that will emerge, will be born, will live."

Then, when André asked him what particular project he was working on at present, Kipper shook his head.

"Oh, I'm chasing several hares at the same time," he said, a trifle sardonically, in the Alsatian manner, "but for the moment, this is what I was doing when you knocked..."

And explaining that he was decomposing metals, projecting the rays of the solar spectrum on the wall, enabling him to calculate the proportion of some particular metal contained in the light of some star, the sun's rays, the heavenly bodies of the infinite and the continents of space—with the result that he had, in that cellar, the secrets of the stars themselves, those infinities suspended in space.

Smiling, he said: "I'm dissecting the stars!"

And the plaintive, tender voice of blind woman interjected: "It would be very pleasant to go there!"

There was so much sadness and poetry in that exquisite music that Fortis was deeply moved by it.

Jean Klipper replied that she made dreams and he made science. Then, turning to his wife, he went on: "You think as a poet, while I calculate and observe as a physicist. A fact, when I can determine it, sometimes arrives at an intensity of astonishment that brings the poetry of science closer, or, rather, makes science itself into the infinite poetry of times to come."

Klipper addressed the poetic creature and Fortis alternately. "The human heart and its coverts, Nature and her mysteries, are two infinities, my darling, which will never, never weary human curiosity. Perhaps I shall have discovered, Monsieur, a few shreds, a few atoms of truth in my long and beloved labor, but I shall die before having found even a hundred millionth part of what generations to come will someday discover. The universe is the infinite, the great limitless sea, the unknown land, more profound than the ether."

Abruptly, he showed André one of his laboratory instruments. "This turning wheel, moved by compressed air, which we can hear humming, and which I hope that you"—he looked at the young woman with the fixed eyes and his voice became clipped—"will see one day, is spinning at a thousand rotations per minute. There is one than can achieve six thousand rotations per minute. Can you believe that it's possible? It is. And the wheel is very small. Well, imagine a gigantic wheel moved by a colossal electrical machine: that wheel could move an entire world! Perhaps it will be built one day, that giant wheel. Oh, we don't know anything, anything at all, yet! But we shall know, we shall! We shall know, know, know!"

151

He repeated the word with a feverish expression. It intoxicated him, like another species of alcohol.

"To know! To know! To live to seek, to learn!"

He was excited, and André observed a kind of flame in his dark eyes that seemed to have the gleam of a madman's gaze. As if the blind woman, rather than divining, had really seen and perceived that morbid flame, however, her voice cut in, gently calming that excitement: "Please, my love..."

"Yes, Martha dear, you're right. Calm. One can do nothing without calm." Vibrant and carried away a moment before, he suddenly calmed down in response to the mere remark of the child-like woman. Taking Marthe's little hands in his, he said to her with a profound tenderness, as infinite as his hopes: "Leave us. I want to talk to Monsieur Fortis."

She turned to André. "Here's the lantern, Monsieur. You have only to pick it up when you come back upstairs."

"But what about you, Madame?"

"Oh, I believe that, not seeing at all, I'm the one who can see the best." She smiled softly at her misfortune.

"And a day will come," said Klipper, firmly, "when the blind will see—when a new eye will replace the closed eyes! Everything comes with patience and faith..."

"When there is genius," said Marthe Klipper, in a tone of limitless adoration, as if in the fervor of a prayer.

André saw her draw away and disappear into the shadow, like a vision in that magical laboratory, with that red patch in the middle of her forehead that gave her the appearance of a living martyr. It seemed to him that the young blind woman with the blonde hair had taken the light with her, the light of her body replacing the extinct light of her eyes.

IV. The Light of Hope

André remembered the strange tale told at Madame de Vernière's house about the experiments carried out on the blind woman: those penetrating jets of light projected on the forehead of a human being with the certainty of causing the hidden pupil gradually to emerge, alive and luminous, to replace the extinct pupils, the dead gleams.

He followed Marthe with his gaze as she disappeared into the blackness of the cellar, and wondered whether that exquisite creature was a victim, pursuing with a maniac whose living experimental subject she was the "dolorous dream" of life, or whether she was, as he was convinced, a martyr destined to be saved, returned to the light by genius.

That word was, for her, as she had pronounced it, Klipper's true name: *genius*. She put all her soul into that hymn of confident tenderness; and André, in his turn, contemplated the strange, alert little man, as if he were confronted by an unreal individual living a chimerical existence.

But what was terribly alive in that singular individual was the fire of his eyes, obstinately fixed on André, who had difficulty sustaining their acuity. Klipper had sat down on a stool behind the electric machine that he had been using when there had been a knock on his door. With his elbows on the bench supporting the instrument, he studied the visitor who had come to disturb him—and that thin face balanced on those body hands, whose phalanges were plunged into the long silvery hair, took on a fanatical, disquieting expression. André imagined him as a bizarre human spider lurking among the electric wires as in the depths of his web, on the lookout for prey—not to devour him, when the ambush was sprung, but to cure him.

"I can't see you well enough," said Jean Klipper, abruptly standing up.

He went to draw the black blind that was blocking the light from outside, and a blue-tinted light filtered through the ventilation shaft that gave the bizarre laboratory an even more fantastic appearance.

"Stand in the light," said the doctor, who had resumed his place behind his instruments. "There's no need to go up to my study for what you have to say to me, and I don't suppose a consultation among my machines will frighten you?"

"On the contrary, my dear Master."

Jean Klipper shrugged his shoulders.

"Don't call me *dear Master*. The term has become utterly banal—it's ridiculous. 'Dear master! Dear master!' Are there any masters? We're all pupils. We're learning to read—poets, the alphabet of the heart, scientists that of science. Masters? There's only one master, who is a cruel and imperious mistress: Nature."

While speaking, he examined André, who was taking pleasure in the conversation as in a performance, mentally comparing the eccentric's scientific lair with Dr. Chardin's luxurious reception-room.

"Monsieur," said Jean Klipper. "Madame Fortis invoked, in order to appeal to me, the name of a man who is very dear to me, and although I don't take on any clients—none at all, having too short a time to live to complete my personal research—he has been kind enough to bring a very interesting case to my attention: yours. It isn't directly relevant to my studies, but anything connected with neurosis, the encephalon, interests me profoundly, and if I can collaborate with Dr. Chardin in our cure, I shall be glad to do so. You're a living problem, and although you're disturbing me slightly—yes, you're disturbing me—I'm delighted to see you."

While he spoke, a little ironic smile lingered on the small man's lips. He still had a characteristic Alsatian accent, pronouncing his *d*s as *t*s and his *g*s as hard *c*s, and the accent gave his words a particular savor.

The "liffing broblem" listened, and studied him too.

154

Klipper then interrogated him, as Chardin had. André described his terrors, the obsession of his anxious life, the heavy sensations in his head, the sudden flashes before his eyes, like the warning signs of a storm—or, rather, a thick cloud—the interruption of his existence...

In the most natural fashion in the world, as if the incredible phenomena in question were perfectly banal so far as he was concerned, Klipper replied, coldly and curtly: "Good, good. It's quite simple."

"Quite simple?" said André.

"Perfectly simple, because it's the confirmation, the proof of a fact that might astonish many people but which, for me at least, is mathematical. Perfectly simple, if you'll forgive the wordplay, because all human beings are double."

V. The Unconscious

He shook his long white hair. "Exactly," he said. "Every human being is double; it's necessary that we get used to recognizing that; yes, it's necessary to admit it, in spite of our stupid pride. Have you read Myers?[35] Evidently not. It's in him that one can see that our *self* is made up of two selves: the supraliminal, which is conscious of everything, and the subliminal, which is unconscious, living an obscure and independent existence...

"These slightly barbaric words tell you nothing, but they have now passed into common parlance. There are two beings in our being: the one that is unhealthy in you, driven to paroxysm, is latent in those with whom you rub shoulders. In me there is an unconscious self that listens to what I am saying to you and which might be dictating my words to me at this very moment. 'I had nothing to do with it,' Mozart said to the people who complimented one of his sonatas. It was the unconscious self that had dictated a masterpiece to his normal self—but you, since you have appealed to me, are double, and you think that you are a unique example of the doubling of the self?

"You have a second life, a second state? But a certain Louis Vidé, studied by Bourra and Barot,[36] had six distinct

---

[35] Frederic William Henry Myers (1843-1901) was one of the founders of the Society for Psychical Research in 1883; when Clarétie story is set he would have been its president. Clarétie could not have read his posthumously-published *magnum opus Human Personality and Bodily Death* (1903) before writing the first version of his novel, but must have come across his version of the distinction between the conscious mind and the unconscious mind in one of his numerous articles.

[36] This combination of names does score one hit on Google, to a publication in Dutch, but the example seems to have gone

156

existences, six different personalities. Six! That can't astonish you, I think—you're not going to cry miracle, you who are a living miracle! A woman studied by Morton Prince, Miss Beauchamp, had three of them. Hélène Smith, a subject studied by Flournoy, and Ansel Bourne, whose case Hodgson has described, had distinct changes of personality, as spontaneous as changes in speech: immediate modifications. You speak to one; it's another that replies.

"Oh, the conscious and the unconscious, the supraliminal and the subliminal! Problems, mysteries! Schopenhauer spoke of certain moments in his life when his will seemed to go to sleep, when his mind was pushed in a direction foreseen in advance. You must have read Schopenhauer? Beautiful ladies have made him fashionable, without understanding him most of the time. 'My person,' he said, in his own terms, 'was like a stranger to the work.' On received his books, he asked himself: 'Did I write that?' It was him, but one might have thought that someone else had dictated it!"

"The Self and the Other!" André said, experiencing, as Klipper talked, all the torments of the anguish of the past. Then, with increasing fury, his anger against that Other, the thief of his self, recovered all of its violence. He asked Jean Klipper, as if he were appealing to a supreme sovereign, to rid him of that obsession, that possession, that torture.

"Oh, your science!" he said, brusquely. "Your science explains everything, but doesn't cure anything!"

---

missing from French sources. As two of the subsequent references are misrendered in the original, however, including the name of Ansel Bourne, a famous patient studied by Richard Hodgson and William James, it may be that one or more of the names is misspelled. The "Hélène Smith" studied by Theodore Flournoy, whose accounts of supposed past lives evoked under hypnosis were popularized in the best-selling *From India to the Planet Mars* (1899), was actually a woman named Catherine Muller.

For a moment, Klipper made no reply. Then, softly, he said: "I've told you that we're only pupils. However, anything can be cured—when one wants to be cured. Would you like me to tell you where your remedy lies? In illusion!"

"Illusion!" André repeated.

"All is illusion down here, in a certain order of things. Happiness? Illusion. One is only happy when one believes oneself to be happy. People condemned to the unforeseen, not to mention the foreseen, which is the inevitable, are only fortunate in imagination. Tell yourself that the Other who is within you does not exist, will not exist any longer, and he will never reappear. Your double is illusory, like your own self. Your art, which consists of putting delicate lies on canvas, is illusory. Joy is illusory! Beauty is illusory!"

"Oh, doctor!" the painter cried. "Beauty is perhaps the most certain thing there is in the world!"

"Who knows?" said Jean Klipper, with his little ironic chuckle. He rubbed his hands together and added: "We find beauty where there is, strictly speaking, nothing but illusion, the phantom of beauty. I could find the Gioconda perfectly ugly, and the frightful Hottentot Venus, who is, at any rate, the ideal of beauty or the Hottentots, perfectly beautiful! Ha ha! If I wanted to!"

"If you wanted to?"

The old Alsatian's dark eyes flashed. "I told you that we're pupils, ignorant and impotent—yes, compared to the absolute; but we can, we can do many things!" He looked André Fortis full in the fact. "You're a painter? I'm a painter too, in my genre. I could..." He hesitated, and then, as if in a triumphal admission of his genius, went on: "I could make living portraits that only have the shadow of an existence. Illusion! Sovereign illusion! Give, for example, a married man with an ugly wife the illusion of having espoused a living beauty. Oh, of course! Of course! It would be an illusion, but so what—love lives on illusions. Illusions! Illusions! Love is just as illusion, like all the rest!"

"An ugly woman can be very pleasing to someone who loves her," said Fortis. "It's quite simple. There's a mystery of attraction involved."

"Oh, that's not what I mean," said Klipper. "I mean that the woman can remain ugly, be perfectly ugly, and that the man can see her as perfectly beautiful, absolutely beautiful, by means of spectacles that I could take responsibility for fabricating myself. Let's see, are you at all familiar with current developments in physics?"

"Hmm!" said André, smiling, all his attention extended toward the confidences of them man who was a kind of priest of the Kabbalah, buried in a Parisian cellar like a Kobold in his somber mine.

"I'll try to explain the problem. You're a painter; once again, it will be easy for you to understand. Mirrors, Monsieur, form perfect images if their form is flat and their surface well-polished; those images are enlarged and deformed as soon as the glass is curved or distorted. You've seen the caricatures that they send back to you then?"

"Yes, of course."

"When the curvature is regular, so is the distortion, and one can vary the resultant effects infinitely. Some skillfully-constructed mirrors show us smaller, as if they were painting an elegant miniature of the face presented to them. Others, easier to construct, alter proportions and produce the caricatures I mentioned, enlarging or stretching the features: incredibly fat Sanchos or fantastically thin and elongated Quixotes. Those are the simplest mirrors. Their effects can be varied infinitely; it's a problem in geometry belonging to catoptrics. But we have dioptrics. Don't be alarmed—I'm talking like one of Molière's pedants now..."

"And I'm as ignorant as Monsieur Jourdain[37]," said André.

---

[37] The socially ambitious but crass title character of Molière's musical comedy *Le Bourgeois gentilhomme* (1670).

"Dioptrics is the science of rays refracted through a transparent medium. It presents more difficult problems and more varied solutions. Every illuminated point, when one looks at it through transparent glass is perceived in a position different from the true one, which depends on the form of the surfaces limiting the various parts of the lens. Well, if, instead of putting one transparent sheet of glass in the instrument, one interposes two, three, four or perhaps six pieces between the eye and the object of the gaze, one can produce the strangest deformations, the most unexpected images, which we call anamorphoses. Understand me clearly: if the observed object is a square, one can render its image circular. Where that square should be, the eye will see a disk. By means of a con-structed instrument, one can produce any illusions, any vi-sions, one wishes. One can cause a living being to see that which does not exist, or at least modify that which exists."

"Really?"

"Oh, the problem would be difficult—but much less so than the problem of squaring the circle. But to change, to mod-ify, to correct a face, by elongating or broadening the oval, giving the forehead more height, diminishing the mouth, etc. etc. would be mere child's play, for an ingenious scientific optician before a permanently immobile bust ever ready to pose. By taking away or adding lenses, polishing them inces-santly and repolishing them without taking off the surfaces, one could—I could—show the spectator the features of a bust completely different from the real one. I could, for instance, give someone looking at Aesop the pleasure of contemplating Plato, someone who had a Megaera before him they joy of perceiving the Venus de Milo."

"Is that possible?"

"Quite possible," said Klipper. "Everything is possible."

It seemed to André that he was living a dream. Was he really awake? Had he not been hurled abruptly into a dream? Was he conscious of himself? Was this strange, ironic, elo-quent, nervous Dr. Klipper, with his dark, seemingly incan-descent eyes, his nostrils aspiring life, fluttering like wings, his guttural accent and curt gestures, a being of flesh and bone?

Of what the man was saying, Fortis retained, above all, the last three words, the prideful affirmation of limitless power: "Everything is possible." The tone in which the scientist had pronounced those definitive words gave André Fortis certainty, absolute faith, in what Klipper represented as the supreme force: illusion.

I shall be cured! I shall be cured! Everything is possible.

What had struck the Alsatian doctor most of all in the painter's confidences was the recent adventure of the duel accepted for the Other: a man rendering a reckoning to an adversary for an insult he had not proffered, a gesture of which he was unconscious. The ceaselessly seething mind of Jean Klipper already glimpsed, in a complication of that episode, a means by which André might perhaps escape the obsession of which he was the victim.

"My God," he said, a trifle peevishly, "I can see that you're going to take up more of my time than I wanted—but you're an invalid who isn't commonplace. Your poor wife touched me, and attracted the sympathy of mine. And then again, even though you're not unique, as I told you...yes, yes, don't have any vanity with regard to your suffering...I believe that we might achieve something!"

"If everything is possible, as you've said, do the possible—and attempt the impossible. Enable me to become myself again—so that I can finally escape the grip of the Other."

"Do, do! I say good, good...it will be necessary to kill the Other, that's all!" Klipper got to his feet and added: "Let me think about it! Come and see me again."

"When, Doctor?"

"Whenever you wish. I'll have reflected, calculated. Come back. You'll always find me here—or almost always. I never go out. Life's too short!"

VI. The Third Eye

André left that poor laboratory with his heart full of joy. Hope is the human viaticum. While he walked he repeated the old Alsatian's decisive words: "Everything is possible." This time, the realization of that possibility seemed to him to be imminent. Of course, he had had the same hope on the day he had consulted Dr. Chardin. He had had faith; he had believed himself to be liberated. Today, however, the man he had just seen inspired more confidence in him. That irregular of science would find the remedy that the official scientist had only enabled him to glimpse.

Why did André have faith in the latter adviser? People need the successive glimmers of light that guide them through the fog and the darkness. One is blown out by the wind; another is ignited—and the journey extends until the final light, the last of all, flickers and dies.

For him, the scientist enclosed in the cellar in the Place de Valois, "dissecting the stars," as he put it, was a living glimmer of light. Those dark, sparkling eyes that had searched and penetrated the depths of André Fortis's soul were stars. The brain of that man, of whom Chardin said "He's a madman, but he has genius," was a star.

When Fortis had gone, Jean Klipper left his laboratory and, after having locked the door to his cellar, went back up to his apartment. He felt tired; he wanted to rest. And his rest, all his joy, was the contemplation of the dear creature who was, for him—along with science—his entire life, and who, as she came and went around him, was the smile, the melancholy smile, of this obstinately austere life.

The blind woman shared all his preoccupations and, in spite of the blindness that seemed to suppress the world, she remained, by virtue of a phenomenon of intelligent bounty, a kind of devoted servant to the scientist, very practical and very aware. She divined everything, knew the place of everything within the apartment; she could find the books that Klipper needed on the bookshelves. She could set the table at meal times better than old Anna, the maidservant. He often said to her: "You have eyes in your fingertips!"

Touch, developed to a hyperacuity, as in many blind people, was like a second sight to her.

"We could live like this permanently, very happily," said the scientist, "but no, I want—do you hear?—*I want* the eye to emerge, to spring forth in your forehead, that beautiful forehead of an exquisite child, that will give you sight!"

And when he spoke thus, his thin fingers caressed the pretty blonde woman's smooth forehead, and marked with the tip of his finger the place from which that hidden, complementary eye possessed by the human race could and would emerge.

Marthe, confident, made no reply. She submitted with complete faith and absolute patience to the experiments of the husband who imposed the torture of his faith upon her, keeping her for hours on end in the dark laboratory, under the projection of intense electric light, the radiation of the infinite power that, according to Klipper's calculations, would enable the germination and the hatching of the third eye, with which the scientist wanted to endow humankind.

And in that old building in the Place de Valois a continual and poignant drama was played, of which Paris was ignorant, the secret of which even escaped reporters as alert as Frédéric Clément: there was a man of genius doggedly seeking the solution of an insensate problem and an obedient young woman sacrificing herself to the doctor's experiments, offering her forehead to the burning rays like an Iphigenia offering her neck to the knife.

Sacrificing herself? No. For Marthe Klipper those long hours spent under the jet of electric light, the slow sessions before the machine from which the lightning sprang forth, stinging and burning, were not a sacrifice but a joy: a hectic joy; the joy of collaborating, albeit as a victim, in a sublime project; the joy of giving her body as subject-matter for study to the great man whose name she bore.

The blind woman remained under the implacable radiation without moving, her forehead curved by the moxa, marked, beneath her beautiful blonde hair, with the stigmata of science, burned—but intoxicated by felicity, by a kind of hysteria of sacrifice, at the idea that if Klipper finally found the solution he sought, it was through her, and in her, that he would have found it.

Oh, it was not her egotism that gave her that cherished intoxication. The recovery of her sight was almost indifferent to her. She was not thinking about herself by about others—or, rather, she was only thinking about him. What if he succeeded in making that incredible discovery? What if humans, condemned to their present form for thousands of years, suddenly recovered, thanks to Klipper, a part of their lost heritage?

To endow humanity with a new means of vision! To render to those who could no longer see the means of seeing! To resuscitate the fabulous Cyclopes by making modern humans into them! Jean Klipper seemed to Marthe to be a diviner of unknown springs, a seeker of buried wealth, who would return to the human race the treasure of which it had been robbed.

And whether the experiment succeeded or not, she experienced a pride at thus being the hostage of the war that the scientist was waging against the impossible.

Anyway, why should the experiment not succeed? The young woman had ended up sharing Klipper's confidence and nourishing herself on his dream, like those individuals who, influencing one another, share the same chimera and live a *folie à deux*.

She sometimes believed that she was already experiencing a kind of hatching, and her imagination showed her a fissure in her forehead, splitting under the fiery radiation like a ripe pomegranate.

If the miracle were to be realized, what joy there would be! And it would be realized, since Jean Klipper had predicted it. Marthe, like a devotee smiling in her faith, would have found the slightest doubted regarding the scientist's omnipotence sacrilegious.

And when she told him, in response to the suggestion of Klipper's own words, that she was experiencing vague hopes, as if the bones of her face were subject to a modification, observed by the cracks that she thought she could perceive, the scientist replied, softly; "When you're able to see me, if I succeeded in enabling you to see, who knows whether you will still love me when your eyes show me to be an old man? I have white hair, Marthe; I have wrinkles; you don't know that!"

Then she took his hands, squeezed them in hers, placed her child-like blonde head on the seeker's shoulder, and said, in a very tender voice: "It's the work that has blanched your hair; it's the search for so many truths that has given you wrinkles. You're not the old man that you say, and I love you, and will always love you, with the same ardently grateful, devoted passion. Oh, Jean, devoted to the point of dying for you, if necessary, if you wished!"

He clapped his hands. "No, fortunately not. It's not a matter of dying, but of living."

And he was excited by his possible discovery, dreaming the dream of correcting Nature, of adding a new instrument to the life of human beings, developing the embryonic eye lost in the human body.

"Yes, I know, they wouldn't believe me if I told them what I was trying to do; they'd talk about Sainte-Anne, and the people who have chairs at the Institute would elect me to a padded cell. I know, I know…but you believe in me, you believe, you understand. And I love you for your generosity as I love you for your confidence. I martyrize you; you suffer under the ray that bites into your flesh!"

"Me? No! I don't suffer." Marthe's voice had caresses of ecstasy when it replied thus, and in the depths of the blind woman's sightless eyes, it seemed that flame ignited, so perfectly were her eyebrows raised to accompany the delightful smile on her lips.

"I bore you by leaving you for hours on end before that electric machine!"

"I'm never bored when I can hear you talking or moving nearby."

"And during those hours of ordeal, what do you think about, my poor Marthe?"

"I think that you're the best and most knowledgeable of the men of this country!"

"Don't say that, Marthe, don't say that. Is it because you know that others are seeking, and that others might perhaps have found? There's so much cerebral effort nowadays; those little ants who call themselves humans expend so much effort in transporting wisps of straw! Perhaps, in some unknown laboratory, an attic or a cellar, there's an unknown scientist who's discovering, at this very moment, some engine, motor or light that will upset the universe. Perhaps there's another finding a powder capable of blowing up the whole world! Who would suspect that in our cellar in the Cour de Valois I'm pursuing the dream of rendering sight to the blind by giving humankind a new eye?"

Then, forgetting that he had already said to the young woman twenty times or a hundred times over what he always repeated with a new fever, he went on, his voice sometimes becoming breathless, emphasizing his words, with his Alsatian accent, returning to his eternal obsession with the fervor of an apostle.

"Everything in Nature has a purpose—everything. The forgotten eye, more or less distinct in all the vertebrates, which is neither a gland nor a nerve ganglion nor a lymphatic ganglion, made of a few nervous fibers and calcareous concretions—the degenerate organ that I want to regenerate—must have a purpose. Reduced to almost nothing in some, more developed in others, no longer receiving, according to Leydig,[38] luminous radiation but only calorific radiation, it's a kind of thermometer-eye in us. At any rate, atrophied or rudi-

---

[38] The German anatomist Franz Leydig (1821-1908).

mentary, it exists! And I want the third eye not only to exist but to serve some useful purpose, to enable it to perceive once again what it no longer perceives. After all, Marthe, our ancestors knew about the pineal gland, considered as a third eye. The anatomists of Galen's time considered it as a tampon, a simple stopper designed to open and close the aqueduct of Sylvius. If the organ moved backwards it could, in fact, obstruct the passage—at least they had that opinion, although Galen himself did not. So he treated them as ignoramuses! And Descartes!"

Jean Klipper opened large book and read to Marthe, ever ready to lend an ear with ecstatic patience, the eternal lesson of the master.

"He didn't say that the eye in question, the third eye, was the seat of the soul. No. This is what I find in the man's thesis. Listen."

"I'm listening."

"'It is the source of the Spirits.' The animal spirits, in Descartes' time. What we call today the nervous fluid. 'The spirits flow from the pineal gland into the concavities of the brain.' It ought to be imagined as an abundant spring. It requires very little to make it incline or lean over to a greater or lesser degree, sometimes in one direction and sometimes the other, and to ensure that in leaning, it disposes the spirits that emerge from it and begin their journey toward certain locations in the brain rather than others. And, quite naturally Descartes' opinion has been disfigured by his commentators, Henricus Regius and Louis de la Forge, and ridiculed by Voltaire, a man of wit.

"Witty people, you see, Marthe, are great flatterers of the stupid and artisans of stupidity. 'The soul would be seated there like a coachman on his bench, from which it directs the impulsions of the brain with the aid of reins!' But he didn't say that, the admirable Descartes, who, finding life too short wanted—you'll find this in the *Vie de Saint-Evremond* by Pierre Desmaizeaux—to prolong it by hundreds of years…yes, hundreds…and would have found the secret if…if he hadn't died at fifty two! Oh, the grain of sand! The grain of sand! The unforeseen! I only fear the grain of sand, you see, Marthe! The accident that lies in wait for us in the shadows. The tortoise that falls on our heads while we doze, like the sleeping poet.[39] That's all I fear...that and witty men, the ironists, the skeptics.

"This is what he meant, the great Descartes, and what he said in many passages: all our organs are doubled, as are the impressions that arrive in the brain, and yet we have only one single and simple thought about one thing at one time. It is therefore necessary that there must be a place where the two images that arrive from the two eyes—or, if you wish, the two other images that come from a single object from the double organs of one of the other senses—can be assembled into a single one, in order that they can reach the soul, in order that they do not represent two objects thereto instead of one. 'There is no other place in the body where they can be combined as they are in this gland.'

"In sum, according to Descartes, that unpaired cerebral organ is absolutely appropriate to combine and fuse the double impressions, and also to direct them via nervous tubes in the form of nervous fluid—animal spirits—toward the particular point in the brain where conscious sensation is formed. I tell you this to prove the importance attached by the great man to that rudimentary organ.

"Thomas Willis and Nicolas Steno, in spite of the evidence, amused themselves at Descartes' expense. It's laughable. The seat of the soul! The seat of the soul! They made the observation that the gland was small in human beings, who have such great souls—ho ho! sometimes; not always—and large in oxen, which have small ones... In any case, the Cartesians refused souls to animals, in which they too were imbeciles. Whether Galen or Descartes made errors, however, if of little importance to me. They observed; that was the important

---

[39] The Greek tragedian Aeschylus was reputed to have been killed when an eagle dropped a tortoise on his head, but the story is almost certainly apocryphal.

thing. And I too observe that the gland is there, the eye is there..."

He touched his wife's forehead with his fingertip.

"Our distant ancestors had it, that eye that has, so to speak, closed over time. It's the atavistic molluskan eye bequeathed by the invertebrates to the vertebrates, which human beings have allowed to atrophy. I've studied and dissected crocodiles and lizards. Well, the globe of the eye actually protrudes through a hole in the skull, and it really is an eye. There's a retina, a lens, a mass of vitreous humor; the epidermis forms a cornea. It's the eye of a cephalopod, the eye of a frog, sand it's a human eye. The hole in the skull through which the pineal nerve emerges is located in an interparietal bone that I've encountered in fossil crocodiles and nothing—nothing—prevents us from believing that that atrophied eye can develop and resume the role in life that it once had, there, where it ought to be, since that is where it is...or will be, tomorrow.

"Tomorrow!"

Jean Klipper seemed to perceive a new humanity before him, equipped with that frontal lantern to guide it in the night of the unknown. Who could tell what triple vision might add to human knowledge?

"Oh, I know, aesthetes will think that it isn't beautiful. The eye of the Cyclops! They'll protest in the name of beauty. But what about utility? Is that nothing? Isn't it life itself?"

It mattered little to him, in any case, what others thought. His goal was, first and foremost, the salvation of the adored being that he subjected to his experiments, to render sight to the blind woman, substituting a living eye for the two dead ones: to extract that martyr from the torment of darkness, and give her light by means of a scientific miracle.

Miracle! "Mirage, perhaps," he said to himself in moments of doubt. "I'm sure that it's true—but shall I ever attain that truth!"

The days passed, long days in which, under the burning rays, before the machine projecting its light on her forehead,

169

Marthe remained almost motionless, dreaming—feeling the fire entering into her skull like a drill, and hoping, and repeating: "Let's go on! You'll find it! You'll restore my sight!"

"What if I ruin our health in the attempt?"

"I never feel as well as I do after the flame."

"What if I don't succeed?"

"You will succeed. It seems to me that it's our lips that are placed upon my forehead, and that the light is you, giving me a kiss."

Thus they intoxicated one another with chimeras, encouraging one another in their dreams, proceeding in the same dream in a communal effort of patience and love.

"You're right," Klipper repeated. "It's necessary to believe, and I do. Even if I only had an illusion, merely the illusion of giving you sight, if death took me that evening, suddenly, I'd die happy. Ah, illusion! Perhaps that's the true light! The star in our darkness!

He deviated slightly from his custom with regard to that obstinately-pursued problem, when he had left André and rejoined Marthe in the apartment.

He sat down in an armchair, looking through the panes of the high windows at the gray walls of the Palais and the gray sky on the far side of the Cour. He liked this peaceful corner of the city. He could believe that he was at Versailles, or further away, on these winter days, somewhere in the North. There were those views of old palaces of the time of Louis XIV, in Strasbourg or Saverne in his homeland, those red, or gray, in the Vosges. And he daydreamed, while Marthe gave instructions for the evening meal to old Anna.

"It's singular, the painter's psychosis," he said, after a long pensive silence. "That very unusual case interests me. The man is handsome, well-endowed, and he's suffering. I'd like to cure him of his suffering. There's no other means than the one Chardin indicated: to convince him that he's cured. How can one prove to him that he's cured? In the Middle Ages, my dear Marthe, the unfortunate fellow would have been considered possessed. The Devil's claw would have been seen in this psychoneurosis: the *signum diaboli!* But it's a kind of twin."

And, giving Molière a vague Alsatian accent, the savant sang, as if to music, lines from *Amphitryon*:

> I am a man of honor; I have given my word
>> And you can believe that of me, if you will!
> I tell you that, believing that I have only one twin
>> I found that there were two of us at home;
>> And of those two selves, pricked by jealousy
> One is in the house and the other with us.

"The two selves! The twin! That devil Molière, who mocked physicians, had divined what medicine ought to study: the doubling of the personality. That doesn't astonish you, Marthe? Except that he attributed to the intervention of the gods, to Seigneur Jupiter, what we attribute to a neurosis. But it's curious, that double self of the good twin!"

Coming back to himself, he added: "Yes, I'd like to cure that man!"

He shook his head, searching for some ingenious method.

"How? Ah, how? It isn't sodium or potassium bromide that will reckon with this mental abnormality. A physician would prescribe some treatment or other—isolation, silence, injections of salt water in an artery. That won't do! It's no good.

"At Bern, there's a certain Dr. Dubois[40] who has seen clearly in similar cases: *a psychic illness, a psychic treatment*, he said—wrote, even. It's by reasoning, by talk, by persuasion, that he arrives at the invalid's intimate self.

"Even if one forbade Monsieur Fortis wine and cigars, and condemned him to a cell, it wouldn't expel the phantom. What's needed...what's needed..."

---

[40] Paul-Charles Dubois (1848-1918), professor of neuropathology at Bern.

VII. Malebranche's Leg of Mutton

"Do you know the story of Malebranche's leg of mutton, Marthe?[41] He was a little crazy, the Cartesian, but he had genius, that other Christian Plato. When he read Descartes for the first time, he had palpitations of the heart and nearly died of joy. *Yes, yes, yes!* Perhaps that's why it's necessary to admire him. Such disciples become masters. And he had his manias, Malebranche. He never drank anything but water, declaring that the hydraulic element is necessary to our organisms, and that it alone is normal. But the maniac was also prone to hallucination. It appears—I can't guarantee the fact, but it's probable—that he imagined that he had a leg of mutton hanging from the end of his nose..."

"A leg of mutton?"

"A leg of mutton."

"Like the character in Perrault's story who had a sausage in the same place?" said Marthe, laughing.

"Exactly. The unfortunate fellow thought he could see, before his eyes, the leg of mutton that was weighing him down, interposed between himself and the paper, and he couldn't read or write. The leg of mutton, the sight of the imaginary leg of mutton, cut a sentence in two or hid the sentence he'd begun. You can understand the torture, the suffering, of the continual hallucination. 'But you don't have any-

---

[41] Klipper (or Clarétie) was not the first person to confuse Malebranche, a fictitious character in Arthurian mythology, featured in the fourteenth-century romance *Perceforest*, who was said to have suffered the hallucination of the leg of mutton and to have been cured in the manner Klipper describes (not by a Oratorian churchman but by a character named Le Tor), and Descartes' follower Nicolas Malebranche, who never had any such problem. The misattribution can be found in several nineteenth-century books of anecdotes.

thing on the end of your nose,' someone said to the poor deformed genius—a superior degenerate, today's official wise men would say. "You have nothing! No leg of mutton! Not an atom of mutton!' 'But I can see it, I can see it—it's there, there!'

"The maniac philosopher dragged that phantom with him everywhere, that spectral leg of mutton, until one day, an Oratorian, who invented auto-suggestion without knowing it, had a very simple but admirable idea. He said to Malebranche: 'I can cure you.'

"'How?'

"'By removing your leg of mutton. Oh, it's a very quick operation, which won't do you any great harm. Just a little incision, right here, at the end of the nose.'

"'Go on! Operate! Cut!' said Melabranche. 'Just rid me of that leg of mutton.'

"'Don't worry,' said the Oratorian. 'I'll choose my moment.'

"One day, when the good Nicolas Malebranche went to sleep by the fire, the Oratorian—who, parenthetically, my dear Marthe, had also anticipated anesthesia and operations carried out during sleep—prepared the coup-de-théâtre, hid a leg of mutton in his jacket and pricked the maniac on the tip of the nose with the point of a dagger. Malebranche woke up with a screech and demanded: 'Who goes there?'

"And the Oratorian replied: 'Me; I've just done the surgery and removed your leg of mutton.'

"'My leg of mutton?'

"'Yes, here it is...' And the operator waved the leg of mutton he had prepared as a hunter might have waved a hare.

"'My leg of mutton!' said Malebranche.

"'Yes, I took advantage of your sleep to do you the least possible damage, and you were so close to the fire that your leg of mutton is half-cooked. We can eat it!' 'With pleasure!' said Malebranche.

"He uttered an *oof!* of deliverance, and was able to return to his papers without anyone ever hearing any more talk of the leg of mutton. The hallucination had been dispelled. It had been proved to Malebranche that the phantom was no longer there. Even if it was not pre-salted—the legend doesn't say— he must have found it delicious. To devour the specter that haunts you is like the Carib Indian devouring his enemy! Well, what I need to do—but how?—is to renew on André Fortis the experiment of Malebranche and the leg of mutton. I need to give him proof that the phantom is no longer there, that the false twin who is persecuting and beating him has been driven away, beaten in his urn. That will be another little problem of psychopathy to add to all those I want to solve. Oh, it's less harmful than the one that's most important to me. I'll find it! I'll find it!"

"You'll find all that you desire," his child-wife replied in her voice made of caresses, whose entire being went out to the scientist like that of a believer to God.

She had settled down quietly, kneeling while he talked, on a stool next to him. She extended her face toward him, in which the sightless eyes seemed to be reading or divining, all the tenderness that Jean Klipper's great dark eyes were pouring down on the dear creature. He spoke to her softly, thanking her so many times, for such devotion and generosity.

"Dear little great soul!"

And in the twilight that was coming through the high windows, among the books with austere bindings, gradually invaded by shadow, the woman kneeling next to the man with long white hair, thin and pensive, enveloped in his black overcoat, would have given the impression of some penitent bowing down beneath the gesture of a priest.

The quasi-paternal gesture of the scientist's hand, caressing Marthe's tilted forehead, was, however, reminiscent of all the human tenderness of an individual devoted to another, and Jean Klipper said, softly, gazing at the houses on the far side of the large Cour, which were fading into the gray dusk: "People have often tried to define happiness. Happiness is laboring beside a beloved woman who understands you: the calm labor

174

continues with an objective in mind. And what an objective! To return the beloved to the light!"

"Let's not be selfish, Jean," she said. "There's also…Malebranche!"

She smiled.

"Oh, André Fortis—him too! I'll return him to himself. I'm seeking and pursuing two lights at the same time: that of your eyes and that of his brain. The more difficult to make appear is there, behind the forehead!"

He leaned over her, gave her a kiss on the very spot where the jet of electricity, as rapid as a short-circuit, had made its mark. He shook his head. "You are…thus far…a stigmatic of science, my poor child! Nothing else!"

"The stigmatized can work miracles, it's said. But the miracle is you—you who will work one, my friend, my master, my God!"

VIII. The Other's Masterpiece

Through the window of the house in the Rue Murillo, André Fortis' wife gazed at the sad landscape of a wintry day enveloping the Parc Monceau. The weather was snowy, the trees powdered with frost beneath a gray sky. The marble statues were clad in cold white cotton wool. In the distance were the roofs of the boulevard, covered in rime. There was an atmosphere of sadness and death.

How many times had Cécile contemplated those same houses, those same trees, Gounod's monument, glimpsed in the distance among the sensitive plants hidden in their armatures of straw. It was her unique horizon, the corner of the world where he thoughts stopped, and which, in the depths of that luxurious house—so empty for her—seemed like a window in a prison...

André was working upstairs in his studio, finishing a canvas into which he was putting, he said, all his fever.

André! Which André? The charmer she had met at Trouville, the lover who had carried her away one evening in her wedding dress, whiter than the snow that was speckled, out there, by the tips of the grass of the lawns, or the Other, the stranger with the grim eyes, who appeared at certain times and seemed to impose a madman's mask over an adored face?

With what work was he busy, the painter who, alternately, evoked dreamy woodland scenes, Venetian canals full of light, or bizarre hecatombs, grim mythologies, compositions of a funereal, frightful, incomprehensible mysticism?

Which André would she see coming down shortly to take his place before her at lunch—or flee and disappear, to return to the dwelling with no distinct memory, a stranger to their common life, looking at her with astonished eyes?

She thought about Dr. Klipper, who had been kind enough to come to see her, and whom Fortis must have consulted in his turn, The doctor had not given her any further sign of life since his visit, and she dared not ask André what the scientist had prescribed. At any rate, nothing in the actions or words of the painter, for some time, had given her cause to fear another crisis. He had been gripped by a kind of frenzy of work, finishing, he said, a vast landscape for the Salon—but not in the hope of a grand medal or any decoration at all, which was of no importance to him. He worked for himself; it was his joy.

By virtue of a coquetry that as unusual in him, however—as a rule, he gladly showed his projects to his wife, consulting her as to the desired effect—he was keeping the canvas in question, which he regarded as decisive, a secret. He replied to Cécile: "When will it be finished? It's my masterpiece. Let me strive until the last moment to make it a masterpiece!"

It was on the "masterpiece" dreamed of by so many artists, who so often fall, crushed, from the height of their dream, that André was working in his studio, while Cécile gazed at the sad grayness of the January sky, the leprous whiteness of the roofs, and the snow hanging from the corners of nearby balconies and the ridges of windows. She allowed her thoughts to wander, to wander far away, losing themselves in the sadness of hopeless skies…

The noise of the door opening behind her caused her to turn her head.

It was Aurèle, André's manservant. He held out a tray to Cécile, bearing a card.

"It's a Monsieur who says that he desires to speak to Madame, not Monsieur."

Cécile picked up the card. *Pétrus Hardy.* She knew the painter well. She admired his portraits. She knew that he liked André. But it was to her that he wanted to speak? What was it about? Her instinct was not deceived. There was some threat in the air, and it concerned André.

"Show Monsieur Hardy into the drawing-room."

Instinctively, she darted a last glance at the park, buried under the snow, and, hearing the drawing-room door open in front of Pétrus Hardy, she went in, greeted the painter, who seemed a trifle embarrassed, and invited him to sit down.

He thanked her, took an armchair, and looked around, as if fearing a sudden visit. "Monsieur Fortis isn't here, Madame?" he asked.

"He's in his studio."

"Definitely? He can't hear us?"

"No, Monsieur," said Cécile, frightened. "But he might come down, naturally..."

"I'll tell you very swiftly what it's about. You'll forgive me, I hope. My action is odd, even difficult, to say the least...for me...for you...but it's a matter of a great artist, his glory, his name... You'll excuse me..."

"Yes, of course," said Cécile, becoming nervous. "But what is it, Monsieur? What is it?"

"We're proceeding, Madame, as doubtless you know, with the arrangements for the Club's Salon. Our private viewing will be particularly well-attended this year. We have works by masters who aren't sending anything to the Champs-Élysées, and we asked André Fortis to end us a series of his latest studies of Venice—his masterpieces. To see the crumbling Campanile again, by way of his canvases, is a joy and a consolation."

"So?"

"Well, Madame, what your husband has sent us is not a series of Venetian impressions; it's a painting that has amazed us all profoundly..."

In a rapid vision, the memory of the strange canvas she had one seen on André's easel returned to Cécile: the terrible apparition of the Golden Calf rolling its chariot over crushed bodies.

"What painting?" she asked.

"My God, Madame, from any other artist than Fortis the canvas might pass for a challenge, one of those pistol-shots one fires at the Salon to alarm the passers-by. From Fortis, if we exhibit the canvas, it will be thought to be a bid for publicity or a scandal."

178

"But what…?"

"Imagine, Madame, an automobile launched in pitch darkness into a crowd. Two huge phosphorescent eyes, a formidable machine, and beneath its rubber tires, a veritable human pulp; women and children crushed; blood and brains; the most horrible of spectacle—and under the painting, on the frame, in red letters, the words *Modern High Life*. There's talent in it, naturally, a great deal of talent, but—how shall I put it?—a talent that seems to be the result of a hallucination. Turner had such visions at the end of his life, and you know that at present, Turner… I beg your pardon…"

Pétrus Hardy stopped, looking at Madame Fortis, whose face expressed a poignant dolor. Then, his gloved fingers mechanically smoothed the hat he was holding on his knees. "We're very embarrassed, you understand. The Committee refuses to exhibit a canvas that seems to be a sort of deliberate protest against many of our colleagues at the Club, members of the Automobile Club—*Modern High Life*, as the title indicates—and which, moreover, in its execution, is gaudy and sinister, with its wounds, its broken limbs, its pools of blood. And before letting Monsieur Fortis know about a refusal that will offend him, I thought, Madame, of addressing myself officiously to the person who is very particularly interested in the success and glory of a master we all love.

"What would be disagreeable, formulated by a Committee, might become simple if the verdict, translated by you, became a cordial recommendation, one of those pieces of advice that women know how to give us better than anyone when we are anxious, when we doubt ourselves—which happens to us all…"

Cécile was convinced that Pétrus Hardy and the Committee must be right. She recalled only too well the painful impression she had felt before the other canvas that disappeared from the studio thereafter—but she could not give André the advice of which Pétrus Hardy spoke, since she had not seen the painting.

"I could only tell him what you have told me."

"What, Madame? Monsieur Fortis hasn't shown it to you?"

"My husband doubtless feared that my impression might anticipate yours—and then, you know, he doesn't take my advice about all his paintings," she added, swiftly, to explain her ignorance of such a work and prevent the visitor from suspected that two different beings were incarnate in the same body, two different painters of almost hostile tendencies, enclosed in the same envelope.

"You could see the painting at the Club. Would you do us the honor of coming today?"

"Yes, Monsieur, I'll go. But I trust you. I know that my husband has been haunted by certain preoccupations of social art. I thank you for having given me your opinion, your advice as a friend..."

"And admirer. But don't say a word about the step I've taken to Monsieur Fortis, I beg you. He might believe it some fit of jealousy on my part, and I'm only jealous of his glory!"

Cécile had but one thought: to go to the Club and judge the truth of Pétrus Hardy's anxieties.

The painting, of unaccustomed dimensions for a Club exhibition, was turned to the wall, among other paintings not yet hung. Pétrus, who was expecting Madame Fortis, gave the order for it to turned round, and before the horror of the spectacle, Cécile uttered a scream.

It was the sinister vision of the Golden Calf, but further exaggerated and exasperated: one of those apparitions in the manner of Chifflart,[42] but even more apocalyptic, in which an appetite for horror, an accumulation of macabre details, give the impression of a murderous hallucination. The giant automobile, a kind of fiery dragon, all red, blood red, was darting

---

[42] François-Nicolas Chifflart (1825-1901) was best-known as an illustrator, particularly for his engravings illustrating books by Victor Hugo, including *Notre-Dame de Paris*, and a series produced in 1859 in association with Gounod's operatic version of *Faust*.

enormous round eyes over the heaped-up cadavers, and the capital letters traced in vermilion on the frame, *Modern High Life*, added a ferocious irony to the terrible vision.

"Do you know," said Pétrus to Madame Fortis, who remained immobile, petrified with terror, "that Dick, the caricaturist, has baptized the canvas—which he has seen, unfortunately—*The Apotheosis of Crushing?*"

Cécile hastened to reply. "You're right, Monsieur. It's necessary that this canvas doesn't appear before the eyes of the public. Keep it, hide it. I don't know how I'll persuade my husband to destroy it, but it's a sick man's dream. I don't want to—I can't—look at it. I can't."

She turned away from the horrible vision. She was in a hurry to get out of the ground floor room to which the immense canvas had, in a manner of speaking, been exiled.

She would tell André everything. And, leaving the Club where *Modern High Life* remained, she wondered, as she went back to the house in the Rue Murillo, who she would find before her at home: the man she loved or the man she feared, the author of so many landscapes impregnated with the soul of things, or the author of that repulsive vision, which resembled a Callot phantasmagoria seen though a skylight in the Morgue. Would it be André, or the man who took André's name? Him, or the Other?

It was André who welcomed her on the threshold of the house, André smiling and amiable, asking her: "Where have you been? Why did you go out? I've had a walk in the park. I'd been working very hard...a headache..."

At first she tried to lie. She had been to visit her parents.

"Ah! How is your father?"

"Well."

"And you mother?"

"The same."

"We don't see them often."

"That's life. The young with the young. And then, my father always worries about disturbing you. A soldier, he respects orders. You shut yourself away..."

She talked for the sake of talking, giving or seeking a reason for going out, but she was not a good liar. She could see that the person listening to her, interrogating her, really was the conscious husband, the great artist whose name she bore.

She did not want to wait, and even if he would suffer in consequence, she would tell him everything—and she dared to do so. Yes, there was at the Club a canvas signed André Fortis, which, if exhibited, would cause a scandal.

"A canvas by me? I haven't sent anything. Nothing! What is it, this canvas?"

At the first words of the description that Cécile pronounced, a cry of desperate dolor escaped the painter's throat.

"The automobile! The iron monster! I know! I've seen it!"

And he did, indeed, see again the bloody canvas, the red canvas that he had hesitated to destroy, the horror realized by the Other's brush!

"Oh, it's enough to drive one mad!" he said, angrily.

Everywhere, then, always and inevitably, like a shadow detaching itself from him, he would find that stranger, that being sharing his life—or, rather, imposing himself on his life—constraining him to countersign actions of which he was unaware and works that he detested: that double bearing the same name as him, lodged within him; that detestable and detested Other, of whom he was a prisoner of sorts, and of whom he had now become the accomplice.

"Responsible for his insults, responsible for his works—and to think that the creature is made of flesh and bone, my poor Cécile, made of *my* flesh and my bone, not...not impalpable but *ungraspable*; that he exists, since he acts, produces, since he's me, and that to get rid of him I would have to put a bullet in my own head, killing myself in order to kill him! No, but it's absurd, idiotic, insane, incredible...and it's true! This arm is his, this hand, mine, is his! This brain, I share with him! Yes, beneath this skull I'm like half a brain, whose other half is someone else! Oh, I've had enough, you see! Truly, it's too much! That I have to ask you once again to forgive me for having associated your life with that of a semi-lunatic! Forgive me, forgive me! Forgive me!"

She had often heard that word, that desperate cry. And she forgave him effortlessly, since she loved him, her love for the unfortunate increasing in her pity.

She calmed him down. She proved to him that this new manifestation of the doubling of his personality would not harm either his reputation or his health. How had the painting been sent to the Club? Doubtless André had sent it while in his "second state." He only recalled vaguely the "aura" of a recent crisis, which had doubtless not lasted very long. Dazzlements, a construction round the skull, and obviously, he had lost his very sense of self. For how long? He did not know. Long enough, at least, to have summoned some porters and sent the canvas to the President of the Club's Artistic Committee.

Aurèle, the domestic, clearly remembered having seen people taking way a large wrapped-up frame, while Monsieur looked on. Monsieur had seemed very anxious. "Be careful with the frame," he had urged the men. "The frame is as important as the canvas, because of the inscription."

Of all that, André had no memory. Instead of the pools of blood painted on an apocalyptic canvas he might really have spilled human blood for which he was not responsible, his fingers having become murderous.

"I can't do it anymore; I can't live like this! Let Dr. Klipper condemn me to exile, to claustration, to solitary confinement, to silence, to everything that soothes or cures madmen; I submit myself in advance to his orders—but it's too many visions and terrors, it's too much. It's no longer living—I'd rather die!"

Softly, Cécile replied: "Then we'll go to see Dr. Jean Klipper."

IX. To Kill the Other

"You'd prefer to die? I understand that, if you were to continue to be subject to the Other's law! It's intolerable...impossible...impossible..."

That was Dr. Klipper, in his study in the Place de Valois, replying, coldly and imperturbably, to Fortis, who was telling him about his latest ordeal and repeated to him what he had said to Cécile. Madame Fortis had accompanied her husband to the doctor's house and she was sitting by the window, looking at the smiling blind woman, who was standing beside the scientist's armchair, leaning her elbow on the back, evoking the idea of a guardian angel.

"You can no longer live in the company of the Other, exposed to the tyranny of the Other? That's quite natural...entirely natural..." The short, thin man's fiery eyes were fixed on André. "Well, then, it's necessary to finish with the Other. It's necessary to kill him."

"Kill him?"

"Quite simply."

"I don't understand," Fortis said.

"It's perfectly clear, however. You are, as you recognize yourself, haunted by a singular being who, like an unexpected guest, takes possession of your own person when you least suspect it. Well, then, expel him! And as the most definite form of expulsion is death, kill him!"

"I've often thought of dying," Fortis replied, with a mournful expression that caused Cécile to experience a frisson.

The little man stirred in his armchair and shook his long white hair. "I'm not talking about you," he said, brusquely. "I'm talking about the one you call the Other and who has a name..."

"A name?"

"Of course. Get used to the idea that this being, this 'sub-liminal,' has a distinct existence within you, living in your brain like a worm living in your gut, and it is through you that it's necessary to reach him. It's necessary to kill him for you to be able to live. Look, until now you have sensed him, sup-ported him, without giving him a name. He is, if you'll pardon the expression, a mental bothriocephalus.[43] He has been, for you, a kind of specter, a mirage, an invisible passenger: the Other! Let us incarnate this Other in a being that will appear to you henceforth in the guise of a man who might resemble you, but is no longer you. Look at me..."

And Klipper plunged the fire of his pupils into André's eyes, like two beams of the electric light he had domesticated in his cellar. He dictated his will, hypnotized by that flame, constraining him to belief the suggestion, insensate in appear-ance but consoling in reality, so thoroughly did it impregnate the troubled brain with his orders.

"Yes, look at me. The being who has shared your exist-ence until now, as if poisoning it, is not called André Fortis; his name is André David."

"André David!" stammered Fortis.

And, imperatively, like the very statue of will, the strange little man began an interrogation.

"David, listen to me carefully, David, and answer me. Da-vid"—he emphasized each syllable—"André, is that really one of your forenames?"

"Yes," said André. "André-Pierre-David."

"Well, he has taken one of your forenames as he had tak-en your name itself—and that André David, on the day he disappeared, would render complete liberty to André-David Fortis, the true Fortis, who is you. Do you hear me?"

"Yes," André repeated.

With his thin hands, the Alsatian had taken the feverish hands of the painter and was squeezing the fingers as if to

---

[43] *Bothriocephalus* is a genus of tapeworms.

break them. With a redoubtable cerebral tension he plunged that almost-crazy conception into the young man's mind.

Tremulously, Cécile contemplated the two men, so very different, sitting facing one another, face to face, not so much a physician and a patient as two adversaries measuring one another for a duel. What gazes, what will-power: the absolute will of Klipper dictating to Fortis the frightful idea than an André David was living within him—and the weaker will of Fortis, tamed by the scientist's eyes, yielded, accepted that fantastic, absurd revelation as if his reason had spoken.

But there was no longer any reason or free will involved: Klipper ordered; Klipper hypnotized; Klipper caused a real being to appear to André's imagination, who, for the painter, suddenly became as real and alive for the painter, even though he did not exist, as the passers-by thronging the street. He was no longer "the Other," he was André David now—and the mere fact of giving a name to that hitherto invisible, ungraspable being rendered André a part of his mental freedom. It seemed to him that this André David was now a sort of adversary that he could fight, a parasite of which he could rid himself.

"On the day when it can be proved to you that this André David is dead," said Klipper, interrogatively, imposing Fortis' response and conviction by the magnetism of his eyes, "you will believe yourself to be free?"

"Yes, certainly," said André, his throat tight.

"You will feel that you are liberated from all constraint?"

"Yes, Doctor, yes—but what if he's still alive? What if he's alive?"

"Only Nature lives forever, because she fattens herself on us. No human lives forever!"

Cécile experienced a sudden terror on hearing those tragic words, coldly pronounced, and Dr. Klipper, with the young blonde woman beside him, now had the effect on her, by virtue of a singular transformation, of some formidable Kabbalist who had evoked a familiar spirit to stand by his side. And it seemed to her, even though that André was, in a sense, a mere phantom, that the scientist was talking, with terrifying impassivity, about the destruction, the killing, of a living being: a real murder.

She did not understand, and yet she had, with a desperate confidence, the vague instinct that André's salvation was at the end of this extraordinary conversation, and she felt joyful as she heard Klipper—over whom Marthe leaned her ecstatic, admiring face—repeat: "You will reckon with this André David. I promise you that, Klipper's word. But first of all, you're fully convinced that he exists, aren't you?"

"Yes," said André.

"Look me again. Look at me. Harder than that. You believe it? You believe me?"

"Yes," André said again, more firmly.

"Well then, we'll send him away once and for all. And if you ever feel again—listen to me carefully, and don't forget a single word of what I'm about to say to you—if you sense, by and kind of warning sign, that this man, the Intruder, the Guest, the Enemy, is threatening to take possession of your being, the moment you feel the merest breath of his presence or the scratch of his claw, sat the first symptom, take the first piece of paper that comes to hand, and with a pen or a pencil, write these simple words: *He is here.* Then send that information to me via Madame."

He had turned to Cécile, who was listening, chilled to the bone, as if those dictated words were the mark of some fatal sentence.

"You won't forget? *He is here.* And be on your guard! That's the entirety of my prescription. Now go. Burn the works that André David wants to exhibit in your name or don't burn them—it doesn't matter. The important thing is to know whether he will come back or not. You're on watch. You alone can warn me about his possible presence. When you have said to me: *He is here*, I shall act."

"But Doctor..."

On last time, Jean Klipper darted his gaze, burning like a ray, into André's eyes; one last time the curt and forceful voice repeated: "You have understood. You will obey!"

Subdued, dominated and hypnotized. André left the apartment, as if petrified by the master's will. When they got into the coupé that was waiting in the Rue de Valois, Cécile was quite astonished to find a little of Parisian life—passers-by, elegant women—after having spent an hour in the company of a kind of mage, a sorcerer of another era.

She could still see the man's ardent eyes, beneath the white hair, fixed on André's dreamy, velvety, wild and obedient eyes.

The painter had no sooner left Klipper's drawing-room than the old doctor rubbed his stiff hands together and said: "My dear Marthe, this is a cure that won't get me into the Institute, thank God, but it will be very curious. That man is now convinced of the reality of this André David. He will see him, in flesh and bone. He is under the influence of suggestion; he will believe that the life of that phantom is graspable. If anyone says to him now that the specter has no normal existence, he will reply that they are mistaken, or lying to him. Now, if I can prove to him that this André David is dead..."

The Alsatian stopped, and began laughing. "Ah! But in fact, my dear Marthe, perhaps killing a man, even when that man doesn't exist, is a case of conscience. Does one have the right to kill a phantom?"

He amused himself in posing the question.

"Bah! The living first, and too bad for the victims!"

Then he passed his fingers over the young woman's stigmatized forehead. "But this is what preoccupies me even more than the second existence of André Fortis, Your life, my poor dear Marthe. Your life! Your salvation! Your light!"

With a slightly feverish haste of a passionate miner racing to a seam or an artist summoned by his incomplete work, he said: "Let's go to the laboratory. It seems to me that the bones are coming apart beneath my hand, and that we're approaching the goal!"

"Yes, perhaps," replied the docile voice of the resigned woman, as always.

They went down the broad stone staircase, and then the narrow spiral stairway to the cellar, and, sitting in her habitual place, motionless, awaiting salvation with her untiring fervor, Marthe Klipper submitted her forehead to the light emitted by the machine, which struck her directly on the forehead, like the thrust of a needle.

The scientist's battle against the impossible continued in the subterranean laboratory, where the doctor worked, full of hope, like a mage, and where his patient remained motionless under the pencil of rays, like a martyr.

X. The Agony of André David

Life resumed for André and Cécile: their habitual, banal, happy life...

The painter had locked the sinister painting, compromising for his name, in the darkness of the loft. Pétrus Hardy had sent it back wrapped in cloth, invisible and hidden, carried by employees of the Club. He had recommenced his labor as if no storm had passed through his existence.

To see him smiling and alert, to hear him talking about all sorts of things like a lively and amiable Parisian, no one, including Cécile, could have suspected that that talented, charming and cheerful individual had been subjected to such ordeals, and was carrying a defect within him. The man had such a faculty of forgetfulness during those brief intervals to which he gave the name of happiness that he lost the memory of what he had undergone, experienced and suffered. The cloud blew away; the weather was fine; it seemed to him that it had always been fine.

It was fine in the house in the Rue Murillo, fine in the hearts of the "loving couple," fine in the park, asleep before their gaze. Sometimes, Cécile, still slightly anxious, went up quietly to the studio in which André was cloistered and listened to see whether any noise might give her cause for anxiety. No, André was working, peacefully. Sometimes, having entirely escaped his anguish, he was singing.

Then she knocked on the door. "It's me."

"Come in."

She gazed at the work begun: sunrises over the lagoon, dusks beneath the trees of Fontainebleau, visions of a poet and a painter.

"Are you content with me? I think it's *going well*," he said, displaying his canvases.

All of André Fortis' talent burst forth in those masterly pages.

It seemed that he had become himself again permanently, free of the terror of old.

The mere fact of Dr. Klipper having personified, incarnated in a determinate being, the kind of phantom that harassed André, gave the painter a sense of liberation.

He was no longer *the Other*—which is to say, another self—he was a living and active individual who persecuted him and took his place. No longer a sort of anonymous shadow but an enemy, having a kind of civil identity, a stranger whom Klipper had baptized with his true name: André David.

And by virtue of a suggestion that became more powerful every day, that André David had taken on substance for André Fortis and gave him the impression not of an inconvenient guest but of some contemporary living a life of his own a long way away, unconfused with his: an annoyance that had been chased away, to sort himself out somewhere else.

The important thing was that he should never come back, and since the old Alsatian had given, or rather imposed upon, his patient that explanation, accepted by André as the final word, the painter had felt strangely relieved, certain that if André David ever reappeared in his life, Jean Klipper would have the means to punish him.

What means? That was the doctor's secret. Fortis did not seek to analyze the matter. He believed. Did he even have to think about Klipper's instructions, if André David had conclusively disappeared?

He had not disappeared.

The precursory dazzling, the unexpected flashes prior to the cerebral storm, passed before André's eyes one evening, during the meal, under the lamp, and Cécile suddenly saw her husband turn very pale.

"What's the matter?"

"Nothing…or rather, yes," said André, still conscious of himself. "Yes, something's the matter A warning... It's *him*."

"Him?"

She was frightened; André's eyes were gazing at an object that she could not see.

"I can see him, as if enveloped in light. I can only see a part of your head now... It's *the Other*...the warning...he's coming. Do you remember what Klipper said?"

André's voice was already changing. It was becoming dull, strangled, as if an invisible hand were griping the young man by the throat.

"Write to Klipper—write, write," he said, curtly.

Cécile, already out of her chair, ran to her room and came back immediately, holding out a pencil and notepad to André. On the top sheet of the pad he traced, with jerky movements, the agreed message dictated by Klipper: *He is here.*

Then laughing dryly, he added his signature: *André Fortis*, and said to the terrified Cécile: "Let's use my name while I'm still me!"

Aurèle came in with the coffee.

"Take that away," said Cécile. "Monsieur is ill."

"Does Monsieur need anything?"

Fortis was already staring at his manservant with eyes that were visibly gazing at and perceiving something else, something beyond.

"No, thank you." She wanted to be alone with André.

"Do you feel better?"

He was there, in front of her, standing up. He made no reply. She recognized the expression on that face; she remembered it. It was the mask: the face of the Other.

"What?" he asked, as if he had not heard.

Oh, the terrible apparition of that frightful first night of their marriage! André, poor André, was once again as she had seen him before her at that tragic moment, sinister and frightening. The "passer-by" was taking possession of his being. The nameless being that the doctor had baptized at hazard, personified as "André David" was about to return—for how long?

She begged the unfortunate to go to his bedroom; she took his arm while he still retained a little conscious will, and went up the stairs with him until the moment when, on the steps, André tore himself away abruptly, saying to her, in a harsh voice: "Let me be! I want to be alone!"

Already, that "let me be" was not pronounced by André Fortis, but the thief of his personality. And the latter, the Other, was in a hurry to go up to his studio; he climbed the flight of stairs that led to it rapidly, and when Cécil, following him with equal rapidity, arrived at the door, she found it shut, and heard André shooting the internal bolt with a violent gesture.

Then she experienced the sensation of infinite terror conveyed by a locked door behind which an individual dear to you is barricaded, desperate or angry. What is happening behind that block of wood, which separates us from the person to whom we are calling? The impossibility of speaking, of explaining, of begging, rises to the brain, blowing like a wind of fear. A drama might be being played out there, to which it is necessary to submit, in anguish and impotence.

Cécile knocked with clenched fists, repeating the beloved name: "André! André!"

How could André reply? If he heard her, he did not understand. That voice could not awaken any emotion in him. Cécile was no longer his wife. He was abruptly living another life, and doubtless at his easel, gripped by the fever of the ferociously symbolic painter who had produced the Golden Calf and *Modern High Life*, hurling some new horror on to canvas. "André! André! It's me, André!"

All of a sudden, as the silence of the locked studio was the only reply to her cries of anguish, she was no longer thinking about anything but Jean Klipper, and the desperate appeal to which André had just signed his name.

It was necessary to inform the old doctor. She instructed Aurèle to watch over Monsieur, to follow him if he went out, and ran to the house in the Place de Valois.

"I've been expecting you," said Klipper. "A more-or-less imminent crisis was inevitable. I've made my battle plan. Let's go—we'll reckon with the Evil One, as they said in olden times."

193

His plan was quite simply. It was a matter of getting rid of the Double who was haunting Fortis.

"An old story," said Klipper. "We thought we'd invented something: the subliminal, the second state. The Egyptians knew that. It's old—as old as the white wolf!"

He had thought at first that suggestion alone might be sufficient to liberate André from his suffering, but the certainty of being subject to so many miseries was so profoundly rooted in the painter's mind that it might be impossible to extract it from him by will-power.

Klipper had found another means. He would suppress André Fortis' normal life to give him the sensation of being reborn into a new life free of all servitude of terror. He would plunge into the sick man's mind the conviction that he was liberated, liberated permanently, from his specter.

And Cécile could be happy. She would no longer know the horror of the unknown.

What he had previously dictated imperatively to Fortis, he repeated to Cécile, with the calmness of certainty: "We shall reckon with this specter."

"Oh, Doctor, how I bless you!"

"Oh, you don't have to bless me, Madame. What's the point of science—which is such a small thing—if it can't do a little good?"

In order to act, however, Klipper had to wait for the new crisis that just gripped André to pass.

XI. Experiments

The painter, locked in his studio, lived there in the fervor of creation, ringing for Aurèle to have his meals brought up, not coming out, seemingly prey to a fury of endeavor that alarmed Cécile.

She went continually to consult Klipper, whom she found with the ever-faithful Marthe, the guardian angel watching over his soul.

"I'm scared," she said. "This fever of labor frightens me. What if he falls ill?"

A bizarre smile then appeared on the little man's wizened face. "Who can tell?" Klipper replied. "That might be an excellent thing!"

He rubbed his bony fingers together, and his blazing eyes seemed to fix upon some distant object imperceptible to Cécile: an unknown goal, a vision.

"The sick," he said, "can be cured. From a typhoid fever, he might perhaps emerge liberated!"

And that possibility, of such a danger—a mortal illness—also taking on a hopeful form for the doctor, amazed Cécile to such an extent that she wondered whether Klipper was really in his right mind.

"Have no fear, Madame. Your husband will find, in this very overexcitement, the strength to resist such a proof, and while André David—since we have named him thus—works, André Fortis is resting. Tell me when he has recovered his own personality. Then I shall act."

"And what will you do, Doctor?"

"Something quite trivial. You'll see." Pointing to Marthe, pale and pensive, with the red patch on her forehead, he added: "What I'm trying to do is much more difficult. And yet, I shall succeed. I shall succeed! One can do anything one wishes. One does everything one wishes, unless an accident, the unexpected—that which destroys all our plans, bringing down the house of cards—intervenes! I fear nothing in life but the unexpected, the atom, the speck of dust, the grain of sand!"

Then, leaving his personal preoccupation and his dream there, he said: "But for your husband, Madame, I'm sure of success. You know that his case isn't unique? A celebrated engraver recently exhibited drawings and pastels executed, he said, by a medium that pushed his hand. All Paris was talking about it. An easily-explicable cerebral phenomenon was attributed to spirit activity.[44] There is no spirit activity. There is the human brain, which can imagine anything and believe anything. I shall focus on André Fortis' brain. I shall take responsibility for his heart!"

One morning, André came back down from his studio, where, condemned to his second personality, he had been living and sleeping for days, taking up his ordinary life at the point where he had left it. It seemed that nothing had interrupted his normal existence. At lunch, what he said to Cécile appeared to be a continuation of the conversation interrupted by the crisis. André asked about the health of General and Madame de Jandrieu—they were spending the winter in Pau—talked about his landscapes for the next Salon, Parisian news, a play performed the day before of which he had just read a review.

"We'll go to see it, that play by Hervieu! I admire his talent."[45]

---

[44] Experiments in automatic writing and automatic drawing were carried out in many French séances, including those hosted by Victor Hugo and Camille Flammarion; the dramatist Victorien Sardou was one of numerous individuals who published work done under such circumstances. Clarétie was not to know that, after the Great War, numerous surrealist artists would develop automatic drawing as a technique without any reference to the suppose mediation of spirits.

[45] Paul Hervieu's drama *L'Énigme*, featuring a ferocious conflict between two brothers in love with the same woman, had

"Whenever you wish," Cécile replied.

Nothing could have made anyone suspect that there had been an interruption of almost a week between their last meal together and this one. Aurèle served the coffee impassively, just as he had served it the other day.

André probably did not even remember that he had written to Klipper, scribbling, like a call for help, the words *He is here.*

He was no longer there, and the painter, having forgotten his crisis, was enjoying life without even wanting to reflect. Instinctively, his brain experienced the feeling of wellbeing that convalescence yields.

"I'd be entirely happy," he said, "if it were spring. I have an appetite for woodland scenes painted from nature in spring." He looked through the window at the damp Parc Monceau, beneath the gray February sky, with the melting snow and the white Gounod monument, sad in the distance... "In April, we'll go to Ville-d'Avray and I'll evoke, if I can, good old Papa Corot on the edge of the pond!"

Cécile remembered Klipper's instruction. As soon as Fortis had recovered his personality, she had to inform the doctor, and the doctor would take action. André have recovered his normal state; the moment had therefore come to attempt the experiment to which the Alsatian had referred without explaining it, and which ought to ensure a cure.

He said so, Jean Klipper. He affirmed it!

She remembered his exact words: "I've made my battle plan." She had the most complete and absolute confidence in that strange man who had scared her momentarily. André would be cured, cured by Klipper—and, then, before him, so many happy years!

---

its première at the Théâtre Francaise, under Clarétie's management, in November 1901. There is an English version known as *Caesar's Wife*.

197

She went straight to the Place de Valois, telling Klipper that the painter did not even remember having had a further attack; if the doctor wished, he could cure him now.

"Let's go," said Klipper.

He seemed a trifle annoyed. It would be necessary for him to interrupt the experiments carried out on Marthe for a few days: to interrupt them at a moment when, under the beams of light, the long-awaiting hatching. The magic, the miracle, might be on the brink of production.

Marthe felt, in fact, an impression in her forehead as if it were cracking beneath the burn. One might have thought that iron fingers were parting the bones of her skull. She too was subject to the ardent faith that Jean Klipper had in the success of his work. In her extinct eyes, which did not perceive any light of life, she had the sensation, the illusion, of glimpsing an expected gleam. Might not that pain that she felt in her forehead be a kind of birth process from which the hidden eye that the heat was causing to develop would emerge?

She believed so. She said: "I'm hopeful."

And Klipper replied: "For myself, I'm sure."

That certainty changed into pious care the torture that he imposed on the young woman, tortured by that immobility before the burning beam that was corroding, almost boring through her skull.

But he was sure—yes, sure—of success, of that triumphant discovery: humans becoming Cyclopes, the power of human sight augmented by a third.

An antisocial recluse avoiding any clientele, he experienced a sort of anger in being interrupted, even for a few hours, in the pursuit of his dream, in order to occupy himself with a stranger, a case that seemed to him to be mediocre and of scant importance by comparison with the stupefying problem that he wanted to solve. But he had promised. He had told Cécile to come. She had come. He would obey.

"Let's go see your husband," he said.

XII. The Salvation

Cécile's carriage was waiting in the Rue de Valois. It transported the doctor rapidly to the Rue Murillo, and André was rather astonished, but not annoyed, to see Jean Klipper arriving at his house. He had a respectful affection for the old man. He found him interesting from the intellectual viewpoint, and very beautiful artistically. He would ask to paint his portrait some day. "I also do faces," he said, smiling, not even remembering the ferocious symbolic canvases fallen from his brush.

On entering André's studio—that was where Cécile took the doctor—Klipper got straight to the point, and, taking an old battered wallet from his long frock-coat, he took out a piece of paper, which he handed to Fortis like a creditor producing a promissory note.

"Do you recognize that?"

André took the piece of paper. It was his own handwriting. Three words: *He is here.*

Cécile was anxious on seeing him pale slightly.

"Yes," he said, "It's me who has summoned you!"

"Well?" said Klipper.

André did not seem to understand what was wanted of him. He remembered having written the words, a few days before, as if he were uttering a cry for help, but everything that had followed had disappeared, so far as he was concerned, into an opaque fog. He no longer remembered anything. Of the suspension of his normal life he retained no memory, no impression. It was as if he had been obliterated. He could not even take account of the parenthesis opened between the moment when he had written to Klipper: *He is here*, and the one when Klipper had appeared, the piece of paper in hand.

The doctor interrogated him, tried to awaken André's memory of one of his thoughts or actions during the second state. Once again, André did not remember anything.

"You have, however, lived a new phase of that existence which superimposes itself on yours," said Jean Klipper, "and André David has retaken possession of the body you share with him."

The old Alsatian gave his words a sort of sacerdotal gravity, and André had the impression of being in the presence of a mage talking quite naturally about the strangest phenomena, which were familiar to him.

Above all, however, the painter felt a muffled grim anger at the thought that the Other—the parasite, the adversary, the mental tapeworm—had made that offensive return, had taken possession of his being once again, without him even perceiving it.

"Thos time," said Klipper, slowly, "it's necessary to finish it."

"Gladly!" said André. "Oh, gladly!"

Klipper's ardent, magnetically imperious eyes—the profound eyes of the visionary that focused on Marthe's forehead and studied the stars—fixed themselves on André's own, enveloping them with light.

"A surgeon is going to perform an operation on you," he said, his Alsatian accent underlining his imperious tone. "Will you allow yourself to be put to sleep? Yes, it's a matter of appendicitis, which is very fashionable, or some tumor...will you surrender your body to the surgeon?"

"Yes," said André, looking at Cécile, who was standing in front of him, trying to smile, or rather smiling, with a desire to faint.

"Well," said Klipper, "I'm a surgeon of another sort. This personality, which is yours, and which another steals from you, I want to suppress temporarily in order to affirm and consolidate it permanently. I want to get rid of the thief of your soul, the robber of your reason, the other André: André David."

"The Other!" Fortis repeated, once again. Then, deliberately: "What do I have to do?"

"Submit to an operation, like any other. Trust yourself to me."

"But I have entrusted myself to you, Doctor."

"Body and soul?"

"Body and soul. Yes, do with me as you please, provided that the specter will no longer torture me—anything that seems necessary to you, however perilous: anything at all."

Cécile stood still, maintaining her tragic silence. It seemed to her that the two men were engaged in a struggle that was a matter of life and death for one of them.

"Do you need to work in the next few days?" asked Klipper.

"I wanted to begin my Salon painting, but it doesn't matter…"

"You'll return to it later with greater joy. I'm asking you, demanding of you, that you abandon life for a few days. Seeing André's interrogative gaze, he added: "That crisis, independent of your will—the interruption of your normal life—I shall provoke myself; and when the crisis has passed, there will no longer be an André David. The Other will be dead, expelled forever. I swear to you—forever."

"Do it," said André Fortis.

Dr. Kipper pointed to a large leather armchair with a high back, near the studio's bay window, "Sit there!"

André obeyed.

The scientist placed his thin hand on Fortis' breast. "No palpitations!" He took the painter's left wrist and placed his thumb on it. "Regular pulse. You're brave!"

"Why shouldn't I be brave? You're here."

"No heart disease," said Klipper. "Let's go."

In the light from outside the man with long white hair standing beside the large armchair in which André was sitting, in the shade, resembled those doctors who surge forth from Rembrandt's gloomy backgrounds. Cécile was looking at him now with a kind of terror, as if the scientist were about to devote himself to some sinister, redoubtable task.

He had taken a bottle from his pocket, with a frosted glass stopper, which he held momentarily in his thin fingers, and then poured a few drops on to a handkerchief, which he raised to André's nostrils.

"Chloroform," he said. "Nothing simpler."

He maintained the handkerchief forcefully, constraining the painter to breathe its evaporations; at the same time, he interrogated the young man's pulse with his thumb on the artery.

André's eyes, open at first, and focused on the doctor with curiosity, gradually closed; the anesthetic took effect and the handsome pale head of the patient slumped on to the back of the armchair, the lips lifting up the black moustache with a kind of ecstatic smile, while the body, languidly extended, took on an abandoned attitude, gradually immobilized as if in sleep or death.

Then Jean Klipper leaned over André's breast, listening to the heartbeat, his fingers still applied to the wrist.

Hs eyes closed, André no longer seemed to be breathing.

"My God, Doctor," said Cécile. "Are you quite sure that there's no danger?"

"None, Madame. The inhalation was prompt; he's now anesthetized."

"Can he hear?"

"No. Perhaps he's dreaming. I thought about giving him hashish, in order for his dream to be better, but one can't control the crazy dreams of *majum*, the green paste. With chloroform or ether, it's sleep. We can control the awakening." The little man added: "Now he has to be carried to his bed."

Cécile pressed an electric button. "Do as the Doctor instructs," she said to Aurèle.

With the help of the porter, the manservant took the sleeping André down to the apartment. Cécile followed them with an anxious heart, watching the two men go down the staircase step by step, carrying the body that resembled a cadaver.

"It's frightful," she said.

202

But the Alsatian smiled, and replied: "It's nothing. You'll see!"

"Undressed and put to bed, André Fortis, beneath the tapestried canopy, seemed even more than before to be sleeping the final sleep. The bony fame of his forehead gleamed on the pillow with a shroud-like whiteness; and, his eyes closed, his lips were parted in an enigmatic smile redolent of the beyond, as if, with his last sigh, he had glimpsed some supreme vision.

"I'm afraid," Cécile repeated, in a whisper. "I'm afraid."

"No, don't worry. You'll see, tomorrow."

"Good God! Are you going to leave him like this until tomorrow?"

"No, no—but tomorrow, I'll repeat the experiment, and tomorrow evening, André David will no longer exist. *Bon voyage!*" And while the young woman approached André Fortis' bed, where he was still asleep, he said: "Nothing is more useful than anesthetization—with chloroform or ether—for extracting mental secrets from the body. Conscripts represent themselves as hunchbacked; one puts them to sleep, and their simulated humps disappear. When madmen can be cured, one subjects them to chloroform. They calm down, and their reason may return. Maniacs who are obstinate in a grim mutism are etherized, and they talk. Guilty men confess; pretended lunatics give themselves away. The truth emerges, not from a well, but from our bottles. You'll see—you'll see tomorrow."

"Tomorrow?"

"Tomorrow I shall bring your husband the proof of his deliverance. Malebranche's leg of mutton, as I think I told you. No? Well, I'll tell you about it..."

The remained at André's bedside until the anesthesia wore off, and when the astonished painter found himself lying in his bed, search the vague confusion of his first impression for an explanation of how he had come to wake up there, with a singular sensation of emptiness in his head, Dr. Klipper was quick to reassure him.

"You're not ill, Monsieur Fortis, but you'll be subject until tomorrow to a very particular regime—not at all painful. I need you to sleep, to sleep for a long time. While you're asleep, I'll be working on your behalf. You know the proverb: good things happen while you're asleep. It not always necessary to believe in proverbs, but they're sometimes true."

André listened, astonished, his mind slightly befuddled, as if in a dream.

"Your husband can drink and eat whatever he likes until tomorrow," Klipper added, holding out a prescription to Cécile, which he had just written on a leaf torn from his notebook, but I want him to take half a glass of this potion every two hours."

"Which is?" André asked.

"Oh, nothing serious. A calming sedative. So, my dear Monsieur, I'll come back tomorrow. Until then, remain in bed. Rest is the best of medicines."

"In bed without being ill?"

"In bed in order not to be ill any longer," said the doctor, smiling. "Until tomorrow."

Cécile accompanied him to the door of the house, slightly anxious and not understanding—but the strange little man did not give her the opportunity to express her anxieties.

"Since I tell you, Madame, that the experiment is necessary. I need a few hours of confusion in that head, which sleep will lull. The potion I've prescribed will continue the state of somnolence I require. Thought, the obsession, the terror of the Double will also go to sleep, and tomorrow..."

That word, persistently repeated, seemed tragic to Cécile, simultaneously full of terror and hope.

"Tomorrow, Doctor."

"Well, tomorrow, you'll see, you'll see!"

And Jean Klipper set off for the Place de Valois, where Marthe, not used to seeing him go out, was waiting for him.

XIII. A Funereal Letter

"It's amusing, science," said Dr. Klipper that evening, at dinner, to the blind woman, who saw in thought—really saw—what the master evoked in her presence. "Amusing, admit it. Pursuing the solution to two problems at the same time, one gigantic and the other curious and paradoxical, and solving them both at the same time. It's exciting!"

"Then Monsieur Fortis…?" Marthe asked.

"Will be cured tomorrow! Asleep for now. Tomorrow I shall bring him salvation, as one presents a baby to a mother after labor, and she smiles. He will be happy."

"And me?" said the young woman.

"You? I'm within reach of success. I sense that soon, dear soul, I shall no longer torture you—no, you hear—and you'll be able to see, to see the vast world!"

"Strasbourg!" put in the old Alsatian woman Anna, who was serving dinner.

And shaking his head gravely at the prayerful tone, Jean Klipper replied: "Strasbourg!" For the old woman, it was the "real world," for Klipper, the cradle.

He repeated: "You'll no longer suffer!"

With her customary softness, however, Marthe smiled and said: "I don't suffer."

"Your forehead?"

"Doesn't cause me any pain."

Klipper's piercing eyes seemed to focus on the burn that marked the place at which the rays of his apparatus converged, seeking the fissure by which the fantastic eye—the complementary, unexpected third eye forgotten by Mother Nature—would appear, and his faith in his discovery was such that, in a kind of hallucinatory certainty, it seemed to him that he saw a pupil emerge in Marthe's forehead, a glimmer for which the scars of the burn formed a kind of red halo.

"Tomorrow," she said to the young woman, as he had said it to Cécile, "tomorrow we shall see, my beloved Marthe. It will be strange if I solve both problems at the same time, tomorrow!"

A smile, which he did not notice, passed over Marthe's lips: a smile that was melancholy at first, as if saddened by a doubt, and then radiant, full of joy, as if, after the thought: *I've been waiting for that tomorrow for such a long time!* she had thought: *Since he says that the day has come, the day has come! A Jean Klipper is not mistaken!*

And the next day, the doctor went to the Fortis house with what he called "the salvation" in his pocket.

"Yes," he said to Marthe. "A definitive remedy."

"Which is?" she asked.

"Oh, the most banal thing in the world: a piece of paper. I have it there, with my bottle of chloroform."

A piece of paper! Marthe did not even ask for an explanation, leaving Klipper, whose confidence she admired, to his projects. In any case, André and Cécile had the same absolute faith in the little man with the blazing eyes.

The doctor found Fortis in bed, as he had ordered, but slightly impatient, weary of lying there. The painter's face lit up on the pillow when he saw Klipper.

"I won't ask you how you are," said the scientist. "You look superb."

"And I have a mad desire to get up, to move. I feel like a prisoner."

"Exactly. A prisoner who will be liberated today."

Cécile had accompanied Klipper to her husband's bedside. She experienced an anxious joy on seeing a glimmer of ardent hope appear in André's eyes. The word *liberated* had lit up the whole of the thin face, still worn by so much anxiety, and which seemed, on the pillow to be the emaciated face of a dying man.

Ah! Finally—finally!—Jean Klipper was about to work the miracle of rendering the unfortunate man the absolute sentiment of the uniqueness of his personality! Liberation! Liberation! The word rang in André's ears like a festival carillon.

"Today?" he asked, again, like a captive who thinks he can hear the bolts of his cell being withdrawn for the last time.

"Today I shall give you the proof that André David..."

"The Other?"

"The Other is no longer to be feared and will never return. Nevermore, as Poe says—but this time, the refrain is consoling."

He had taken from his pocket the bottle of which he had made use the day before, and, asking Cécile for a handkerchief, he impregnated the batiste with a few drops, counted one by one; then, leaning over the bed, he swiftly applied the chloroform-soaked cloth to André's lips and nostrils.

And, his ardent eyes fixed on the young man, who gradually became drowsy again, he held his writing, counting the pulsations. As if he were driving the words into André's ears one by one, he said: "You know that André: the persecutor, the enemy; André David? He's ill—very ill. He's doomed."

Beneath the handkerchief that was compressing them, André Fortis' lips murmured vague words, repeating, then stammering, the words that Klipper had pronounced: "...ill...very ill...doomed..." And his haggard eyes appeared to be searching the shadow of the alcove for some disquieting image: a phantom."

It seemed to him, while he fell asleep, slowly and gently, as if sliding smoothly into the void by night, into the darkness, that it was suddenly traversed by strange sounds—sounds that he had heard before, and recognized: the satanic voices of *Manfred*; the *Manfred* that had jangled his nerves and caused the phantom, the Other, to appear for the first time.

And it was to those distant echoes of Schumann, mingled with a memory of Charpentier's *Vie du poète*:[46] the shrill, sar-

---

[46] Gustave Charpentier's symphonic drama *La Vie du poète* (1888-89), a product of his youth, was subsequently adapted into the opera *Julien* (1914), but Clarétie could not know that.

castic shrieks of madness of drunkenness cutting through the final bacchanal, underlining the delirium and despair of the poet fallen into his dream, killed by omnipotent doubt. And while the chloroform did its work, in the drowsiness provoked by Klipper, André perceived, leaning over him like an incubus, stifling him like Smarra,[47] the face of André David, his second self, obsessive and ferocious, whose sniggering laughter resembled the sarcasms of *La Vie du poète*, and the diabolical ironies of *Manfred*.

Then, André Fortis had a bitter desire to struggle, to sit up and chase away the specter, to extend his arms in front of him, to try to seize him, to sink his fingernails into his eyes—the disquieting eyes that seemed to be watching the recumbent Fortis, And as if Dr. Klipper had divined, by an intuition of genius, what was happening within his skull, having deciphered the very thought through the bones, the old Alsatian, letting the words flow into the painter's ear, as of to leave him one last sensation before going to sleep, repeated a supreme affirmation.

"All that you can see is nothing but lies. The real truth, you shall know when you wake up. Sleep, sleep, sleep! The evil dream is over, word of Klipper. You shall see!"

Then the sleep rose up, like a benevolent tide, and Fortis felt, as the chloroform took effect, a sensation of appeasement and freshness in the confused hypnagogic images that were dancing before him, as pale as ghosts and sparkling like luminous atoms...

Then, the eyelids descended over the frightened, troubled pupils, and gently, under the action of the chloroform, André Fortis went to sleep.

When the anesthesia was complete, the little man shook his head and his long white hair, took his worn leather wallet out of his frock-coat pocket and took out a piece of paper bor-

---

[47] The vampiric spirit in Charles Nodier's *Smarra ou les démons de la nuit* (1821).

dered in black—a letter of mourning—which he unfolded, read in a low voice, and then showed it to the terrified Cécile.

The unfortunate woman had perceived André's name on that half-glimpsed letter!

She recoiled in fear, and, pointing at the lugubrious paper with her finger, she said in a strangled voice: "What's that?"

"Read it," said Klipper, coldly.

Cécile's trembling hand took the black-bordered letter that the doctor was holding out to her and, her eyes wide with fright, the young woman spelled out the words printed beneath a black cross that formed a heading and surrounded the M of the address.

M

You are invited to attend the procession, funeral service and burial of

Monsieur André David
Painter
Deceased 20 January 1901 in his thirty-second year.
Which will be held on the 22nd of the same month, at one o'clock precisely, at the Église de Saint-Étienne-du-Mont, his parish

De profundis.

The letter, at which Cécile started fearfully, also contained a list of relatives, whose names were unimportant, and the indication: *After the ceremony, the body will be transported to Saint-Laurent-du-Pont, his birthplace.*

And the poor woman, holding the funeral invitation between her fingertips, interrogated the scientist with her gaze. His eyes were shining now with a strange, ironically joyful gleam.

"There it is, the salvation," said Klipper, finally. "The persecutor is dead. When your husband has in his hands the proof that André David is dead, he will no longer fear the apparition of the Other. I'm killing the phantom. No more phantom! And André Fortis will be able to live happily.

"So," said Cécile, her gaze not quitting the letter, "it's you…?"

"Me, who, in order to materialize the confidence that I want to drive into André Fortis' brain, has imagined the death and burial of André David, who only exists in the imagination of André Fortis, and who I am killing. But the most astonishing thing"—the little man had a sardonic smile on his clean-shaven face—"the most curious thing, which proves that everything is possible and that anything might happen, is that André Fortis can. If he has any subsequent doubt, make the journey to Saint-Laurent-du-Pont. There he will find the grave of one André David, and will be able to read the name on the tombstone, as you are reading it on that funeral notice. I didn't want to leave anything to chance. I wrote, enquired, questioned, and only situated that tomb of an initially-non-existent dead man when I had been given the very place where your husband can decipher, if necessary, the name of André David. I've put in action some undertakers I know. Although I never leave my cellar, I have my acquaintances too, and undertakers and physicians, naturally, have connections; the former live on the latter. They searched, searched, searched…and found, in the Dauphiné, the tomb of an André David, a painter—yes, a painter; everything happens, everything is possible—who had just died. The Maire and the Prefect will certify the fact. And there you are! Scientists, eh? Scientists can sometimes do as much as novelists! And what is science, Madame, but a novel?"

Cécile listened, and wondered whether she might be dreaming, whether the man might be mad, who was playing thus with life and death, suppressing by anesthesia a living being, slaying with a stroke of the pen, a fictitious letter, a person who did not exist…

She looked at Klipper in bewilderment—and yet, she had the very clear impression that the scientist was risking an experiment in psychotherapy, and not overstepping his rights as a savior.

"It's by mental means that one treats and cures psycho-neuroses," he had said to her more than once.

The sublime deception of André David was, for the doctor, one of those mental means that he had at his disposal.

But what if André, woken up, recovering himself, did not believe in the definitive disappearance, the death of the specter, the disappearance of the Other?

He was there, in his bed, motionless, plunged in sleep, and Klipper waited until the chlorcform had completed its work in order to set that evidential proof before the painter's eyes.

The minutes seemed like centuries to Cécile, infinitely long hours of torture, until the moment when André opened his eyes, emerged from sleep as if dazed, and looked around, seeking to understand...

His gaze went from Klipper, sitting next to him, to Cécile, standing at the foot of his bed; his ideas were drifting, confused.

Finally, he said: "What's the matter? What's happened?"

Cécile waited for the doctor's response, as if it were a verdict.

"Something very important," said Klipper, slowly.

Slightly fearful, André Fortis almost screeched: "What? What is it?"

"What? But you're a fortunate mortal, my friend. Your enemy, your shadow, your double, you know well..."

André looked alternately at his wife and the doctor.

"Well, Doctor?"

"Well! In fact, read it!" said Klipper, holding out to André, who sat up in bed, the black-bordered letter that he had handed to Cécile a short while before.

The husband's question was the same as the wife's: "What's that?"

"Look."

In his turn, André began to read the letter. He read aloud: *"You are invited to attend the procession, funeral service and burial of Monsieur André David, painter, deceased..."*

Then, suddenly interrupting himself, leaping out of bed, half naked, with a great exclamation of surprise and almost of triumph, he said: "What? André David? *Him*? The *Other*? Dead?"

"And buried," said Klipper, coldly.

Cécile felt her heart beating like the iron weight of a clock.

"Dead?" repeated André Fortis.

He continued reading and rereading the letter, taking note of the dates. "Today is the twentieth of February..."

"The twentieth of February, eleven-twenty in the morning," said Klipper. "For a month the Other has been resting beneath his tombstone in his birthplace. And you know the famous saying: *It's only the dead who don't come back!* False in politics, of course—the dead come back and are known as martyrs.

"André David, painter, deceased the twentieth of January 1901, in his thirty-second year..." Fortis reread, and said to Cécile: "My age! He was my age, just as he had my face!"

"Now, replied the Alsatian, mockingly, "he no longer has anything. You'll never see him again. Finished! Pfft! Smoke!"

"Smoke!"

"Or putrescence. Don't think about that. You're free!"

André Fortis came back, as if obsessed by those magnetic lines, to the black-framed letter, and repeated as if to engrave them on his mind the words, the name: "*You are invited to attend the procession, funeral service and burial of Monsieur André David...*

"But why," he said, suddenly, "didn't I know a month ago?"

Still retaining his mocking expression, Klipper said: "Remember, this isn't the first time I've put you to sleep! I'll reply to you like the *Légataire universel*: 'It's your lethargy.' The essential thing is that *he*'s no longer there."

"The Other!" said André. He added: "At Saint-Laurent-du-Pont. I saw that corner of the earth, once, on the way to Chartreuse! That's where he's sleeping?"

"And don't go to wake him up, or to plunge a sword in his heart, like a vampire," said the doctor. "Peace to the dead, and life to the living!" He extended his thin hands to the young man, who shook them with an effusive ardor.

"Well," said the doctor then, darting into André's eyes pupils that were almost had burning as the spark in his laboratory, "do you believe me now; do you feel liberated?"

"Yes," André replied.

"You're you! The other has disappeared! Go on, kiss your wife! Now you'll be happy forever."

"Forever, yes—I feel it, my love! Forever!"

He put his arms around Cécile's neck; he held her in his arms; he caressed her forehead with his hand, and he kissed her closed eyelids, as he had on the evening of their engagement. And it really was a new engagement that was beginning, a life without terror, confident and free—the life of the prisoner who sees the clear sky, the open road, space...

"Oh, how I adore you, my Cécile!"

"My good André!"

"And how I love you too, Doctor, for having given me the strength to live!"

"And the joy of seeing *him* buried!"

André, who was radiant, became serious. "That's true," he said. "All this joy is founded on someone else's death!"

"Oh, don't feel sorry for the dead," said Dr. Klipper. "They're travelers who have arrived. We still have a way to go. Let's do it as people who know the price of happiness. Its fragments are still rarer and more expensive than those of radium."

He was in haste to leave Cécile and André alone. He was also in haste to rejoin Marthe. Since he had a fortunate hand today, he wanted to take his laboratory research further.

"Now," he said, "I'll abandon you to your privacy. Be certain that the Other will never—*never*, you understand—reappear! He's asleep, and sleeping soundly! You're convinced of that?"

"Absolutely," André replied, in the certainty of faith.

"You'll no longer be afraid of anything?"

"Nothing," said the painter, again. His eyes never left the funeral notice, from which, by a singular irony, an impression of fortunate deliverance radiated.

With a handshake into which she put her whole soul, Cécile thanked the doctor in a fervent voice. His smile underlined that joy with a sort of irony, and she asked: "Will you permit me to kiss you, Doctor?"

"With pleasure," said the Alsatian, offering his meager cheeks to the young woman's lips.

"Relay that kiss to your dear Marthe—a saint!" said Cecile. In a whisper, without André hearing, she added: "And here too, you have returned a human being to the light!"

Dr. Klipper put a finger over her lips. "I've killed a parasite, that's all," he said. "It's my profession. But confess that it required patience, research and luck—the great collaborator, luck!—to find in a distant cemetery a dead man who bore the same name as the man I wanted to exile, and exile permanently. The real André David was not, however, the same age as the André David of my funeral notice; he was much older. But funeral notices are not compelled to tell the whole truth...coquettish females do not frame their age in black. The important thing is that the name André David is on this piece of paper, and the name André David on the stone out there, and that André David will not reappear again in the Rue Murillo. Adieu, Madame!"

XIV. The Grain of Sand

Dr. Klipper went out of the house full of joy, leaving André in the plenitude of confidence, the Other flattened, expelled and buried—almost forgotten already, like all the dead—and he took a fiacre in order to get back more rapidly to the house in the Place de Valois, the cellar where his instruments were waiting for him.

Lunch was also waiting for him out there. He ate with a hearty appetite, humming old Strasbourgian tunes learned in childhood.

"It's a good day," he said to Marthe. "I want to complete it! I've worked for someone else; now I want to work for myself. For you, my love! You're not tired?"

"No."

"Well, perhaps Madame Fortis is right; I've returned her husband to the light with confidence. Perhaps, today—today!—I'll arrive at the result for which I'm ambitious in your case. For you! Oh, what a dream!"

"And Monsieur Fortis is cured?"

"Cured, because he believes it. Cured, because I have killed, not the mandarin who is making him rich, but the phantom who made him doubt himself; cured because I have substituted one illusion for another. *Ecco!* That's life. But no, it's not an illusion. Has not André David lived his actual life, has he not had a funeral, and does he not have a tomb at Saint-Laurent-du-Pont? Does he not really exist, since the imagination has created him? His life was a fact, since André Fortis suffered from it. His death is a fact, since the funeral notice is there. *Requiescat!* And henceforth, reassured, reinforced, his phantom surgically excised like a cancer, André Fortis will live again! As you will live again, dear creature, with that new eye that I want to see emerging from your forehead—yes, yes, today, Marthe, today! Today!"

He was exultant, speaking and gesticulating, and while serving dessert, old Anna said to him: "Be careful, Monsieur. Calm down. You'll give yourself a fever."

"Fever?" asked Marthe, anxiously.

"Yes, Madame, fever. Madame can't see Monsieur, but Monsieur's ears are all red, and he's congested. That's not good!"

But Klipper interrupted the maidservant. "I'm not red at all! Don't believe it. *Madame can't see Monsieur. Madame can't see!* Well, she *shall* see, Madame! She shall see Monsieur! She shall see us, Anna! She'll see that I don't have red ears. She'll see everything, Madame! And perhaps today! Yes, yes, today! Today! I'm lucky today! Go for today!"

Klipper's voice, like a clarion sounding the charge, gave the blind woman an absolute confidence. Marthe was convinced that she was within reach of the conclusion of the long ordeal that brought her every day beneath the projection of electric light, as if under the jet of a blowtorch. Of the fact that she suffered, that she felt the burning bite on her forehead, she did not complain. She obeyed; she hoped. *The master has spoken.* But it was a joy nevertheless to hear Klipper speak of the end of the experiment and to believe success to be imminent, perhaps immediate.

"We're going down to the laboratory," he said.

And with a feverishness that he did not usually have, he picked up a candle to illuminate the dark stairway, and held his hand out to Marthe.

"Lean on me!"

Her hand in the doctor's hand, the blind woman slowly went down the steps leading to the cellar. Klipper opened the door. Feeling the stone steps with her feet, she used her free hand to guide her along the wall. Her other hand never quit Klipper's. They walked in that manner under the vault, whose damp odor also served to guide Marthe. She counted the steps one by one, plunging into the darkness, which was no blacker for her than the eternal night that surrounded her.

Suddenly, she experienced a sensation of terrible cold. She felt Klipper's hand escape hers. She heard a cry in the darkness, and then the dull, muffled thud of a falling body—and nothing more.

Nothing: silence. She groped in search of the hand that had been guiding her a moment before. She found nothing: emptiness.

She called out: "Jean? Where are you, Jean?"

Jean Klipper did not reply. Was it him who had just fallen down a few steps, whose fall she had heard?

She still had that sinister sound in her ears, as if in her heart.

Thud! Thud!

Oh, it was him, it really was him, having made a false step, who had just fallen down the stone steps. Where was he? How could she help him?

Marthe called out again, but Klipper's instructions were strict. No one was to go down there while he was working. No one responded to Marthe's shouting. Could anyone even hear the blind woman's cries up above?

She bent down, and slid down the steps in a sitting position, interrogating the darkness, searching with her hand to see whether she might touch a recumbent body.

The silence—the deadly silence—frightened her. What if he were dead?

Her hands felt boldly, searching every time she moved a step closer to the place where the cry had come from—and still nothing.

Although he was not answering, though, he was there, in the darkness.

"Jean! Jean!"

A vague, distant echo came back of that name uttered in anguish: "Jean!"

She cried out in her turn when she encountered an obstacle under her feet when she slid to the next step. The blind woman leaned forward, interrogating with her hand. It was a body. Klipper was lying there, doubtless at the bottom of the staircase, motionless.

She ran her fingers over the body, found the shoulder, touched the head, the forehead—and started violently in horror. The hair that her fingers reached was sticky, with a warm liquid: blood! Blood was running down the adored forehead, the august forehead of the scientist. She could feel the blood beneath her trembling hand.

She called for help. An atrocious thought came to her.

What if he's dead? He's dead!

Dead!

And in the night, in the darkness to which she was condemned, the unfortunate woman tried to lift up the body, which was perhaps no more than a corpse. Her lips sought for the face that she could not see, the ears into which she repeated her desperate appeal: "Jean!"

He did not move. The body lay there in the darkness, inert. She could not lift him up, soothe him. And if Kipper, fallen thus, were dying beside her, she could not do anything to dispute that atrocious death.

Then the frail creature, the timid little blonde, found an unexpected, superhuman energy within her. She crawled back up the stairs, groping her way, until she found herself at the door giving access to the ground floor. Then, pushing it brusquely, she called out, uttering a loud cry of distress, which was heard by the porter, and by old Anna, who was coming downstairs at that moment.

"Help! Help! The doctor is dead!"

They came running. Dr. Klipper, picked up sat the foot of the stairs, was brought up, bloodied, to his apartment.

He was not dead. His foot having slipped on one of the steps, he had struck his head, and was badly injured. Anxiously, Marthe, condemned to darkness, asked questions. They reassured her.

A physician who lived nearby soon arrived, and bandaged the wound. He was a young man who knew the reputation of the Strasbourgian doctor, and who, on seeing him lying there, said: "What a loss that would be!"

Klipper recovered consciousness, however. At first, he stammered a few words, and then called out: "Are you there, Marthe?"

"I'm here, my friend!"

Jean took the hand that he had released a little while before, when he fell.

"What's happened to me?" Then, he suddenly remembered. "Ah! Yes, we were going to work..." Abruptly, he went on: "There's a fable by La Fontaine: 'The Astrologer who fell into a Well.' Yes, yes...one studies the stars...the star!...and one stupidly falls into a cellar!" He seemed astonished to see a new face at his bedside. "Who are you?"

"One of your admirers, my dear Master," the young doctor said.

"Ah! My admirers! Not very numerous, my admirers! But when I've endowed humanity with the third eye...! Today, perhaps, today, Marthe!"

He became excited. He was feverish.

"Calm yourself, my dear Master."

"No, no, today; I want my final experiment to take place today. You don't believe in the third eye?"

"The pineal gland? Indeed, my dear Master. You will find it! If you seek, you, of all people, will find!"

An expression of intense pride had overtaken the scientist's face. He saw that he was understood, understood by a man of the new generation. "You see," he said to Marthe. "He has faith in me."

And she, believing him, put her lips to the scientist's hand and kissed it, as she might have done the hand of a prophet, or her God.

Then the injured man became drowsy, and a kind of prostration, a coma, overwhelmed his body and his brain. The young doctor became anxious, allowing his fear to show in the words that he repeated while shaking his head.

"It will be a great pity!"

XV. Disappearance

An item in the newspaper, in the miscellaneous news section, informed André Fortis and Cécile of the accident to which Dr. Klipper had fallen victim. They hurried to the Place de Valois, but no one was being allowed in to see the injured man.

Marthe came to thank them, however, and André said to the poor woman: "That man has saved me! He will be saved in his turn."

Every say, André and his wife came in search of the latest news. Sometimes it was alarming, sometimes reassuring. Nothing was certain. Mystery was hanging over the invalid, floating around him.

André had the impression that there was something that he was not being told.

What was not being said was that the fall down the staircase had caused a lesion in Klipper's brain, such that the light of reason that he had shown after recovering consciousness had darkened. An opaque fog now enveloped that admirable divinatory intelligence. The young doctor, a distinguished psychiatrist, had summoned experts. Their verdict left no hope. The great Jean Klipper was doomed to progressive deterioration, destined for dementia—worse than that, to be no more than an individual living a purely animal, bestial existence, like the idiots that wander in the courtyards of asylums.

Marthe—who could not see anything, but demanded that she be told everything—did not want any human eye to perceive that degradation of an adored, venerated individual; a genius with a great heart. She hid that human wreck, whom she held in her arms, fighting his illness, from any visit, and any questions. His body was healing, but his reason did not return.

One day, when André Fortis came to the house in the Place de Valois to obtain news, the concierge said to him: "There's no one there any longer."

"What do you mean?"

"Monsieur and Madame Klipper have left."

"Left? Where have they gone?"

"We don't know."

"Strasbourg?"

"I don't know."

"Can I talk to old Anna?"

"No. She's no longer here. She went with them. Oh, she loves Monsieur Klipper too much, and Madame Klipper, being blind, needs her too much for her to leave them. She's a woman deserving of the Prix Montyon, that worthy Anna!"

"What if I want to write to the doctor?"

"He won't receive your letter."

"If I were to write to him here?"

The concierge showed him the notice that he was about to attach to the door of number 4: *Apartment to let.* "The house is empty, and Madame Klipper didn't want to leave us her new address."

"No one knows, then...?"

"No one."

"Not even me!"

André went home, very sad. It seemed to him that he had lost a lifelong friend. An affection had been stolen from him, a reason to show an eternal gratitude to a fellow human being.

When he told Cécile what had been said to him, with the admirable instinct that women have when they are in love, Cécile guessed the truth. She guessed that Marthe wanted to hide a diminution in Klipper's genius, as she herself had hidden André's sinister crises when he was the Other—the Other, whom Klipper had expelled permanently.

"If they don't want anyone to know where they are, it's necessary not to try to find out," she said. "Misfortune has its modesty, like love."

One morning, however, with a sob punctuating his words, André held out a newspaper to Cecile, in which his fingernail indicated a passage, saying: "Look at this!"

Frédéric Clément announced in the *Boulevard* the death, in an outlying district of Paris, of a man unknown in the city, but who, if he had lived, would have brought about a revolution in science, Dr. Jean Klipper, one of those irregulars of genius who are the pioneers of the future.

The doctor had died ordering that his funeral be unobserved. No letters of invitation had been sent, Madame Klipper respecting, as always, the wishes of her husband. The journalist added:

There is less talk of the disappearance of the scientist—about whom we once said a few words in one of our articles, who dreamed of adding a supplementary eye to humankind by rediscovering the eye of the Cyclopes—than the première of an operetta that is taking place this evening. That is perfectly natural. The operetta will amuse people with its music and waltzes. The death of a scientist causes less of a stir. Make way for the theater! But the man of genius will have his revenge, and we are taking it upon ourselves to work to that end.

Cécile had read the reporter's article though her tears. She handed the paper back to her husband.

André shook his head, his heart aching, his eyes red.

General de Jandrieu and his wife, paying a surprise visit, found their children in the sadness of that news.

"What's this?" said the general, trying to laugh. "A family scene? You've had a quarrel? You, a model household?"

"No," said Cécile. "There's nothing between the two of us but joy—but we've lost a man to whom we owe the best of that joy!"

"A man of genius," said André.

Surprised, the general shrugged his shoulders. "I've seen so many men die—so very many! I was thinking that just this morning—the eighteenth of August, the anniversary of

Gravelotte![48] It's necessary to be an old fogey to remember Gravelotte, eh, my dears! At any rate, I remember it. Dead, your Dr. Klipper! Everyone has his turn. It's always necessary to be ready, packed, sealed and trussed up...when one's time comes."

But that man didn't kill, he saved," said André, repeating: "A man of genius."

"I've often wondered what people mean by a man of genius," said the general, ironically serious. "Would you like me to tell you what a man of genius is? It's a man one doesn't understand."

---

[48] The Battle of Gravelotte, on 18 August 1870, was the largest of the Franco-Prussian War, fought near Metz in Lorraine. The Prussians, under the command of Helmuth von Moltke, annihilated what was left of the French troops they had been harassing for several days.

XVI. The Statue of the Living Dead

Death resembles the darkness that causes the stars to come out. The name unknown the day before suddenly begins to sparkle. An unexpected light emerges from tombs.

Scarcely had the news of the tragic death of Dr. Klipper begun to spread than laudatory biographies informed the crowd of the extraordinary worth of the unknown man that science had just lost. Special reviews listed the seeker's endeavors, and official scientists celebrated the discoveries of the independent mind that had fought in the advance guard, working alone and in the shadows. And the great public learned, to its amazement, that it had been rubbing shoulders, without suspecting it, with a man who merited a statue.

A statue! The idea did not fall into the void. The *Revue des Sciences Nouvelles* having printed the suggestion under the signature of Dr. Chardin, Parisian gossip took up the subject. Frédéric Clément, the chief reporter of the *Boulevard*, began with a moving preface and a series of interviews about the life and works of Jean Klipper, and, after having rallied, like a good journalist, the statue fever—statumania—prevalent in our era, he interrogated the majority of great scientists as to whether the son of Strasbourg, having devoted his entire life to science, living and suffering for it, merited an image on a pedestal in a public square; and almost all the responses published by the Boulevard concluded in favor of honoring Klipper. Bust or statue, the Alsatian merited a tribute.

For an entire week, Paris, between two conversations about the latest première and the latest scandal, forgetting temporarily the wings of the theater, fashionable comes and the investigations of examining magistrates, was occupied with Dr. Jean Klipper, as if it were a matter of a star actor, a recidivist apache or a heroine of the restaurant booths.

Frédéric Clément had, moreover, presented as possible, even probable, Dr. Klipper's extraordinary discovery, promising to endow humankind with a third eye, a third window to the life of the universe. The journalist had entitled his series of articles and interviews *A Magician of the Nineteenth Century*, and thanks to him, so far as the crowd was concerned, the figure of the seeker had taken on the fantastic aspect of another Dr. Faust, leaning over his alembics. The public, taking an interest in the life and death of Klipper, had read that dramatized biography as if it were devouring a *feuilleton* novel, a book by H. G. Wells or Rudyard Kipling.

How was such a man able to live in the heart of Paris without the glory that immediately accrues to political or literary hams having given to that now-cold head, that now-famous name, a radiance of the renown that it lavishes upon mediocrities, social climbers and adventurers?

Frédéric Clément developed that theme vehemently, thus shaking opinion. People became irritated with the injustice of fate. All the misunderstood, the vanquished, and those whom fortune had left by the wayside, saw their own claims incarnated in that that ignored genius Jean Klipper. And quite naturally, anger against human injustice and the injustice of fate echoed all the way from Paris to Alsace. Klipper's compatriots felt both prouder and sadder than the Parisians themselves of that destiny, the glory of which rebounded on to the cherished homeland.

It is in France that he struggled, said the *Journal d'Alsace, but it is in Alsace that he was born.*

Then the idea was born, initially expressed by the *Alsacien-Lorrain*, of erecting a monument in Strasbourg to the scientist that the French academies and periodicals were hailing as a precursor. A committee was rapidly formed, which launched an appeal for funds, and in the emotion provoked by Frédéric Clément's investigations, the subscription rapidly rose to a rather considerable sum. Enough money to erect a statue was soon raised.

A statue for Jean Klipper in Strasbourg, which had not erected one to Koeberlé![49] Now the polemics began. Patriotic rivalries were concealed by singular pretexts. The German authorities dreaded that students of the Alsatian race and the French soul might profit from the inauguration of that statue to lift up significant crowns and render homage that those young people were already inclined to offer, at midnight every Christmas, to the image of Kléber. And truly, did Jean Klipper, with his perhaps admirable, but simple, visions of the future, merit the same honor as Jean Gutenberg, whose bronze had once been solemnly saluted as "from the French times"?

In the final analysis, an understanding was reached by accepting a compromise. The partisans of the status renounced the pedestal; their adversaries accepted the idea of a bust: a bronze bust encased in the wall of the house where the scientist had been born, with an inscription beneath the effigy indicating to passers-by that Jean Klipper had been born there. The homage was just as solemn, but, for the German government, the ceremony did not have the same popular—and hence perilous—character. The inauguration of a bust in a small street in Old Strasbourg would not attract as big a crowd as a statue erected in a public square.

It is a danger halved, said the German newspapers.

And half a concession, replied the Alsatian committee, resentfully.

The bust of Klipper, wrought by a young Strasbourgian sculptor, from an admirable drawing once made from life by J.-J. Henner,[50] was exhibited in the Salon. It was a god rendering of the strange physiognomy, the pensive thinness of that face in the manner of Michelet or Mommsen. The critics had no difficulty in divining, at a glance, behind the pensive forehead, the man of genius.

---

[49] The Strasbourgian surgeon Eugène Koeberlé (1828-1915), who also wrote poetry and carried out studies in archaeology.

[50] Jean-Jacques Henner (1829-1905) was a noted portrait painter.

The Strasbourgians, as ignorant as the Parisians regarding Dr. Klipper's research, merely saw the homage rendered as a memorial to one of their compatriots living and dying "on the other side," a son of Alsace transplanted to the great city. It seemed to them that from beyond the frontier, Paris was sending back to them, glorified and magnified, a child of the homeland. And it was, indeed, the homeland that had recollected, if not acclaimed the scientist bent over his research. It was Paris that had subsequently discovered Jean Klipper and returned him to Strasbourg enveloped in glory—albeit belated and posthumous glory. You take what destiny gives you.

And it was a great day of celebration when the Committee escorted the Parisian delegates who had come to salute the image of Jean Klipper from the railways station to the Rue de la Mésange. The Strasbourgians decked the windows of the neighborhood with the colors of their region: red and white. The color that the Strasbourgian flag lacked was worn by young women in their corsages, by adding cornflowers to poppies and white daises, but at least Alsace was fêting an Alsatian with its own flag fluttering in the sunlight.

Dr. Chardin had come from Paris, intent on paying the late scientist the debt of science. He would speak, not in the name of the Académie de Médecine, but on his own personal behalf. The testimony of an official representative of French science was no less important; it was one master saluting another.

The *Boulevard* reporter Frédéric Clément, having been unable to make the journey to Alsace because a Théâtre de Nature in the Greek Style was being inaugurated on the same day in a seaside town, on reading the proofs of the speech sent to the newspaper, telegraphed: *A masterly page, my dear doctor. When one can talk like that, one is ripe for the podium!*

Chardin was perhaps of the same opinion.

André Fortis had piously wanted to make the journey to Strasbourg with Cécile; for him it was a pilgrimage of gratitude. All his peace of mind, his liberation, his deliverance, the joy that he now had in experiencing life, in living his youth, in loving the exquisite creature who was his wife, in hoping for children, in giving himself entirely to his art—all of that new existence—he owed to Jean Klipper. The devotion that he could no longer testify to the scientist, since death had overtaken it, he wanted to bring, transformed into grateful admiration, to the natal house. The painter was in the first row of the audience, in front of the crowd, with his wife beside him.

The veil that covered the bust placed above the main door of the old house, like a shroud, only allowed a confused, somewhat ghostly, perception the features. Crowded in the street, controlled by the police, the people gazed, impatiently, at that hidden bust, which was about to show them the unknown features of a compatriot whose story—or, rather, whose legend—they were telling one another.

The "old folk" had known little Klipper when he was a boy, playing outside his father's cutlery shop. Since then, it appeared, he had become a great scientist far away in Paris! A member of the Institut, some said—"like Pasteur," said others. They did not know that Klipper was nothing but Klipper.

Beneath a beautiful clear spring sky, André gazed at the picturesque scene in the street, the crowd with its pretty blonde girls with placid faces and tall, thickset, square-shouldered lads; the flags fluttering at the windows; and the curious faces at those windows, as in paintings of the Middle Ages, the silhouettes of old women and the chubby cheeks of infants, avidly watching the spectacle in the street.

But suddenly, André thought he had been dazzled.

XVII. The Apotheosis

He said to Cécile, squeezing her arm: "Look! Look!"

At one of the windows of the house opposite the birthplace of Dr. Klipper, he had just seen—yes, the closer he looked, the more he seemed to recognize—a man with emaciated features framed with long white hair falling over his shoulders: a man with a bony face whose eyes were fixed immovably, as if hypnotized, on the dwelling on which all the attention of the crowd was concentrated; and that man—an incredible encounter!—resembled Jean Klipper, feature for feature. Yes, it was another Klipper: the visionary poet's black-clad brother, with the resemblance of an identical twin.

"It's impossible! But if Klipper weren't dead, I'd say: *It's him!*"

And what rendered the apparition utterly implausible, and frightening, was that beside that pale and thin face, like Klipper's, with hair perhaps a little longer than before, another face was framed in the open window: the face of a young blonde woman, also thin, sad and very pale, reminiscent of Marthe's face.

Or rather, no, not reminiscent; it really was Marthe: Marthe, with that red patch on her forehead that was like the admirable stigma of her devotion and her martyrdom. Only one woman in the world resembled the woman perceptible there. Only one woman wore that scar of science on her forehead. There was no doubt about it; the woman who was there was Marthe Klipper.

But in that case, the man who was leaning on her shoulder, the man who was visible beside her, the living specter, beneath the old man's hair, was Jean Klipper himself, Klipper alive, the Jean Klipper whose image an entire people was about to salute, whose memory they were about to acclaim.

"I'm not mistaken, Cécile," Fortis whispered, his voice strangled like that of a child who has seen a ghost.

229

"No." Cécile replied. "It's incredible, but one would swear that it's him!"

"And her—her forehead, the red patch. It's Jean Klipper, and his wife!"

"It's frightening," said Cécile.

They were not the victims of a hallucination. They could both see the couple that no one else had noticed, at whom no gaze but theirs was directed. From the height of the window, overlooking the crowd, his gaze was riveted to the green serge veil, while she was parading over the crowd of curiosity-seekers and strangers an unseeing gaze that seemed to be searching in the darkness for familiar faces.

And behind Marthe, another face appeared: a woman who was looking and could see; old Anna, the faithful and devoted...

Then, André and his wife, in order to attract the attention of the maidservant—it really was her!—detached themselves from the line of spectators and took a few steps into the empty space between the crowd and the natal house.

No one took account of the fact that they were raising their heads toward a window on the other side of the street—but as they interrogated with a visible attention the man and the woman leaning over the balcony, old Anna met that gaze, amazed and yet meticulous.

The maidservant whispered a few words in Marthe's ear, as if she were pointing out someone in the crowd.

André saw Marthe blush and step back slightly, while the man, motionless, his eyes still staring obstinately, had not made any movement, remaining there as if petrified.

And as André's and Cécile's eyes remained fixed on those two individuals, the woman, to whom old Anna was still talking, gently raised her hand to her mouth, placed two fingers over her lips, and, with a gesture replacing an expression, which, had she been able to express her thought in that way, would have been pleading, the poor martyr made the sign of silence, begging from afar, as if, through the crowd and above the crowd, Monsieur and Madame Fortis had just discovered some lugubrious secret.

Those fingers over the mouth, and even those dead, seemingly-staring eyes, as if petrified by fear, all seemed to be imploring, saying: "Not a word! Let us be! Incognito, forgetfulness, is what we're asking of you, please!"

Then, André saw the wife's small hand settle on the old man's shoulder and draw him into the room. Slowly, the widow closed, only allowing the perception, through the pane, between the raised white curtains, two pale faces framed there as if by the folds of shrouds.

The maidservant vanished into the shadows.

"It's him! It's Jean Klipper!" André repeated.

"It's definitely him," said Cécile.

Abruptly, they divined a terrible drama: the tempest that must have blown within the skull of Marthe Klipper when the disaster had occurred: the scientist, the adored and venerated man, the glory of her life, only getting up from his fall to drag out a heart-rending existence, surviving in a phantom state: a ghost, a human rag, devoid of ideas, perhaps of speech, the brain empty, the lips mute, abolished, brutalized, relegated from the world of thought, trailing his cadaver through the world of the living.

Yes, that was it; that had to be it. Klipper had survived and Marthe Klipper had not wanted anyone to know how he had been able to survive. And the incredible spectacle displayed in the broad daylight of a public celebration: a man who was believed to be dead, whose death had been recorded by the biographical dictionaries, giving the precise date, had survived his necrology, reappearing in the flesh, not as a phantom, but alive, from head to toe, and watching his own apotheosis.

Alive? The ravaged face, the staring eyes, the air of distraction that gave the thin face the appearance of an immobile mask—were they really those of a living being?

No, no—the soul was absent; the brain was no longer thinking; and the person who was standing there, who was still

231

perceptible through the window, a pale and haggard mask—Fortis could divine it, from afar—was no longer anything but the specter of Jean Klipper.

A stumbling misstep in the darkness, and perpetual night had fallen on a being marked for immortality.

Suddenly, a cortege appeared in the distance, with flags fluttering above the crowd. It was the Committee of the Klipper Monument arriving, old Strasbourgians marching at the head, contemporaries and comrades of the scientist's childhood; Dr. Chardin was among them, wearing a white cravat but not even having donned his Academician's uniform, where the Alsatians would have found a hat with a tricolor cockade. He was not there officially, the solitary traveler who was about to be welcomed.

Trumpets sounded a poignant march, *Sambre-et-Meuse*. One might have thought it a festival of old, a day of yore...

The cortege stopped in front of the old house. The crowd drew as close to the threshold as possible, and André found himself pushed, with Cécile, until they were close to Chardin, who had bowed to them, a smile on his rosy lips, his face amiable and calm, so different from Klipper's tormented visage.

Then, at a gesture from the Committee's chairman, the serge veil, pulled by a rope, slowly fell away, while a brass band, massed near the door, played an old Alsatian tune.

The bust of Kipper was resplendent, sealed in the wall in a recently-hollowed niche; and André rediscovered in the strangely lifelike work of the young sculptor the features, the expression and even the gaze—a dark gaze hollowed in the bronze—of that singular man of genius, whom he had seen in the cellar in the Cour de Valois, in his subterranean laboratory, like a kobold of science.

The bust had the same poetry, a trifle singular and seemingly fantastic, as the inspired little man. The hair seemed to be floating, the lips seemed to be animated, the pupils seemed to be seeing. It was a masterpiece of life: a resurrection, said Dr. Chardin, who was already unfolding a piece of paper taken from his pocket, and beginning his speech.

At the base of the bronze bust, an inscription in golden letters was displayed on a marble plaque:

TO JEAN KLIPPER
Doctor and Philosopher
Born in Strasbourg 3 December 1840
Died in Paris 31 October 1903
To the Son of Alsace
From his Grateful Compatriots
To the Scientist,
From this Faithful Admirers

"Resurrection!" That was the word that Chardin pronounced; that was the impression that the few members of the audience who had known Jean Klipper received.

André Fortis heard, adding their fraternal commentaries to the cheers that greeted Dr. Chardin's eulogies, regrets and expressions of sadness. "What a pity that such men must disappear!" And Chardin insisted on the disaster that the death of Jean Klipper had been for science.

"At his age, Messieurs, the human brain is far from giving given its full measure. Imagine Pasteur, our admirable Pasteur, ending his life at the same age as Klipper. How many discoveries unmade! How many lives lost! And yet, Pasteur was almost lost to the fatherland and to humanity entire. Suppose, when he had his first attack, that a single droplet of blood, one more atom, had reached that admirable brain: so many discoveries, so much genius, would have been abruptly suppressed. The clearest, the most vivid, the most profound—I might say the most divinatory—of intelligences, would have sunk into darkness.

"Jean Klipper did not fulfill his destiny. A banal accident, a vulgar fall on a staircase—a wretched misadventure!— has brutally terminated a life still so full of projected endeavors, glimpsed, or even indicated discoveries whose realization would have been pursued. Klipper lived in obscurity. The time would have come when he would have been illustrious, and when honors would have succeeded ordeals. But he died!

"Honors! I am pronouncing there, Messieurs, a word that our dear and great compatriot would have rejected. Jean Klipper only sought the harsh duties of labor. Honors, for him, were in his dark laboratory, the instruments of labor that he fabricated himself, including the ingenious construction of a photographic apparatus to analyze the light of the stars in space.

"He could have been rich; he might have had titles and grants; but he never asked anything of anyone. But the present, and what is known as 'the glory of ready money' were not for him; for him, there was the future, and it is posterity that is saluting him today in this ceremony, simultaneously solemn and cordial, in which Alsace is recovering the image of one of her glorious sons, who left this corner of the earth at a tender age, and in which France salutes the child who became an immortal old man in her bosom!"

Dr. Chardin's speech ended in a tempest of cheers. The hurrahs underlined the scientist's words celebrating a forerunner, and the brass band struck up the chorus from Gounod's *Faust*: "Immortal glory to our ancestors!" And while Cécile, closing her eyes, recalled the marble image of the composer glimpsed so many time through the trees of the Parc Monceau—how many memories left behind!—André gazed at that pale face glued to the high window: the face of Jean Klipper, which reappeared, immobile, with its staring eyes.

Then, when the ceremony was over, when the official cortege had drawn away and there was no one left in front of the house but idlers and passers-by pausing to read the plaque and examine, criticize or praise the bust, André thanked Chardin, who rolled up his manuscript and slipped it into his pocket.

"I was certain that I'd find you here," the physician said to the painter.

"Of course. I haven't forgotten what I owe you, and what I owe him. It's said that invalids are forgetful; not at all. I'm not an ingrate."

André was tempted to question Chardin, to speak to him about the apparition that had just given the ceremony a fantastic character, but Chardin was doubtless unaware of anything, since he had come officially, to deplore Klipper's death with sincere emotion. The white face was no longer visible at the closed window. In any case, what virtue was there in betraying such a secret?"

"I'm going back this evening," said Chardin. "Will you travel back to Paris with me?"

"Yes, Doctor, but I have to visit someone first. We'll meet you on the train."

The visit in question was—like a pilgrimage to a tomb— a halt at the house in which, on the day of the triumph, the specter of Jean Klipper had just put in an appearance.

André and Cécile, as emotional as on the day of their first visit to Dr. Klipper, went up the narrow stairway of the Alsatian house, where Marthe had come to stay for a while with the illustrious man whose name she bore.

André rested his hand on the wooden banister, saying: "Do we have the right to disturb their silence?"

He hesitated momentarily before ringing the bell of the first floor—the one from which Jean Klipper had followed the ceremony uncomprehendingly. What if Marthe said to them: "By what right have you come to spy on our suffering, to diviner our secret?"

"Let's go!" he said. A rather long time went by before the door, sculpted with eighteenth-century woodwork, opened. Then Marthe Klipper's face, appeared, lamentable and fearful. Behind her was old Anna, who said to her mistress: "It's them."

The poor blind woman with the stigmatized forehead put a finger over her lips again, as she had done before, and then said: "Come in."

Her voice was low, as if broken and extinct.

Anna invited Monsieur and Madame Fortis to sit down in a small reception room whose curtains she had drawn. Then Marthe said, softly: "You saw?" And in those two words there was an entire poem of dolor, an infinite distress.

André's only reply was a nod of the head,

"Then…?" said Cécile

"Will you swear to me to keep the secret?"

"What affects you affects us," said André. "Your duty is our duty. I owe my life to Jean Klipper."

"And it was in saving others, in trying to render light and sight to me, that he foundered…"

Then the blind woman related the drama of that destiny. A lesion of the brain had deranged the mind of the old seeker of the impossible. After his fall, he had remained motionless for hours, his pupils fixed, as if looking into the beyond, interrogating something with his eyes that could not be seen. Then, one day, in a fit of sudden fury, contrasting strangely with that sort of gently resigned torpor, as if self-consciousness had returned to him, and with that revelation of his state of terror and distress, racked by grief and fear, shaken by a bitter desire to put an end to it, to escape from stupidity and unreason via death, he had opened the window with the gesture of a madman, and, shouting: "I'm free!" had hurled himself on to the cobblestones of the courtyard. A broken body had been picked up, and the newspapers had then announced the death of the scientist—but the details had been drowned in the racket of a dispute in the Chambre and the publicity of a sensational première. Obituaries had swiftly buried Jean Klipper, to whom the biographical dictionaries of Leipzig and London had devoted extended notices, mentioning the list of his works, the date of his first experiments and the date of his death.

Officially, therefore, he was dead, Jean Klipper, the avant-garde soldier of science—and yet, he was alive. He survived, leading a vegetative existence, and in a refuge in Montrouge, Marthe Klipper, liquidating al her savings, selling everything, including clothes and books, had succeeded in finding a boarding house where, after having converted her meager resources into an annuity, they lived under the names of Monsieur and Madame Durand, in order that it would not be said that Jean Klipper, whose genius had suddenly been discovered and praised, in the funereal light of posthumous glory, was no longer anything but an incurable senile old man, babbling inconsequential words, as far from humanity as beasts of burden and idiots.

Oh, rather than admit to that disaster. That loss of reason, that horror, Marthe, proud of Klipper's renown, would have opened a gas tap by feel, and asphyxiated herself along with that adored individual thus reduced to being nothing but the phantom of himself. She had thought about that, but then had said to herself: "Patience; everything happens in time, and death is inevitable."

And then, one morning, she had learned that Strasbourg was about to celebrate the memory of its son. The information regarding the ceremony and the program for "the inauguration of the bust of Doctor Klipper" had been read to her in the boarding-house in Montrouge. She had experienced horrible suffering in repeating what she had learned to Klipper , who could not hear and did not understand, having been brutally relegated from the world of the living.

No matter what dolor she would feel, however, she had wanted to be there when the image of Jean Klipper appeared triumphantly to the eyes of his compatriots. She wanted him to be present too, a living dead man in attendance at his own apotheosis. And, guided by old Anna, who often came to the boarding house to see her former employers, and who had traveled with "Monsieur and Madame Durand," she had left for Strasbourg, dragging the unconscious man whose genius was absent, with the staring eyes, as incapable of judging what he saw as the blind woman's own pupils. And Marthe Klipper realized that incredible and frightful living irony: a man who was believed to be dead witnessing—not, alas, cognizant of what has happening, but present in the flesh—the inauguration of his image, to the glorification of his memory.

"It's terrible," Cécile repeated.

"I don't know of any torture simultaneously as cruel and as sweet," replied the blind woman "When the band was playing there was a moment when I said to myself: *Finally, finally, they're doing him justice!* And then: *But he can't hear, he doesn't know...he's here without being here.* And again: *Perhaps it's me who's the cause of that horror! It was for me that he wore out his brain, found madness, sought suicide, encountered the death that has left him alive!*"

And, just as the relatives who have just lost a loved one take you to the deathbed. Marthe asked: "Would you like to see him?"

Cécil shivered. What if that apparition reawakened a past crisis in André?

But Fortis' voice was calm, and Cécile was reassured when he said: "Yes, I'd like to thank him once again!"

Leaning on Anna's arm, the blind woman went to a door, which she opened.

Jean Klipper was still standing at the window, his face against the pane, gazing...at what? The plaque, the bust, the streets, the passers-by...but seeing nothing, not thinking about anything.

"Jean!" Marthe called.

He turned round mechanically at that soft familiar voice, and André and his wife went toward him. He bowed to them. He bowed to them without recognizing them, letting guttural sounds fall from his lips.

"You have all our gratitude, Doctor." It was André, grave and emotional, who spoke.

The old man, moving aside the white hair that had fallen over his forehead, interrogated with his dull eyes. Where was the bright and penetrating gaze of old?

"It's me, Doctor—André Fortis. Fortis, whom you cured, saved..."

The aphasic lips tried to repeat the name. Nothing emerged but disconnected syllables: "An... An... Fo... For..."

"You see," said Marthe, in her poor broken voice.

Than Cécil knelt down in front of the man, whose brain was empty and his great heart extinct, took the thin hand with the protruding veins that Jean Kipper was allowing to dangle by his side. Gently, she raised it to her lips, gazing, through her tears, at the man who was no longer anything but an inert creature devoid of reason, and she said to the unfortunate, lost in darkness, drowned as in a sea: "May your great name be blessed, you who have sacrificed your life for others."

But Klipper withdrew his hand, like a fearful child, and looked at the kneeling woman as if she might do him harm. Then he ran to Marthe and took refuge in her arms, alarmed and frightened by the presence of stranger that he did not recognize.

The spectacle was too cruel. Never, perhaps, had the ferocious irony of Nature devised a more atrocious torture—and it seemed that she was taking her revenge, irritated and implacable, on the human being who had wanted to tame her. She struck at the brain like a headman at the neck, and the practiced murderer the heart.

"Let's go!" said André Fortis, his throat tight.

"Let's," said Cécile.

She kissed poor Martha on the forehead, on the red stigma of Klipper's experiments. The blind woman repeated: "You won't say anything?"

"Nothing."

"To anyone?"

"To anyone."

"You swear?"

"We swear to you, Marthe."

And they left Marthe and Klipper in the little house that they were about to quit in order to return to Montrouge to the boarding-house apartment of "Monsieur and Madame Durand": the martyr and the man of genius, two vanquished individuals united in the same grief.

In front of the old natal house, people were still pausing to contemplate the bust of the son of Strasbourg that Paris, great Paris, had blessed as a "great man."

XVIII. And Life Goes On

That evening, in the train that took the back to France—
and they shook their heads as they repeated the words "*to
France*"—Doctor Chardin and his former client talked about
the man, the bust that had just been inaugurated, and the inci-
dents and emotions of the day, while vague landscapes, sta-
tions and towns flew past outside the windows. And Chardin
repeated, familiarizing the expressions that he had expressed
more academically that morning in his official speech: "In
truth, no, I don't know of any brain more astonishing than
Klipper's. He had genius. I've said it and I'll say it again: genius."

"So, if he had lived, Doctor..."

"He would have amazed us with his discoveries. His
third eye would have come back, you see, and perhaps Klipper
would have been saluted one day with the name of Klipper the
Cyclops. Oh, that marvelous brain! Admirably organized, solid, imperturbable. He's not the man—oh, not him—who might
have been afflicted by the famous modern neurosis..."

Cécil and André exchanged glances in the electric light
of the carriage.

"There are brains, then," André said, "that disease never
afflicts?"

"Oh, never is a word that doesn't belong in any language," the scientist replied. "But Klipper was one of those
who defeat disease and don't even know it! Look at the differ-
ence: I soothed you, he cured you. A genius, I repeat, a genius! And where does genius get you, alas?"

André replied: "Science has its hostages. He was one.
Bah! Paris waits us, and we too are the hostages of toil. *To
arms!* as Julien Sorel said.

And while the train moved on, the painter thought about
the work to be done, the entire life of joyful labor—of labor,
and also of love—that was before him, and that grave in Saint-

Laurent-du-Pont, where the Other was asleep: the one whom
Jean Klipper had sealed up forever, like those vampires into
whose hearts a sharpened stake has been plunged, to prevent
them from ever reappearing.

Afterword

When *feuilleton* fiction first became a commercially-important popular fad, in the 1840s, in the Parisian daily newspapers, works were routinely contracted on the basis of an idea or a few sample episodes, and then made up as they went along, never more than a few days ahead of the most recently-printed episode, and often with no margin at all, ever ready to be curtailed or further spun out in response to reader and editorial reaction. Under those circumstances, it is hardly surprising that many feuilleton serial wandered away from their initial direction, losing coherency along with consistency and underwent strange and sometime paradoxical metamorphoses.

There was no need for that custom to be maintained by writers of weekly and monthly serials, and many reasons why it was far from the ideal way to proceed, but the custom persisted, mainly because it was a custom. Its effects were muted when the original versions were read one episode at a time, over a period of months, but it inevitably became obvious when feuilleton serials were reprinted in book form, and consumed all of a piece, perhaps in a matter of hours. The inconsistencies and incoherencies then became glaringly obvious—but that did not prevent the book versions from selling, and maintaining the stories in a strange afterlife quite different from the one for which they had been designed and shaped.

L'Obsession is one of the stranger manifestations of the perils of that mode of composition, and also one of the most ironic, as its narrative comes to mirror its own theme. It is a narrative with a multiple personality, in which the story that begins is gradually taken over, at first intermittently and then almost entirely, by another story, which is just as crazy in its own internal nonsensicality, but which has a markedly different personality. That was not the initial intention—the reference to Dr. Chardin's laboratory offered in the early chapters

243

makes it clear that he had been planned as André's savior and that Klipper's invention was a belated improvisation—but Clarétie was probably quite proud of his ingenious variation when he thought of it.

There is, of course, little or no point in asking questions to which the narrative itself remains stubbornly blind, especially in respect of the particular representations it contains of multiple personality and scientific method, which are bound to see extremely odd to the modern eye. It would be tiresome to list all the narrative's inconsistencies and peculiar assumptions, or to wonder what buried memory it was that Schumann's *Manfred* triggered in André mind in order to conjure up his alter ego, but there is one point that is so striking in its oddity that it is perhaps worthy of a little further speculation, and that is the matter of the Other's third painting, the masterpiece with which he attempted to follow up *Modern High Life*. No mention whatsoever is made of that painting, although its absence from the plot is surely far more remarkable than any failure of a fictitious dog to bark or the remarkable dearth of toilet facilities throughout the entire universe of fiction.

The reader is surely entitled to wonder whether it might not have been a mistake on Dr. Klipper's part, even if his absurd plan ever had the remotest chance of working, to inform André that his alter ego had died a month before, immediately after he had suffered a lacuna of several days in his ordinary life—apparently the longest one he had ever endured. Surely, if and when André had become aware of the magnitude of that lacuna, he would have realized that the apparent death of "André David" had been no barrier to the repossession of his body, and perhaps the opposite. André would not, of course, have "remembered" the lacuna, even as an absence, but surely, at some point, if not for some time, he would have found the work that the Other had done in that interim, which must still have been somewhere in the studio, like the misanthropic symbolist's other efforts.

André, Cécile and Jules Clarétie, of course, had not the slightest sympathy with the symbolist's apocalyptic visions, being the kind of dull-as-ditchwater characters who prefer sentimental landscapes, but it seems highly probable that not all of the novel's readers would have felt the same even in 1905, and it is inconceivable that all readers of this translation will agree. Some contemporary readers would surely have thought the depiction of the Golden Calf and *Modern High Life* more interesting by far and anything André produced while in his "right" and terminally tedious mind. Such readers surely could not help but ask the question of what the theme of the third element of the triptych, on which the Other labored so long and so hard, might have been.

We cannot know, alas, any more than we can know what André's reaction when he finally found the painting in question, hidden behind a dresser or slipped into a folder—because he surely would have found it, eventually, and recognized its talent...perhaps its genius. The fact that we cannot know, however, only adds more spice to the game of speculation. Anyone's guess is as good as anyone else's, of course, so any suggestion I might make is of no particular value, but that that does not make the temptation any less irresistible, so...

The Other's final masterpiece, the summation not merely of his intermittent career but of his entire potentially-doomed existence (for he could not know for certain that he would survive Klipper's experiment, however daft it must have seemed to him) would surely have been a reaction of sorts, just as *Modern High Life* was a reaction to his brush with the appalling Monsieur de Morlière's wretched automobile. Given that, it would surely have been a reaction to the threat to his existence that he must have glimpsed, refracted through André's consciousness, of Dr. Klipper's intervention, firstly when the doctor visited the house in the Rue Murillo and secondly when André visited him at the Cour de Valois. The automobile of the second painting and the Golden Calf of the first would therefore have been replaced by a different symbol of apocalyptic mass-destruction: science in general, and the science of the mind in particular.

That third and final masterpiece, secreted somewhere in André's studio, awaiting discovery, must be a "portrait" of Dr. Klipper—but a symbolist portrait, in which the "kobold of science" martyrizing his poor, blind, trusting wife with his searing radiation becomes an incarnation of a much vaster project, in which, while pretending—and believing—to be working for the betterment of humankind, the juggernaut of scientific ambition is driving the word inexorably to the brink of destruction, not merely burning a hole in a single victim's head in quest of a hypothetical "third eye" but setting fire to the entire world with all manner of newly-discovered and recklessly-deployed radiations, and all manner of other means of heating up the atmosphere and the fevers of the human brain—including, but no longer limited to, the blazing lust of avarice and the fervent infatuation with speed. The depiction would, of course, go beyond the crude pulping of bodies featured in its predecessors, to symbolize, by some more subtle means, the destruction of minds rather than bodies, the devastation of souls rather than flesh: the crucial labor of the twentieth century, and beyond.

Like Dr. Klipper, the Other is a person who does not care at all about present glory, but is focused entirely and obsessively on the future, on transformation, and transfiguration, on death in life and life in death, on the vision of the mind's eye as well as, and beyond, quotidian sight. They are both insane, of course, but in an insane world, sanity is merely the choice of the most familiar form of insanity, and has nothing much to recommend it but the timidity of tedium. Does their insanity really amount to genius? Probably not—they are both deeply flawed individuals who could not be trusted as far as one could throw a feather into a headwind—but that is a matter of scant concern, and would be, even if genius were all that it is cracked up to be by boggled minds like Chardin's and Clarétie's. Of the two of them, however, the Other is undoubtedly the one who sees more clearly and further, and expresses what he sees more graphically and more cleverly. His oblivion, if we could believe in it, would be a far greater tragedy than Klipper's, the good doctor having at least been saved by that deadly slip from the agony of killing his beloved patient with misguided kindness.

Fortunately, we cannot believe in the Other's oblivion. Even those timid souls who like conventionally insipid happy endings in which soppy love conquers all cannot really believe that the Other has gone for good, and must realize—as Jules Clarétie surely did, if only secretly or subliminally—that when André eventually finds the Other's final masterpiece, there will be Hell to pay.

And that, for any reader who appreciates symbolism, truth and recklessness, would surely be the authentically happy ending.

SF & FANTASY

Henri Allorge. *The Great Cataclysm*
Guy d'Armen. *Doc Ardan: The City of Gold and Lepers*
G.-J. Arnaud. *The Ice Company*
Charles Asselineau. *The Double Life*
Cyprien Bérard. *The Vampire Lord Ruthwen*
Aloysius Bertrand. *Gaspard de la Nuit*
Richard Bessière. *The Gardens of the Apocalypse*
Albert Bleunard. *Ever Smaller*
Félix Bodin. *The Novel of the Future*
Louis Boussenard. *Monsieur Synthesis*
Alphonse Brown. *City of Glass; The Conquest of the Air*
Emile Calvet. *In a Thousand Years*
André Caroff. *The Terror of Madame Atomos; Miss Atomos; The Return of Madame Atomos; The Mistake of Madame Atomos; The Monsters of Madame Atomos; The Revenge of Madame Atomos; The Resurrection of Madame Atomos*
Félicien Champsaur. *The Human Arrow; Ouha, King of the Apes; Pharaoh's Wife*
Didier de Chousy. *Ignis*
Jules Clarétie. *Obsession*
Michel Corday. *The Eternal Flame*
Captain Danrit. *Undersea Odyssey*
C. I. Defontenay. *Star (Psi Cassiopeia)*
Charles Derennes. *The People of the Pole*
Georges Dodds (anthologist). *The Missing Link*
Harry Dickson. *The Heir of Dracula*
Jules Dornay. *Lord Ruthven Begins*
Alfred Driou. *The Adventures of a Parisian Aeronaut*
Sâr Dubnotal *vs. Jack the Ripper*
Alexandre Dumas. *The Return of Lord Ruthven*
Renée Dunan. *Baal*
J.-C. Dunyach. *The Night Orchid; The Thieves of Silence*
Henri Duvernois. *The Man Who Found Himself*
Achille Eyraud. *Voyage to Venus*
Henri Falk. *The Age of Lead*
Paul Féval. *Anne of the Isles; Knightshade; Revenants; Vampire City; The Vampire Countess; The Wandering Jew's Daughter*
Paul Féval, *fils. Felifax, the Tiger-Man*
Charles de Fieux. *Lamékis*

Arnould Galopin. *Doctor Omega; Doctor Omega and the Shadowmen* (anthology)

Judith Gautier. *Isoline and the Serpent-Flower*

Léon Gozlan. *The Vampire of the Val-de-Grâce*

G.L. Gick. *Harry Dickson and the Werewolf of Rutherford Grange*

Edmond Haraucourt. *Illusions of Immortality*

Nathalie Henneberg. *The Green Gods*

V. Hugo, P. Foucher & P. Meurice. *The Hunchback of Notre-Dame*

Romain d'Huissier. *Hexagon: Dark Matter*

Michel Jeury. *Chronolysis*

Gustave Kahn. *The Tale of Gold and Silence*

Gérard Klein. *The Mote in Time's Eye*

Fernand Kolney. *Love in 5000 Years*

Paul Lacroix. *Danse Macabre*

Louis-Guillaume de La Follie. *The Unpretentious Philosopher*

Jean de La Hire. *Enter the Nyctalope; The Nyctalope on Mars; The Nyctalope vs. Lucifer; The Nyctalope Steps In; Night of the Nyctalope*

Etienne-Léon de Lamothe-Langon. *The Virgin Vampire*

André Laurie. *Spiridon*

Gabriel de Lautrec. *The Vengeance of the Oval Portrait*

Alain le Drimeur. *The Future City*

Georges Le Faure & Henri de Graffigny. *The Extraordinary Adventures of a Russian Scientist Across the Solar System* (2 vols.)

Gustave Le Rouge. *The Vampires of Mars; The Dominion of the World* (w/Gustave Guitton) (4 vols.)

Jules Lermina. *Mysteryville; Panic in Paris; To-Ho and the Gold Destroyers; The Secret of Zippelius*

André Lichtenberger. *The Centaurs; The Children of the Crab*

Jean-Marc & Randy Lofficier. *Edgar Allan Poe on Mars; The Katrina Protocol; Pacifica; Robonocchio; Tales of the Shadowmen 1-9*

Xavier Mauméjean. *The League of Heroes*

Joseph Méry. *The Tower of Destiny*

Hippolyte Mettais. *The Year 5865*

Louise Michel. *The Human Microbes; The New World*

Tony Moilin. *Paris in the Year 2000*

José Moselli. *Illa's End*

John-Antoine Nau. *Enemy Force*

Marie Nizet. *Captain Vampire*

C. Nodier, A. Beraud & Toussaint-Merle. *Frankenstein*

Henri de Parville. *An Inhabitant of the Planet Mars*

Gaston de Pawlowski. *Journey to the Land of the 4th Dimension*

Georges Pellerin. *The World in 2000 Years*

Ernest Pérochon. *The Frenetic People*

Pierre Pelot. *The Child Who Walked on the Sky*

J. Polidori, C. Nodier, E. Scribe. *Lord Ruthven the Vampire*

P.-A. Ponson du Terrail. *The Vampire and the Devil's Son; The Immortal Woman*

Edgar Quinet. *Ahasuerus*

Henri de Régnier. *A Surfeit of Mirrors*

Maurice Renard. *The Blue Peril; Doctor Lerne; The Doctored Man; A Man Among the Microbes; The Master of Light*

Jean Richepin. *The Wing; The Crazy Corner*

Albert Robida. *The Adventures of Saturnin Farandoul; The Clock of the Centuries; Chalet in the Sky; The Electric Life*

J.-H. Rosny Aîné. *Helgvor of the Blue River; The Givreuse Enigma; The Mysterious Force; The Navigators of Space; Vamireh; The World of the Variants; The Young Vampire*

Marcel Rouff. *Journey to the Inverted World*

Han Ryner. *The Superhumans*

Brian Stableford. *The New Faust at the Tragicomique;The Empire of the Necromancers (The Shadow of Frankenstein; Frankenstein and the Vampire Countess; Frankenstein in London); Sherlock Holmes & The Vampires of Eternity; The Stones of Camelot; The Wayward Muse.* (anthologist) *The Germans on Venus; News from the Moon; The Supreme Progress; The World Above the World; Nemoville; Investigations of the Future*

Jacques Spitz. *The Eye of Purgatory*

Kurt Steiner. *Ortog*

Eugène Thébault. *Radio-Terror*

C.-F. Tiphaigne de La Roche. *Amilec*

Théo Varlet. *The Golden Rock. The Xenobiotic Invasion; The Castaways of Eros; Timeslip Troopers* (w/André Blandin); *The Martian Epic* (w/Octave Joncquel)

Paul Vibert. *The Mysterious Fluid*

Villiers de l'Isle-Adam. *The Scaffold; The Vampire Soul*

Philippe Ward. *Artahe*

Philippe Ward & Sylvie Miller. *The Song of Montségur*

MYSTERIES & THRILLERS

M. Allain & P. Souvestre. *The Daughter of Fantômas*

A. Anicet-Bourgeois, Lucien Dabril. *Rocambole*

A. Bernède. *Belphegor*; *Judex* (w/Louis Feuillade); *The Return of Judex* (w/Louis Feuillade); *The Shadow of Judex*

A. Bisson & G. Livet. *Nick Carter vs. Fantômas*

V. Darlay & H. de Gorsse. *Arsène Lupin vs. Sherlock Holmes: The Stage Play*

Séamas Duffy. *Sherlock Holmes in Paris*

Paul Féval. *Gentlemen of the Night; John Devil; The Black Coats ('Salem Street; The Invisible Weapon; The Parisian Jungle; The Companions of the Treasure; Heart of Steel; The Cadet Gang; The Sword-Swallower)*

Emile Gaboriau. *Monsieur Lecoq*

Goron & Emile Gautier. *Spawn of the Penitentiary*

Rick Lai. *Shadows of the Opera: Retribution in Blood*

Steve Leadley. *Sherlock Holmes: The Circle of Blood*

Maurice Leblanc. *Arsène Lupin vs. Countess Cagliostro; Arsène Lupin vs. Sherlock Holmes (The Blonde Phantom; The Hollow Needle); The Many Faces of Arsène Lupin*

Gaston Leroux. *Chéri-Bibi; The Phantom of the Opera; Rouletabille & the Mystery of the Yellow Room; Rouletabille at Krupp's*

Richard Marsh. *The Complete Adventures of Judith Lee*

William Patrick Maynard. *The Terror of Fu Manchu; The Destiny of Fu Manchu*

Frank J. Morlock. *Sherlock Holmes: The Grand Horizontals; Sherlock Holmes vs Jack the Ripper*

Antonin Reschal. *The Adventures of Miss Boston*

P. de Wattyne & Y. Walter. *Sherlock Holmes vs. Fantômas*

David White. *Fantômas in America*

Pierre Yrondy. *The Adventures of Thérèse Arnaud*

www.ingramcontent.com/pod-product-compliance
Lightning Source LLC
Chambersburg PA
CBHW060350030726
47497CB00003B/659